Here's what critics are ~~saying about~~
Gemma Halliday's books:

"A saucy combination of romance and suspense that is simply irresistible."
—*Chicago Tribune*

"Stylish...nonstop action...guaranteed to keep chick lit and mystery fans happy!"
—*Publishers' Weekly*, starred review

"Smart, funny and snappy...the perfect beach read!"
—*Fresh Fiction*

"A roller coaster ride full of fun and excitement!"
—*Romance Reviews Today*

"Gemma Halliday writes like a seasoned author leaving the reader hanging on to every word, every clue, every delicious scene of the book. It's a fun and intriguing mystery full of laughs and suspense."
—*Once Upon A Romance*

BOOKS BY GEMMA HALLIDAY

High Heels Mysteries
Spying in High Heels
Killer in High Heels
Undercover in High Heels
Christmas in High Heels
(short story)
Alibi in High Heels
Mayhem in High Heels
Honeymoon in High Heels
(short story)
Sweetheart in High Heels
(short story)
Fearless in High Heels
Danger in High Heels
Homicide in High Heels
Deadly in High Heels
Suspect in High Heels
Peril in High Heels
Jeopardy in High Heels

Wine & Dine Mysteries
A Sip Before Dying
Chocolate Covered Death
Victim in the Vineyard
Marriage, Merlot & Murder
Death in Wine Country
Fashion, Rosé & Foul Play
Witness at the Winery

Hollywood Headlines Mysteries
Hollywood Scandals
Hollywood Secrets
Hollywood Confessions
Hollywood Holiday
(short story)
Hollywood Deception

Marty Hudson Mysteries
Sherlock Holmes and the Case
of the Brash Blonde
Sherlock Holmes and the Case
of the Disappearing Diva
Sherlock Holmes and the Case
of the Wealthy Widow

Tahoe Tessie Mysteries
Luck Be A Lady
Hey Big Spender
Baby It's Cold Outside
(holiday short story)

Jamie Bond Mysteries
Unbreakable Bond
Secret Bond
Bond Bombshell
(short story)
Lethal Bond
Dangerous Bond
Bond Ambition
(short story)
Fatal Bond
Deadly Bond

Hartley Grace Featherstone Mysteries
Deadly Cool
Social Suicide
Wicked Games

Other Works
Play Dead
Viva Las Vegas
A High Heels Haunting
Watching You (short story)
Confessions of a Bombshell
Bandit (short story)

DEADLY BOND

a Jamie Bond mystery

GEMMA HALLIDAY

DEADLY BOND

CHAPTER ONE

"Is it an animal?"

"Nope," I replied, idly picking at the cuticle on my ring finger as I sat in the driver's seat of my Roadster in the parking lot of the Sunshine Inn in North Hollywood.

"Vegetable?" the woman in my passenger seat asked. Samantha Cross. She was tall and lean with mocha skin and dark doe eyes that she was currently adding an extra layer of eyeliner to, creating a smoky effect that was pretty impressive considering the only light she was working with came from the blinking neon sign to our left touting *No vacancies* and *Free Wi_i*. (Their *f* was busted.) Sam had the style of Foxy Brown, the sass of Beyonce, and the aim of Dirty Harry. While Sam was technically my employee, she was the closest thing I had to a best friend, which at least made the cramped car bearable.

"Not a vegetable," I told her. I stretched my arms up above my head, skimming the ragtop roof of the car and stifling a yawn.

"Okay then tell me this—can I see it right now?" Her eyes went out the windshield, taking in the two-story motor inn in front of us. The name was deceptive, as there was nothing sunny about its appearance. The paint was peeling, the pool was a murky green color, and the rates were charged by the hour and usually paid in cash. The Beverly Hilton, this was not. Then again, for North Hollywood, it was par for the course.

"Yes, you can see it from here."

"Is it smaller than my—wait, is that him?" Sam sat forward in her seat, squinting through the night as a short, portly guy in boxers and a tank top emerged from one of the rooms, ice bucket in hand.

I gave him a quick glance. "No." I tamped down the flutter of anticipation. "I think he came from 105."

Sam made a disgusted sound and sat back in her seat. "Could this guy just do it already? I'm dying of boredom."

We'd been waiting for Igor Plotnikov to come out of room 103 with his mistress for the last three hours. Which was actually kind of impressive. I'd originally pegged Igor as a fifteen minutes kind of guy.

The Starbucks Sam and I had bought on the way over had long since been consumed, the dregs now cold. Sam had caught me up-to-date on all the cases currently under contract with the agency—which hadn't taken long since Igor was only one of two still unresolved. We'd already both counted out six degrees of separation from the president, debated whether the streak of light in the sky was a shooting star or a jumbo jet leaving LAX, and we'd finally resorted to twenty questions to pass the stretching time.

"We just need one picture of them together," I said, unable to keep the yawn at bay this time. Mrs. Irina Plotnikov had found the matchbook to the Sunshine Inn in her husband's pants pocket and put together where he *really* was every Saturday when he said he'd been playing *durak* with the boys. While the matchbook was a good clue, Irina's lawyer had said photos would go a long way toward getting her their beach house once she filed for divorce. So, she'd done what every reasonable wife in LA did when suspecting their husband of stepping out on them—she'd called the Bond Agency.

Namely, me. My name was Bond. James Bond.

Yeah, I know…trust me, I was *not* the person who picked that name out. The blame for that cruel and unusual punishment lay squarely on the shoulders of my father, Derek Bond. Hoping for a bouncing baby boy, he'd insisted on the name, thinking it was some sort of cool tribute to his childhood hero. In reality, he was the only person who called me James. Well, the only one who called me that and lived. Ever since I'd been old enough to voice an opinion, I'd gone by Jamie.

In addition to the name, my father had also given me his other legacy—the Bond Agency, a small PI firm in Los Angeles specializing in what we liked to call domestic espionage. Or catching cheating husbands. I'd spent more childhood nights than I cared to count falling asleep in the back of my father's Bonneville while on stakeouts at cheesy motels very much like the one I was currently sitting in front of. When Derek had been injured in the line of duty, he'd reluctantly passed the reins of the business on to me. And while it might not have been my first career choice, I'd grown into the role. Even if moments like this did remind me of my childhood and why Derek Bond would never win father of the year.

I shifted in my seat, wiggling some feeling back into my left foot, which was starting to grow pins and needles.

"How much is the wife paying us?" Sam asked, finishing the smoky eyes and moving on to refreshing her lipstick.

"Not enough," I mumbled, slipping the red pump off my foot and massaging some sensation back into it.

"Then tell me why we're doing this?"

"Because business is slow and we need the money," I told her frankly.

Sam paused, lipstick hovering over her bottom lip. "How slow?" she asked with a frown.

Usually I didn't bother my girls with the financial end of things. And, truth be told, the last couple of years had been good for us, bringing in enough profit to pay the bills, upgrade our computer systems, and even tuck away a little extra for a rainy day. But then the pandemic shutdown had hit, everything had closed down, and the cases had stopped coming in. While husbands and wives everywhere had been cooped up with each other long enough to triple the divorce rate, very few had been slipping out the back door to cavort with the opposite sex on the sly. Even though the world was cautiously getting back to something like normal now, it was still making for a very slow season for adultery. Slow enough that our rainy day fund had been wiped out several monsoons ago.

"Don't worry," I told her with false optimism. "I'm sure business will pick up in the spring. Warm weather always makes people frisky."

"Hmm." Sam didn't sound convinced. "Well, I wish Igor would hurry up and get frisky." She puckered her lips in the mirror, blotting red lipstick with a tissue.

"You have somewhere to be tonight?" I asked, noticing for the first time that her dangling earrings and leather jacket did seem a little put together for an evening sitting in NoHo counting bottles of beer on the wall.

She gave me a coy look. "Maybe."

I raised one eyebrow. "Maybe? Is this *maybe* a date?"

Sam scoffed and shook her head. "Hardly. Junior's bowling with his dad. I said I'd join them if I got off early enough."

Julio Jr. was Sam's twelve-year-old son, and Julio Sr. was the baby-daddy who had knocked Sam up, ruined her modeling career with stretch marks, and promptly taken off. Sam had been a struggling single mom when I'd hired her, though recently Julio had come back into the picture, paying up on child support and spending more time with his son.

And, I noticed, more time with Sam too.

"Didn't you guys just go mini golfing together last week?" I asked.

She nodded. "We did." She paused. "And I know what you're thinking."

I grinned. "I'm thinking that's a lot of smoky eye to impress your twelve-year-old."

Sam gave me a playful smack in the arm. "Okay, okay, yes. Julio and I have been spending more time together lately. But this"—she gestured to her face—"is not to impress anyone."

"No?"

"No. It's to keep the goodwill coming. Did I tell you Julio showed up at my place with a steak dinner last week?"

I shook my head.

"Yeah, and he paid for Junior's little league season coming up, and he bought me these earrings for Christmas, and he even offered to get my transmission fixed on my car."

"Sounds like he's really stepping up," I noted.

Sam shrugged. "Hey, if Julio wants to make up for lost time by showering me with gifts, I'm not gonna stop him."

I smirked. "Work it, girl."

"Trust me, I will." She paused. "So, what was it?"

"It?" I asked around another yawn. I must be getting old. It was only eight. Or maybe boredom was aging me.

"Not animal, vegetable, and where I can see it. I give up. What is it?"

I pointed across the parking lot. "Ice machine."

"Ah." She nodded. "That was my next guess."

"Look, if you want to go meet up with Julio, I can watch this place alone—" I started, prepared to take one for the team.

But I didn't get to finish as Sam grabbed my arm. "103! The door just opened."

She was right. I watched as a redhead in thigh high boots and a tiny tube dress emerged from the room, giggling and grinning. Right behind her was the large, bulky frame of Igor Plotnikov. He was wearing a bathrobe, loosely knotted around his ample middle. He had thick dark hair, beady dark eyes, and a wickedly dark smile on his face as he gave Boots the up and down. Even from across the parking lot, the look suddenly made me feel like I needed a shower.

I grabbed my camera, zooming in as far as my expensive lens would allow out my open window as I trained the view on Igor and Boots. I watched him mumble something in her ear—more giggling on her part—then she leaned forward and planted her lips on his.

Bingo.

I popped off a series of shots that would make Irina Plotnikov's lawyer do a celebratory *cossack.*

"Did you get that?" Sam asked excitedly in the seat beside me.

"Oh yeah," I told her, the camera still at my eye as I watched the amorous couple. Boots pulled back and winked at Igor. Then he watched her walk away with a slightly glassy look in his eyes.

That is, until his gaze roved the parking lot and settled on me.

And my camera.

Pointed at him.

"You!" He stabbed one hairy finger in my direction, and I immediately dropped the camera into my lap.

Uh-oh. Time to go.

"I think he spotted us," Sam said unnecessarily as I handed her the camera and turned the car on.

"I think so too. Let's get out of here."

Only, for a big guy, Igor was surprisingly fast. In seconds flat he was across the lot, his bathrobe flapping against his sides, revealing a whole lot of hairy naked skin.

I tried to avert my eyes as I put the car into reverse.

"Who are you?" Igor yelled, bearing down on us. "Why you taking pictures? My wife send you?"

I backed out of the parking space. But as I switched gears to pull forward, a pickup darted out from nowhere, and I had to slam on the brakes to avoid it.

"Jamie!" Sam said, a note of urgency in her voice as the hairy Russian caught up to us. He slammed one gigantic fist down on my hood, and I cringed, praying it didn't dent.

"You spying on me?!" he shouted.

Yeah, kinda.

"I'll kill you!" he threatened, standing in front of my car, banging the other fist down for emphasis.

At the very least, he was killing my paint job. I quickly put the car in reverse again, spinning around to check behind me before stomping down on the gas, sending us rocketing backwards through the parking lot.

Igor stumbled forward at the sudden shift in weight.

"Hurry, hurry," Sam chanted beside me, her eyes on the guy as he caught his balance again and started running after us, his bathrobe flying behind him like some sort of cape.

I hurried, making it all the way out of the lot and onto the street, where a Prius laid on its horn as I backed into traffic.

I waved an apology, changed gears, and merged over a lane.

Just as Igor came running out into the street.

"I kill you! I kill you, you hear!" he yelled, punctuating that last statement with a string of Russian insults that were lost to the night as I surged into traffic.

"Well, that was fun," Sam breathed, leaning her head back on the seat with a sigh.

I nodded my agreement. "Let's just hope normal people start cheating again soon."

* * *

The next morning, armed with my briefcase in one hand and a caramel macchiato in the other, I pushed through the etched glass doors of the Bond Agency.

As mentioned, as a child I'd never had any aspirations of being a PI. In fact, after a lifetime of watching Derek work, I'd wanted to get as far away from the seedier side of human nature as possible. As a teen I'd yearned for the glitz and glamour the world could offer and found my way toward getting a taste of it as a teen model. I'd been discovered at a mall one day by a talent agent who'd taken me out of the Valley and onto the runway.

I'd spent the bulk of my teens and twenties strutting down the catwalks of Paris, Milan, and New York, and while I'd never made supermodel status, I'd had enough of the taste of the good life that I'd been heartbroken when, at the age of twenty-six, I'd been deemed too old and unceremoniously dropped by my agent. With few options, I'd reluctantly come home to take over the family business.

Shortly afterward I'd hired on a small crew of other former models. While their looks often aided in catching cheating husbands with their boxers around their ankles, they'd also possessed hidden talents that made their brains much more of an asset to me than their beauty.

"Morning, boss," Maya Alexander said, rising from the reception desk to greet me. Maya was a former Playmate and PI in training who kept the agency running like a Swiss clock. Her slim frame was encased in a tasteful pencil skirt and low heels today, accentuated by a soft sweater that looked to be cashmere. Her long dark hair was pulled into a ponytail that swished behind her as she moved.

"Morning," I said, nodding her way. "What's on the agenda today?"

"Well," she said, grabbing her phone and scrolling as she followed me to my office. "Mrs. Duffy called last night."

"Oh?" I asked, hearing the note of hope in my voice. Mrs. Duffy's husband was a talent agent who she suspected was doing more than just casting the young starlets who came through his offices. "She ready to give us a retainer?"

Maya's frosted pink lips puckered into a frown. "No. Sorry. She said she decided to go with another PI firm."

"Rats." I tried to hide my disappointment behind my coffee cup as I sipped. "Any other good news?"

"Well, your accountant, Mr. Levine called. He said the fourth quarter losses don't look *quite* as bad as he'd feared."

I cocked my head at her. "You're sugarcoating that, aren't you?"

"A little," she admitted.

"Thanks." I dropped into my desk chair. "Anything else?"

"We did get a request for a new client meeting through the website." Maya sent me a hopeful smile. "A guy named Drake. Wants to come in at ten, but I wasn't sure you'd be ready by then."

I nodded, sipping from my cup again. "Absolutely. Tell him to come on in."

Maya's face brightened. "Great, I'll let him know." She turned to go. "Oh, and I almost forgot. There's a voicemail on the system from Aiden." She gave me a wink before shutting the door behind her.

Oh boy.

Aiden Prince was the Los Angeles County Assistant District Attorney, and our relationship was complicated at best. Aiden was tall, blond, tanned, and as close to physical perfection as you could get outside the pages of a GQ magazine. His suits were Brook Brothers, his aftershave was subtle, and his morals were unshakable. His wife had died of cancer a few years earlier, prompting him to leave his native Kansas City and start over on the West Coast, where he worked tirelessly bringing the bad guys of LA to justice.

Aiden and I had first met when I'd been a fugitive from the law and he'd been determined to track me down and turn me in. Somehow in the thrill of the chase, he'd realized I wasn't guilty and I'd realized he was more than just a handsome face. Mutual attraction had blossomed into mutual respect, and eventually the two had been much too enticing of a combo to keep us apart. While I had firsthand knowledge of whether he was a boxers or briefs man (silk boxers, in case you're interested), our relationship was still hovering in that indefinable area between sexy encounters and serious commitment.

I was personally fine with hovering, but I feared a commitment being forced soon. Aiden had said the *L* word to me recently, and it had been hanging in the air between us ever since, waiting for me to reciprocate. Aiden was great, and I wasn't quite sure what was holding me back from jumping in with both feet, but somehow I hadn't been able to force my mouth to form the word yet.

Though, an evening of lust was definitely still on the table.

I picked up my extension and keyed in my code to retrieve my voicemail. In addition to Aiden's, there were two earlier ones. One was a reminder from my landlord that rent on our office space was due last week. The other one was from my father Derek, first giving me some really unnecessary details of his latest colon checkup from his doctor and then an invitation to join him and his girlfriend, Elaine, for dinner that weekend. I made a mental note to call back as Aiden's voice came over the line.

"Hey, beautiful. Sorry I missed you."

I grinned, feeling warmth spread through my belly at the deep timbre of his tone.

"Thought maybe I'd swing by and we could catch a late dinner, but it sounds like you're not at the office. Call me tomorrow if you're in the mood. Until then, I'll be thinking of you."

When the beep told me the message was over, I barely resisted the urge to replay it. I set the lovely thought of calling Aiden later aside as I booted up my computer to get to work.

* * *

"Jamie?" Two hours later, Maya stuck her head in my office door. "Your ten o'clock is here. The website client?"

"Perfect," I told her, hitting *ctrl S* and saving the file I was working on. A detailed account of our evening at the Sunshine for Irina Plotnikov.

"Should I show him into the conference room?" Maya asked.

I nodded, rising from my chair. "And ask Sam and Caleigh to join us, would you?"

Maya nodded, slipping back out as I grabbed a yellow legal notepad and pen. I gave her a moment to get him settled, smoothing down any wrinkles in my burgundy blouse and throwing my black blazer over it. I'd paired it with dark jeans and tall black boots that went up to my knees, which gave the outfit just enough edge to be business with a kick. Then I exited my office, taking a right down the short hallway to where our small conference room sat, overlooking a view of the parking lot behind us and the roof of the KFC to our left. On a really clear day, you could just barely make out the shape of the *oo*'s in the Hollywood sign between the two buildings to our right. On a really smoggy day, the scent of fried chicken and biscuits was overwhelming. Today the *oo*'s were hidden and the eleven herbs and spices were making my stomach grumble.

In the center of the room was a polished wood table, and seated at the end of it was my potential client. I wasn't sure what I'd expected from the scant details Maya had gotten from our website contact form, but what greeted me stopped me in my tracks.

Slumped in a tall chair was an older man dressed all in black, from his shaggy black hair sticking out in frizzy tufts, to the black shirt with a black leather vest over the top of it, to the black jeans and black motorcycle books on his feet. Even his fingernails were painted black, and his eyes were rimmed in black eyeliner, making them look dark and saggy. From the loose jowls at the side of his face and stooped hunch to his posture, I put his age somewhere in the AARP range, despite his rock 'n' roll attire. If Ozzy Osbourne had a skinnier American cousin, I was looking right at him.

As I walked into the room, the man raised one hand, four of the five fingers encircled by large silver rings with skulls on them. "Hey, man."

"Uh, hey." I cleared my throat. "I mean, hi. I'm Jamie Bond."

He shrugged. "Cool. I was expecting a dude."

"Well, you got *me*," I said, pulling out a chair and sitting opposite him as I regained my professional composure. "Maya said your name is Drake?"

"Drake Deadly."

I paused. "Drake...Deadly?"

Drake opened his mouth and cackled, sounding a lot like a Disney villain. "I take it you're not a Deadly Devils fan?"

"Deadly Devils...the band?" I asked, the name ringing some faint bells. I seemed to remember my father listening to them years ago. Back in the MTV days, when big hair and guitar solos reigned supreme.

Drake nodded. "You *have* heard of us."

I licked my lips, not wanting to wound the ego of a potential client. "Of course." I smiled. "My dad's a fan."

"Oh yeah?" He raised one eyebrow at me, the gesture creating a network of wrinkles in his pale forehead. "Well, I'll have to give you an autograph for him."

I had high hopes his autograph would be on a retainer check, but I just smiled and nodded. "So, what can I help you with, Mr., uh, Deadly?"

He cackled again. "Call me Drake, man. I ain't formal."

"Sure. Drake. So, how can I help you?"

But that was as far as I got before a high-pitched squeal came from the doorway. "Ohmigosh, you're Drake Deadly!"

I swiveled in my seat to see Sam and my other employee, Caleigh Presley, come into the room. The squeal having come from Caleigh, who rushed forward to greet our potential client.

"Wow, I am such a fan!" she gushed. She grabbed one of Drake's ringed hands in hers and pumped it up and down so hard that I feared the man's arm might crack right off. "Caleigh Presley," she told him. "Of the Memphis Presleys. Ohmigosh, it's such an honor to meet you. My older brother had all your music back in the day. I think I even lost my virginity to your 'Jugs & Gin.'"

Drake got a dreamy look on his face. "Wish I'd been there."

"Uh, these are my associates. Caleigh Presley," I said, indicating the bubbly blonde as I steered her to a seat farther down the table. "And this is Samantha Cross."

Sam gave a discreet wave, sitting opposite me.

Drake gave her a healthy up and down. "Wow. This place is fulla hotties, huh?"

I bit my tongue, giving him a wan smile instead of the several feminist replies running through my head. "Was there something you thought we could help you with?" I asked the man.

Drake tore his eyes from Caleigh's low-cut blouse to meet mine. "What?"

"The reason you contacted us?" I prompted.

"Right, right." He nodded, as if suddenly remembering where he was. "Yeah, man, I do think you can help me. You like, follow people, right?"

I nodded slowly. "We do. If the investigation warrants it."

"Well, this one warrants it. I want you to follow my wife."

Now we were getting somewhere. "Do you suspect your wife has been unfaithful to you?" I asked, pen hovering over my legal pad.

"She told me she wants a divorce," he said slowly, eyes on the table. "And I want to know if there's someone else."

"You're married to Jenna James, right?" Caleigh piped up.

He nodded. "That's right."

"Jenna James?" I asked, sending Caleigh a questioning gaze. She was clearly more up on aging rock star culture than I was.

"She's a dancer," Caleigh explained.

"Was," Drake corrected. "Quit when we got married."

Caleigh nodded. "But she used to be a backup dancer for J.Lo, though, right?"

Drake nodded. "That's how we met. She was performing at the VMAs. I was getting a lifetime achievement award, and she was doing some sort of twerking thing." He grinned, eyes getting a far-off look, as if reliving the romantic moment.

"So, I'm guessing Jenna is a bit on the younger side?" I asked, getting a clearer picture of the dynamic.

Drake laughed again, years of smoking who-knows-what crackling in the back of his throat. "She ain't a *bit* younger. She's a *lot* younger. Twenty years. And hot. Stacked." He put his hands out in front of his chest as if to illustrate.

"I see." I discreetly wrote down *trophy wife* on my legal pad. "And she told you she's seeking a divorce?"

His eyes narrowed. "That's right. Talk about ungrateful. I've given her everything. Cars, jewelry. Even upgraded her a couple of cup sizes."

Some girls had all the luck. "Uh, how long have you been married?" I asked.

"Five years," he said, his eyes going to a spot on the floor. "She couldn't get me to the altar fast enough. Did the Vegas thing just a few weeks after we met."

I added *possible gold digger* to my notes. "Any kids?"

Drake shook his head vigorously. "No way. I been shooting blanks long before I met Jenna." He grinned. "Thankfully! Or, lemme tell you, there'd be a whole lotta little Drakes running around out there, if you know what I mean?" He waggled his eyebrows and stuck his tongue out in what I assumed was supposed to be some sort of sexual gesture. In reality, it just made me nervous he was going to drool on my conference table.

"Uh, okay, so what makes you think Jenna has been unfaithful?" I asked.

Drake put his tongue away. "What do you mean?"

"I mean, has she been secretive? Taking private calls? Hiding her activities from you?"

"Yeah." He gave me a blank look. "Sure. Maybe."

I shot a look to Sam, wondering if our potential client was high. He seemed to be having as hard a time focusing as I was having taking his dyed hair and elderly guyliner seriously.

"Look, I just want you to follow Jenna, okay?" Drake said, leaning his elbows on the table. "Tell me who she sees, where she goes. Everything."

His meaning was starting to sink in. "Did you have Jenna sign a prenup before you married?" I asked.

"Of course. I ain't stupid."

"Mind if I ask the terms?"

Drake's eyes went around the table before he answered. "Standard. Anything I came into the marriage with is mine. We split ways, she only gets alimony on what I made while we were together."

"In dollars and cents, how much are we talking?" I asked. The man in front of me had *has-been* stamped all over him, but if he'd been that popular once, royalties could still be coming in.

Drake's eyes did more pinging around the room, as if he were trying to gauge whether he should try to impress us or play his cards close to his vest. Apparently ego must have won out, as he answered, "Maybe a million."

I heard Sam do a low whistle beside me.

"A million in alimony?" Caleigh clarified. I could see her mental wheels turning, going down the same path mine had started on at Drake's lack of conviction in his wife's extramarital affairs.

"So, I'm guessing this prenup has an infidelity clause?" I said, eyes cutting to my associates. "Meaning, you offer proof she's been unfaithful, and you avoid paying that alimony."

Drake grinned. "That would be nice."

I pursed my lips, wondering if there actually was someone else in the trophy wife's life or if Drake was just fishing.

"Look, just follow her, okay?" he said, clearly picking up on my hesitation. "Just…tell me everything she does, everyone she sees." He pulled a piece of paper from his pocket, sliding it across the table toward me. "Our address. Make and model of her car. Some places I know she goes a lot."

I glanced down at the paper, surprised to see the very organized-looking list in neat handwriting. "Does your wife work?" I asked, scanning the list of places she frequented. It appeared to be largely nail salons, estheticians, and clothing boutiques.

Drake scoffed. "No. Like I said, she quit dancing when we met. Her only job for the last five years has been spending my money." The resentment in his tone was unmistakable.

"What's this?" I asked, stabbing my finger at an event it appeared the wife was due at that evening. "AAA? Is this a substance abuse program?"

Drake's cackle cut through the air again. "Nah, man. It's Alien Abductees Anonymous."

I thought I heard Sam snicker, but she was professional enough to cover it quickly.

"So, she's been abducted by aliens?" I asked, trying to keep the disbelief out of my voice.

"Look, I didn't marry my wife for her stunning intellect," Drake said. "What can I say? She's a ditz."

I shook my head. While I didn't know about the aliens thing, Jenna James couldn't be too dumb if she was effectively making a million dollars off a five-year investment. Wall Street had nothing on those kinds of returns.

"Well, we can certainly look into the matter and see what we can find," I said. "Check into her phone records, see who she might be spending time with, where she goes when she's not with you."

"Great." Drake nodded, his jowls lifting as his mouth attempted a smile. "I'll be back tomorrow morning for a full report."

"Tomorrow?" I glanced from Sam to Caleigh. They both wore frowns that mirrored my own thoughts. "Uh, Mr. Deadl—er, Drake, we're going to need a bit more time than that to thoroughly look into the matter. I mean, just doing background research alone is going to take us a good portion of the day."

But Drake shook his head. "There's three of you, right?"

"Well, yes, but—"

"So you background or whatever," he said, pointing to Caleigh, "and you just follow her." He pointed to Sam before turning his eyes on me. "And you put a rush on it and gimme a report tomorrow."

I silently searched for a delicate way to tell him that we couldn't very well put a rush on Mrs. Deadly's libido happening to carry her to a lover's arms.

"Look, I'm happy to give you a retainer for your services," Drake said, pulling a check from the fringed pocket of his leather vest. "Would this cover it?" He slid the paper along the table toward me.

I peeked at the amount and had to fight to cover my reaction. It had a couple more zeroes than I was used to working with.

I shot a glance at Sam.

She sent me a small shrug.

"Okay," I finally said. "We'll see what we can dig up."

CHAPTER TWO

———

As soon as Drake Deadly left, I did as he suggested—putting Caleigh on background info and records for the wife and putting Sam on the address he'd provided for his house in Brentwood where she could find and follow Mrs. Deadly. On the chance that Jenna was planning to meet up with a secret lover that day, Sam would be there to catch it.

And, because I rarely liked to rely on chance, I grabbed my purse and jumped into my car, heading toward Hollywood, where I knew I could find the perfect bait to interest a young, bored trophy wife.

The first time I'd ever used my feminine wiles as bait to entice the husband of a wealthy senator to step outside of his marriage, I'd felt a little dirty—like I'd somehow trapped the poor guy. However, as his wife had happily pointed out to me as she'd shuffled through the 8x10 glossy photos of her husband slipping me the key to his hotel room, if he had been a faithful loving husband, he never would have taken the bait in the first place. It wasn't as if I'd faked the evidence she planned to use against him in their divorce proceedings. I'd just provided an ideal situation for him to show his true colors.

And in a time crunch, that was just the type of situation I needed to create for Mrs. Deadly.

Which is why half an hour later, I was standing outside Danny Flynn's apartment. I gave a sharp shave-and-a-haircut knock on the door marked 3C, listening as I heard bare feet padding across hardwood on the other side. A beat later, the door opened, and I looked up into a pair of sleepy blue-green eyes topped by tousled sun-streaked brown hair. A dusting of stubble ran across his jaw line, and he was dressed in a pair of jeans, still unbuttoned, and nothing else, as if he'd hastily thrown on the first thing he could lay hands on before answering the door. On anyone else, the look might have felt unkempt. On Danny, it just made a girl envision what he'd been doing all night to look so tousled.

He gave me a slow smile, leaning on the doorframe. "Hey, Bond. Aren't you a lovely way to wake up."

"It's almost noon," I told him, pushing into his apartment. A tan leather sofa, a sturdy wood coffee table, and a bunch of camera equipment took up the bulk of the living room. The shades were still drawn against the light, and two empty wineglasses sat on the table, noticeable lipstick stains on one. I inclined my head toward the glasses. "Late night?"

Danny shrugged. "Or early morning. Depends on your point of view."

"Don't tell me she's still here?" I asked, peeking around him toward the open bedroom door.

His face broke into a wide grin. "Late *photo shoot*," he clarified. "Strictly professional."

I glanced at the lipstick. "Uh-huh."

I'd met Danny Flynn on my first professional modeling gig, when I was just a teenager—all gangly legs and awkward self-consciousness. He'd shown me the ropes and stepped into a sort of big brother role, putting me at ease. We'd worked so well together that the photos had ended up in *Seventeen*.

Danny was old enough that fine laugh lines had formed at the corners of his eyes where the sun had kissed his skin one too many times, but young enough that his swinging bachelor life was still charming and not yet veering into the realm of lonely and sad. I'd never known a time when Danny's little black book of numbers hadn't been overflowing, and being in his line of work, most of those ladies were young, eager models who were ripe for the plucking. Whether Danny ever chose to pluck, I didn't ask. But I knew it wasn't for lack of opportunities.

Over the years, my relationship with Danny had gone from big brother to best friend to something that was a whole lot more grown up and a whole lot less definable. There'd been a point when I'd been pretty sure Danny had been interested in me in ways far beyond friendship. And I knew for a fact there was a time—not so long ago—that I'd thrown caution to the wind to pursue more intimate feelings for him. Unfortunately, neither of these times had coincided, and what we'd been left with were missed opportunities and a lot of unresolved emotions that no one liked to talk about.

Instead, we usually just teased each other and flirted and occasionally worked together when we were feeling really risky.

Or desperate.

"Just tell me this photo shoot of yours last night was done clothed?" I told him, eyeing a pile of discarded garments on the back of his sofa.

"Now what fun would that be?" Danny joked.

I rolled my eyes. "Men. You're such pigs."

"Don't tell me you're jealous, Bond," Danny joked, sinking down onto the sofa and leaning back to display his toned abs.

I glanced away, trying not to let him see the heat filling my cheeks (and various other parts of my body) at the sight. I grabbed a T-shirt off the back of the sofa. "Put something on, Danny." I threw it at him.

He laughed, complying as I averted my eyes. "Coffee?" he asked, getting up and walking into the kitchen.

"No. Thanks. I've had my caffeine fix for the day already."

"Okay, so if this isn't a social call, what's up?" Danny opened a cupboard, pulling out a box of pods and inserting one into his Keurig.

"Actually, I came to ask you a favor."

He glanced my way as the machine made all kinds of gurgling noises and started processing a heavenly scent that had me rethinking my answer about a cup. "Oh? Is this favor of the business or personal nature?"

"Business," I said decidedly.

"Bummer." He shot me a wink before turning to the fridge to pull out a carton of creamer.

I ignored the flirting, clearing my throat. "I have a new client," I told him. "A celebrity of sorts." I gave him a brief rundown on Mr. Deadly's dilemma.

"So, he wants fuel to bust the prenup and leave her with nothing?" Danny surmised.

"Well, to be fair, she had nothing before she married him," I pointed out. "She's been living a nice life off his royalties for the last five years."

"Doesn't sound terrible. You're sure *she's* the one who wants the divorce?"

"That's what Drake said."

Danny shrugged. "Okay, so where do I come in?"

I paused, licking my lips. "Bait."

Danny let out a bark of laughter. "So you *do* just want me for my body."

I rolled my eyes. "Look, she's planning to be at this…support group…meeting tonight," I said, hesitating to share too many details, lest I give him more reasons to say no. "I figured maybe you could show up, work your magic on her, see if maybe you can drum up any interest in her coming back to your place for a…" My eyes went to his lipstick stained wineglass again. "…*photo shoot*."

"So you want me to sleep with the wife?" Danny teased.

"No! Geez, do I look like a pimp?"

"Well, those are some boots." He looked down at my leather knee-high footwear.

I swatted him on the arm. "Do *not* sleep with the wife. Just flirt. Invite. Get her on camera accepting." I paused. "Look, the girls do it all the time. Just, this time, they're not exactly Mrs. Deadly's type."

Danny sipped from his coffee, leaning his back against the kitchen counter. "And what makes you think I'll be her type?"

"Danny, you know you're every woman's type."

He threw his head back and laughed. "Flattery will get you everywhere, Bond."

"Here's hoping." Oh, geez, was I flirting back now?

I pulled my phone from my purse, scrolling to a photo of Jenna James that Caleigh had texted me. I turned the screen so Danny could see it. "This is the wife."

Danny looked from the screen to me, raising both eyebrows up into his messy hair. "Well, why didn't you say so?"

He nodded at the phone. "That's the kind of favor I don't mind doing for a friend."

I hoped he was at least halfway joking. "Flirt. Just flirt and invite, yeah?" I cautioned.

"Sure." He glanced down at the phone screen again. "Whatever you say, boss."

* * *

About half an hour later I was driving through Del Taco to pick up a quick lunch when Maya's face lit up my phone.

"Hey," I answered, putting her on speaker as I exchanged my credit card for a pair of chicken soft tacos and a handful of Del Scorcho sauce. "What's up?"

"Someone is here at the office asking to see you," Maya's soft voice came in my ear.

"Oh? A client?" I asked, ever hopeful.

"Uh, sort of." She paused and lowered her voice. "It's Kendall Manchester."

I frowned. Kendall Manchester was the daughter of a prominent movie producer, Wendell Manchester, who lived in a small castle in Bel Air and had a thing for ladies of the evening, large parties, and grey areas of the law. I'd first met the Manchesters when Wendell had thought Kendall had been kidnapped, and in the ensuing investigation I'd ended up spending a frustrating week prying half-truths from Wendell and an even more excruciating night with the spoiled-more-rotten-than-a-month-old-banana Kendall. When we'd finally cleared the case, we'd all left on civil, if not besties, terms, and I'd happily imagined I'd never hear from either one of them again.

Which is why I was surprised Kendall was in my office.

"What does she want?" I asked.

"I don't know. Said she wanted to talk to you about family troubles."

"Great. What has Wendell done now?"

"One can only imagine," Maya said. She paused. "What should I tell her?"

While I was tempted to tell her I'd left the country, the truth was the Manchesters might be pains, but they were very rich pains. And if Kendall had a problem she was willing to *pay* me to deal with, I figured it was worth at least listening to. "Tell her I'll be right there," I said around a bite of taco as I pulled out of the drive-through.

"You sure about that?" Maya asked, her thoughts clearly going along the same lines as mine.

"Yes." No. "Fifteen minutes," I promised.

* * *

Fourteen minutes later, I was sitting across my desk from Kendall Manchester. Her long dark hair shone with salon created highlights, her manicure was chip-free and flawlessly on-trend, and the number of diamonds shining in her ears could have paid my rent for a year. And that's talking California real estate prices. She was dressed in a pair of loose, black silk palazzo pants that billowed around her red soled Louboutins, and she'd topped the luxurious look with a deceptively simple looking white T-shirt and a faux fur jacket that kept slumping down her shoulders as if she were posing for the paparazzi right there in my office.

"What took you so long?" she asked, scrunching up the nose Daddy had bought for her as I settled into my desk chair.

"Sorry. Traffic," I said, even though I was technically thirty-three seconds early.

"Ugh, isn't there always like, so much traffic?" she said, the Valley Girl thick in her accent. "It's so stressful. I keep telling Daddy I need one of those self-driving cars."

"Wouldn't they still have to go through the traffic?" I reasoned.

"Well, yeah, but then the *car* would be stressed, not me." She nodded sagely.

I had no argument for that, so I just smiled and nodded. "So, Kendall, what can I do for you?" I asked.

She let out a deep, dramatic sigh. "Well, like I told your secretary out there, I have some family problems."

I cringed at the outdated term, glad Maya was out of earshot. "Okay, shoot. What has Wendell gotten himself into now?"

But Kendall shook her head, her hair swooshing prettily behind her. "It's not Daddy. It's Gammy."

"Gammy?"

"My grandmother." Kendall did another deep sigh for drama's sake. If she wasn't careful, she was likely to hyperventilate. "She's like, really old and lives in this retirement village called Sunset Acres in Culver City."

"Really old" in Kendall's world could be anywhere from thirty-five to a hundred, but I just did more smiling and nodding. "Go on."

"Anyway, Gammy is…" She wrinkled up her nose again. Though I could see the expression didn't reach her forehead. Apparently she'd been investing in Botox already. "…is seeing someone."

"Seeing, as in dating?" I asked, still trying to get at the issue.

Kendall nodded. "I know! Totally indecent at her age!"

"Okay, so your grandmother has started dating." I paused, waiting for the punch line. "You're concerned about this because…"

"Because of who she's dating." Kendall leaned forward. "He's a lying, cheating creep."

"Cheating?" I said, jumping on the word. That was something I could work with.

Kendall nodded vigorously. "Yes! I think he's seeing other women behind Gammy's back."

"What makes you say that?" I asked.

She leaned in as if telling me a secret she didn't want the walls to hear. "I saw him with a blonde."

"Where was this?"

"At Sunset Acres. I was there to see Gammy, and as I was arriving, I saw him with another woman near the clubhouse."

"Is it possible she was just a friend?" I floated.

But Kendall shook her head. "Unh-uh. I saw him lean down and *kiss* her as she was leaving. On the lips!"

That was pretty convincing. "Any idea who this other woman is?" I asked, thinking that would be a good place to start.

She shook her head. "No, I only saw her from behind. After the kiss, she took off. But she had blonde hair about this long"—she held her hand to her shoulders—"and she was dressed all skanky. You know, like in really tight clothes and cheap animal prints."

Which could describe a lot of woman in LA, but I noted it down.

"Look, he's just too into Gammy to be real, you know?" Kendall said. "Says all the right things, does all the right things, flatters her nonstop."

"Sounds like a doting boyfriend," I noted.

Kendall shook her head. "Sounds like a load of bull to me."

I stifled a grin. "So what do you think he's using her for?"

"Gammy is wealthy and has a heart condition." Kendall gave me a knowing look.

"And you think he's after her money?"

"Duh!" Kendall rolled her eyes. I knew for her it was a reflex action to just about any situation, so I didn't take it personally. "I mean, why else would he be with her?"

Love? Companionship? But those might have been foreign concepts to Kendall, so I kept that to myself. "What does your father think of this guy?" I asked.

"Daddy's not here." She pouted, looking much more like a two-year-old than her actual twenty-five years. "He's doing a movie in Australia. I can hardly even get him on the phone these days."

I chewed my lower lip, wondering how involved I wanted to get. "Okay, tell me about this guy your Gammy is dating."

"I would be happy to," Kendall said, looking like she was ready to dish the dirt, mean-girl style. "His name is Alejandro Tenasco. He says he's from Spain."

"Where did Gammy meet Alejandro?"

"It was at a mixer at the retirement village. But, like, he doesn't even live there. I think he was just there trying to pick up some rich old ladies."

"Has he asked your grandmother for money?"

"Well, no. Not exactly. But Gammy buys him all kinds of stuff."

"Like what?"

"Well, for starters there was the Rolex she gave him for their one month anniversary!"

I gave her a raised eyebrow. "That's a nice gift."

"Right? I mean, it was my birthday last November, and I didn't get a Rolex." She did some more pouting.

"Has she bought him other gifts?" I asked, thinking maybe Kendall actually had a valid concern.

She nodded vigorously. "Tons. Like, all the time. She's always spending money on him."

"So, what is it exactly you think I can do to help?" I asked.

"I need you to find proof that Alejandro is cheating on Gammy. It's the only thing that will convince her that he's just using her. You know, before things get too serious." Kendall leaned forward, sincerity etched on her young features for possibly the first time since I'd met her. "Please, Jamie? The last thing I want is for my Gammy to have her heart broken."

Or spend Kendall's inheritance on someone else.

But, as the girl's big brown eyes blinked at me, I found myself nodding. "Okay. I'll look into it."

Kendall smiled, showing off a flashy set of white veneers. "I knew I could count on you."

* * *

After I got some details from Kendall about where I could find Alejandro and Gammy, I checked in with Caleigh. She'd put together a good background profile on Drake's wife, Jenna James, so I told her to run one on Alejandro Tenasco and possibly add a visit to the retirement village to ask around about his blonde.

Then I called Sam's number, putting it on speaker. Three rings in, she picked up.

"Hey, boss," she answered. I could hear the sound of cars in the background.

"Hey. Where are you?"

"Brentwood. I'm sitting in front of Jenna and Drake's place. Followed her home about an hour ago."

"So, what was the wife up to today?" I grabbed a pen and pad of paper from the corner of my desk.

"Sadly, nothing adulterous. We hit Fernando's salon in Beverly Hills, where she spent two hours getting her color touched up. And, I might add, emerged looking just about the same."

"I'd guess several hundred dollars poorer though."

"At least. The place looked ritzy. Anyway, she did lunch at Spago and then a little shopping along Rodeo."

"Rough life," I commented, noting all of this down. "She meet up with anyone for lunch?"

"Just a couple of gal pals. Sorry."

"Me too. She head home after shopping?"

"Dermatologist. If the swelling in her lips was any indication, she had a little Restylane refresher. Then she went home. I've been sitting on the place since, and no movement."

I blew out a breath. Sounded like a typical afternoon for the Trophy Housewives of Beverly Hills. "Okay, well, why don't you call it a day. She's got her AAA meeting in a couple hours, so I'll pick her up there."

"You think she might be meeting some guy at the meeting?" Sam asked.

"I think she will be tonight. I'm bringing Danny."

Sam was quiet for a moment. She knew my complicated history with Danny better than anyone. "You think that's wise?"

"Well, unless she swings both ways, he's got a lot more chance at baiting her than I do alone."

"I meant, do you really want to spend the night with Danny?"

"I'm not *spending the night* with him."

"You know that's not what I meant," Sam said, ignoring my attempt at humor. "You know that whenever you spend time with Danny, you get all funky and flirty with him again."

"I do not get funky," I protested, glossing over the accusation of flirty. Considering I had, in fact, accidentally gone a little flirty at his apartment that afternoon. "Look, we're both professionals. He's helping me do a job. That's it."

I heard her suck in a breath on the other end, like she had more protest in her, but I didn't let her voice it.

"Go home and give Junior a hug from Aunty Jamie. I'll call you in the morning." Then I hung up.

CHAPTER THREE

———

Alien Abductees Anonymous held their weekly meetings at the Jewish Community Center off Briarwood in one of their meeting rooms on the second floor. As Danny and I made our way down the corridor, we passed by a room on the right full of Cub Scouts, noisily shouting and gluing feathers to pinecones, and a room on the left where I could see a woman in a blazer demonstrating CPR on a dummy for a handful of twenty-somethings. At the end of the hall, a printed paper sign was taped to a partially open door reading *AAA*.

I pushed in ahead of Danny, entering a room that looked like it served several different purposes throughout the week. An upright piano was tucked against one wall, along with a couple of bookcases filled with various art supplies. A long folding table had been laid out along one wall, laden with trays of cookies, snacks, and a box bearing the Starbucks logo next to a stack of paper cups. Folding chairs were set up in a circular pattern in the center of the room, though only a few were occupied at the moment. A tall guy with a green mohawk sat in one, chatting with an elderly woman in support hose. A few more people mingled near the snacks, though I could tell the meeting hadn't gotten underway yet.

"Welcome to AAA!" A man in a loud Hawaiian shirt and Birkenstocks with black socks approached us. "I'm Dave."

I looked down to give him a smile. Way down. The guy had to be under four feet tall. His dark hair was pulled back in a ponytail at the nape of his neck…that is, where a neck should be. His chin seemed to blend seamlessly right into his chest. "Hi. Jamie," I told him. "And this is my friend Danny."

Danny raised one hand in greeting. "Hey."

"Nice to meet you both," Dave said, grinning. "I don't recall seeing you here before. Is this your first time?"

I nodded. "Uh, yeah. We're new."

"Well, we have lots of literature for you to take a look at," Dave said, gesturing to a small wooden table by the door that was covered with a smattering of pamphlets. *Aliens of the Past. Your Abductees Rights. Surviving Extraterrestrial Intervention PTSD.*

"I usually suggest newbies start with this," Dave said, handing me a glossy brochure with a picture of a saucer shaped UFO on the front.

I glanced down at the title. *So you've been abducted. Now what?*

I bit my lip, thinking it would be rude to laugh. "Uh, thanks."

"What's this?" Danny asked, pointing to a stack of paperback books at the back of the table. He picked one up, turning the cover so I could see it.

A half-naked man was wrapped in the embrace of a green, scaly looking creature with huge, exposed breasts beneath the title: *My Lover from the Stars*.

That laugh bubbled up in my throat again as Danny waggled his eyebrows at me.

"That's my latest novel," Dave said, pride unmistakable in his voice.

Danny turned the book over, and sure enough, there was Dave's bright smile on the back.

"It's a slightly fictionalized account of my erotic encounter with a Reptilian."

"*Slightly* fictionalized," I repeated as Danny thumbed through the pages.

"It's in its third printing. Sold almost a million copies in digital."

I blinked, my eyes going from him to the naked lizard girl on the cover. "A million copies?"

Dave smiled and nodded. "Amazing how many people can relate to my experience."

"Yeah, it looks super relatable," I mumbled, thinking I was totally in the wrong business.

"So, what kind was yours?" Dave asked.

"Mine?" I asked.

"Your ET," Dave said. "The one who abducted you?"

"Oh, uh, it was…short. With a big nose. And…hairy?" I said, suddenly wondering if maybe I should have done a little research before coming here.

Dave's eyes narrowed. "Hairy?"

"Uh, maybe it was fur," I said, trying to cover. "But, I-I didn't really get a good look at him."

"Him?" Dave said, eyebrows going into his hair line. "Well, that is quite unusual. The short, hairy ones are almost always female."

"Well, I assumed it was male. I-I don't know."

"It was all so harrowing that she's blocked a lot of the details out," Danny jumped in. "She's still working through it."

"Ah." Dave nodded, giving me a sympathetic smile. "I understand. Start with that." He gestured to the glossy pamphlet in my hands. "A lot of us have repressed memories. You're not alone."

"Thanks," I mumbled, grabbing Danny by the arm and steering him away from the info table.

"You're welcome," Danny said.

"Welcome?"

"For the save." He shook his head at me. "You were describing Alf, weren't you?"

I shrugged. "E.T. seemed too obvious."

Danny laughed. "Hey, the book looked like interesting reading at least."

"Please don't tell me you're into lizard girls," I mumbled back, my eyes searching the rest of the room's occupants. While we'd talked to David, a few more people had trickled in, mostly converging on the snack table.

"I don't know," Danny joked. "Who knows what a lizard girl could do with a quick tongue like that—"

"There she is!" I said, cutting him off before his imagination wandered into too-graphic territory. "Jenna James."

I nodded toward a blonde standing near a tray of cookies in the shape of little green men. She was petite, at least six inches shorter than my own 5'9", and slim through the waist and hips, which were shown off in a tight white skirt with a hem several inches shy of her knees. Tanned, toned legs ended in stiletto heels in a leopard print that perfectly matched her top, straining to hold in a pair of breasts that were much farther down the alphabet than my own. Her hair was a pale bleached platinum, her skin a tanning salon gold, and her eyes big and bright blue, giving her a look of childlike innocence that I had a hunch was a complete illusion.

She was chatting animatedly with a guy in a pair of corduroy pants and a comb-over holding a paper coffee cup in his hands. She seemed completely oblivious to the attention he was giving her cleavage.

"Go work your magic," I prompted.

"On it." Danny gave me a wink, and I waited until he was getting a paper cup of coffee next to the chatting pair before I edged around the other side of the table, pretending to be interested in the finger sandwiches in the shape of pyramids instead of the conversation.

"...so that's when I knew it was in the Orion constellation," the guy in the corduroy pants said to Jenna. "I mean, clearly the three mounds were a representation of the belt, pointing to their home planet like a map."

Jenna nodded, her hair not moving an inch. "So amazing. You think they were here as teachers or researchers?"

I watched Danny step closer to the pair.

"Well, if I had to guess, I think they were here to study us. We are a fascinating species to the ET of the outer belt systems, and—" The guy broke off abruptly as Danny bumped into him, spilling coffee on his cords.

"Oh, wow, I'm so sorry," Danny said, making a show of looking around for napkins.

Jenna grabbed a handful from the table and quickly shoved them at Cords.

"I'm so clumsy. I didn't see you there," Danny continued.

"It's fine," the guy said, frowning in a way that said the interruption was really anything but fine.

"I think I saw a restroom on the way in," Danny offered.

"Uh, yes." Cords' frown deepened. "I'll, uh, just go clean up."

"Sorry, again," Danny said as he and Jenna watched Cords walk away.

As soon as the guy's back was turned, Danny wasted no time.

"Hey, I'm Danny, by the way."

"Hi. Jenna." She gave him a friendly smile. "You new here?"

He nodded. "My first meeting. I'll admit, I'm a little nervous." He flashed her a grin that was all boyish charm.

I turned my back to them, trying to look like I wasn't listening in.

"There's no need to be nervous at all," Jenna assured him, putting a hand on his arm. "We're all survivors of the same thing here. I mean, sure our stories are different, but we all made it home, right?"

"Right," Danny said, though I could tell his grin was holding back a snicker.

"So, was it a Grey?"

"Excuse me?" Danny asked.

"Were you taken by a Grey?" She munched on a cookie, biting off the alien's bulbous head. "With guys, it's usually the Greys. Martin, over there"—she gestured to the guy with the green Mohawk—"he has a theory that the Greys are a predominantly female race."

"Really?" Danny asked, leaning in closer. "You know, I'd love to hear more about your experience, maybe over drinks—"

But before Jenna could reply, a loud voice boomed across the room. "Okay, everyone, let's take our seats and get started," David called out, waving people to the circular ring of chairs.

Jenna gave Danny a smile, then took a seat in a white folding chair near the windows. Danny quickly deposited himself on the one next to hers, and I noticed Cords return from the restroom to take the chair on her other side, giving Danny a dirty look.

I slipped between Mohawk and a quiet woman in mom jeans clutching a purse on her lap.

"I'd like to get started by welcoming those of you who are new to the group." David gestured first toward Danny then to me. "I hope we can help enlighten you about your personal ordeals and provide some comfort in our shared experiences."

Jenna gave Danny a wide smile and patted his hand.

Physical contact. This was an encouraging sign.

Danny scooted his chair just a little closer to Jenna's.

"I'll be happy to start us off tonight," David said, standing and addressing the group. "Hi, I'm David, and I'm an alien abductee."

"Hi, David," the group said in a synchronized monotone.

"I was first abducted seven years ago," David went on, "and it's been a recurring phenomenon in my life, leading to many encounters with otherworldly beings." He sat in his chair and folded his hands in his lap. "Would anyone here like to tell their story tonight?" His eyes went around the circle, pausing when they met mine.

I shook my head.

David cocked an eyebrow at me.

I shook harder.

"I'll go," Jenna said, saving me. She rose from her seat awkwardly, in a shimmy designed to keep her short skirt from riding up to reveal the color of her panties. "Hi, I'm Jenna."

"Hi, Jenna," we all said.

"I was first taken when I was a little girl, but my encounters with the otherworldly really picked up when I got married."

I pictured her husband. I could only imagine.

Danny put a comforting hand on her leg as she sat down, and I noticed Jenna did not brush it away.

Okay, hardly a smoking gun to infidelity, but it was a start.

* * *

Unfortunately, as the evening dragged on, with stories from Cords about his encounters in the Orion constellation and

Mom Jeans with how she suspected her daughter's karate instructor was a Reptilian in disguise, our good start fizzled before it ever went anywhere. By the time the meeting ended and abductees dispersed to finish off the alien cookies and coffee dregs, Danny didn't seem to be any closer to winning Jenna's affections.

"Your story was so interesting," Danny said as Jenna shimmied out of her seat again, hoisting a designer handbag onto her shoulder to leave. "I'd love to hear more about your experiences."

Jenna gave him a smile. "I'm always happy to share if it helps out a fellow abductee come to terms with his journey."

"Maybe we could go grab a drink?" Danny offered.

She frowned. "Sorry, I've actually got plans tonight."

"Oh?" I could see Danny's eyes cut to mine over her head. "I'm sorry to hear that. I was really hoping to connect with someone like you who really gets what I'm going through."

Jenna melted under his crooked grin, like I'd seen so many women do before. "You're so sweet. I see why the Greys were drawn to you."

Danny's smile faltered as I could see him trying to make out if that was a compliment or not. "So, what do you say? Rain check on the drinks? Maybe tomorrow night?"

"Jen?" Cords hailed Jenna from the door. "Walk you to your car?"

Jenna nodded. "So nice to meet you," she told Danny, quickly moving past him and toward the exit.

"No luck, Casanova?" I asked, coming up beside him as we watched the wife leave.

He frowned, shaking his head. "I thought I was close, but no."

"Maybe you're losing your touch, Flynn."

"Ouch." He put a hand over his heart in mock pain. "Or maybe I'm just not her type."

"You think Cords is?" I asked, inclining my head toward the door he'd just exited.

Danny shrugged. "I don't know, but she said she had plans tonight. I'm guessing they're not with her husband."

"Or a little green man?" I joked.

Danny laughed. "I don't suppose her being made love to by an existential being will hold up in divorce court."

I shook my head, grabbing him by the arm as I headed for the door. "Let's see what the wife's plans are this evening."

* * *

We followed Jenna's mint green Jaguar out of the parking lot of the JCC and onto the main road, keeping a car length behind her. While it was dark out, streetlights, brightly lit storefronts, and billboards illuminated the road almost as if it were daytime. Danny fiddled with my radio, settling on some jazz station, as I merged into the left lane, staying close enough to Jenna that a red light wouldn't derail us.

"I'm sorry, I don't get jazz," I said as he leaned back in the seat.

"It's music. What's not to get?"

"All that skiddly this and skattily that. And there's no melody. It's just all over the place."

Danny laughed. "That's the beauty of jazz. You never know where it's going to go."

"My life is enough chaos. I don't need it in my music." I watched Jenna make a right at the next light and signaled to do the same.

"So, what's your music then, Bond?"

"Something I can sing along to." I made a right just in time to see Jenna turning again at the next intersection.

"Don't tell me you're the Harry Styles type?" Danny joked.

"Hey, Harry is adorable! There's nothing wrong with Harry." I hung a left at the intersection, following Jenna's lead. "But no, I'm more into the classics."

"Bach? Beethoven?"

"I was thinking more like McCartney and Dylan, but yeah, those guys are good too." I saw the Jaguar turn onto a side street. "Did you ever listen to the Deadly Devils?" I asked Danny.

He nodded. "If I recall, they wore a lot of leather and used a lot of innuendoes in their lyrics. Why?"

"I'm trying to figure what Jenna would see in Drake."

"I'm guessing a fat bank account."

I shot him a glance. "So, maybe that's Jenna's type."

"Dang. I'm outta luck, then."

My phone pinged with a text alert from my purse, and I dug around by feel for it as I followed Jenna's taillights. A quick glance at the readout showed Aiden's name. I swiped it on, eyes pinging between the road and the screen.

Free for dinner?

"No texting and driving, Bond," Danny said, reaching over to grab the phone from my hand before I could stop him.

"Hey, that's private," I protested.

He raised his eyebrows at me. "That sounds exciting." He looked at the screen.

And all the humor in his demeanor faded.

"So, we're still seeing that guy, huh?" He handed the phone back to me.

I shoved it into my purse. "It's complicated," I hedged.

Danny nodded but turned his head so I couldn't see his expression. "Love always is."

His use of the *L* word made me uncomfortable enough that I shifted in my seat. "I think Jenna's heading home," I said, glad for the distraction as I followed her to the left again and recognized the street name from the address her husband had given me earlier that day.

"She said she had plans," Danny said. "You think she's having someone come over?"

"Either that or she was just blowing you off." I watched as she pulled off the road, onto a short driveway filled with stone pavers leading through the trees. I hesitated a moment, letting her headlights cut a swath through the darkness ahead of us before slowly going past the driveway and making a U-turn to come to a stop across the street where there was a break in the tree line. Through it, I could see Jenna park her Jag outside a large, two-story colonial revival style home, complete with white columns and gawdy statues guarding the door. Lots of uplights highlighted the artful landscaping as well as provided enough illumination to clearly see the blonde make her way to the front door, pull a key from her purse, and go inside the house.

A series of lights turned on, first in the front rooms then slowly trailing up to the second floor as Jenna made her way through the house. I could see a faint silhouette moving against the large window at the front right, which seemed to be where Jenna settled.

"Maybe she's changing to hit the town?" Danny said.

"Maybe." I glanced over at him. "Or maybe—"

"I know, I know. She blew me off."

"I was going to say she's waiting for her ET lover to show up, but that's a possibility too." I leaned over and changed the radio to a station playing oldies. Danny shot me a look but didn't protest.

As the two of us sat in silence, watching Jenna's window, I itched to text Aiden back. But as much as I hated leaving him hanging, it felt mean to do it in front of Danny. While I had no idea if Danny's flirtatious nature with me was old habit, a rekindling of feelings, or just his way of teasing me, the jealousy in his voice had been unmistakable. Part of me loved it. Part of me hated it. All of me didn't know what to do with it. So, I sat in silence, trying to ignore my phone as Elvis sang about his blues and Sinatra crooned for me.

Finally, after about twenty minutes, we watched the lights go out in Jenna's room. No one left the house. No one arrived.

"I think she's gone to bed," I told Danny, stating the obvious.

He shook his head. "Maybe I really am losing my touch."

"Or maybe the wife is faithful," I said, not liking that idea at all. I tried to put thoughts of how unhappy my client would be in the morning out of my head as I turned on my car and pulled away from the curb.

* * *

"Give me some good news," I said, pushing through the glass doors of the Bond Agency the following morning. I noticed Caleigh had beaten me there, already sitting on the sofa in reception with coffee in hand.

Maya popped up from her desk, dressed today in a pair of white capri pants, suede ankle boots, and a loose green blouse that brought out her eyes. "First up, you have a meeting with Drake Deadly. At nine."

I blew out a breath. A meeting at which we had nothing to share with our client other than his wife liked to shop. "I said *good* news," I mumbled, glancing at the wall clock. Eight fifty. Precious little time to stall.

Maya shrugged. "Well, Caleigh got coffee?" She held a paper cup out my way.

"Thank you." I took a grateful sip, loving that the girls knew just how I liked my coffee. Strong and loaded with flavored syrup and whipped cream. "Anything from Sam this morning?" I asked hopefully.

Maya shook her head. "Not really. She's been at Jenna's place since dawn, but she said the only activity was the housekeeper arriving."

"Well, it's only been a day," I reasoned. "Drake can't expect miracles." At least I hoped not. "Have her stay on Jenna this morning, and maybe we'll get lucky."

Maya nodded. "Will do."

I turned to Caleigh. "Wanna update me on Gammy Manchester's case before Drake gets here?" I asked.

She nodded, rising from the sofa and following me the few paces to my office. "I ran a background check on the boyfriend," she started, sitting in one of the club chairs in front of my desk as I sank into the office chair behind it. "He's pretty clean."

"*Pretty* clean?" I asked, jumping on the word.

Caleigh shrugged. "A couple speeding tickets, and a bankruptcy a few years ago."

"I like the sound of that. So he needs money?"

"Maybe," Caleigh hedged. "The bankruptcy was in 2017, so he's had a little time to recover. Looks like he went to work for a real estate developer after that, and now he's got a condo in Manhattan Beach and drives a late-model BMW."

I sipped from my cup. "Okay, so not destitute."

Caleigh shook her head. "But not living life in the Manchester style."

"Go on," I said, glancing at the clock. Drake was due any minute. "Any leads on the blonde he was seen with?"

"Not yet. I did visit the retirement village and talk to a few people in the commons and at the clubhouse. I told everyone I was Mary's granddaughter."

"Who's Mary?" I asked.

Caleigh shrugged. "Doesn't every retirement village have a Mary?"

I chuckled. "Okay, so anyone feel chatty with Mary's granddaughter?"

"They were *all* chatty. I heard about Barb's surgery, Bill's good-for-nothing son-in-law, and the orderly who Sally thinks is stealing from her." She paused. "But no one seemed to know a blonde in animal prints who might be friends with Alejandro."

"But they did know Alejandro?"

She nodded. "By all accounts, he and Gammy are joined at the hip. Janet, who lives in the Tulip block, told me he even took her to dinner last weekend at the country club."

"Sounds nice."

"She also said Gammy paid." Caleigh shot me a knowing look.

"Sounds like what Kendall was describing." I tapped my pen against my desktop. "Still. Being a cheapskate is one thing. Gold digging cheater is another."

"I can see if I can look into his finances more," Caleigh offered. "Maybe see if he's in debt or in need of quick cash."

I nodded. "Do that. And see if you can find out anything about his past relationships too."

"Like who he dated prior to Gammy Manchester?"

"Right. Is there a pattern of dating wealthy women and profiting from it, or is it just his luck Gammy's the generous type?"

Caleigh shook her head as she rose from the chair. "Janet told me about the diamond tie pin Gammy bought him. That's really good luck."

I had to agree with her there. "See what you can find and keep me posted."

"On it," she promised, heading back out to reception.

I glanced at the clock again. Nine ten. I peeked out the open office door, but Maya and Caleigh were the only ones in the lobby. No sign of Drake. Then again, rock stars weren't usually known for their punctuality.

I sipped my coffee, getting as much caffeine fortification as possible before my client showed up. I booted up my computer and checked my emails. Mostly advertisements. No new clients. Nothing that needed my immediate attention. There was one forwarded cat meme from my father's girlfriend, Elaine, but other than that, things were conspicuously quiet.

I sighed, finishing my coffee as I held on to my hope that the warm weather would bring out the naughty side in spouses again. If everyone kept wearing their masks and staying faithfully cooped up together, I'd be out of a job.

I tossed my cup into the trash and checked the time again. Nine twenty. Drake was now officially late. While I hadn't been necessarily looking forward to telling him we had nothing for him, I was starting to wonder if I was being stood up. I was just about to call him, when I heard Maya's voice from reception.

"Jamie! I think you need to see this!"

I got up from my desk and went to the open door to find Maya and Caleigh both staring down at something playing on Maya's computer screen. Whatever they were watching had them totally engrossed, wearing matching looks of concern as they frowned at the screen.

"What is it?" I asked, a small niggle of dread taking hold in my belly as I crossed the room.

"I don't think your nine o'clock is going to show up," Maya said quietly, eyes still on her screen.

I came up behind her and glanced down to find a live news clip playing on her browser. It was a local channel, and a perky redheaded reporter was talking into a microphone, a scene playing out behind her with flashing police lights and lots of guys in LAPD blue.

Maya leaned in and turned up the volume.

"...scene at the Beverly Hotel this morning where a tragedy has struck," the reporter said.

I felt that dread kick up a notch as the scene switched to another view. This one was of the entrance of the posh hotel in

Beverly Hills, where police were wheeling a gurney covered in a black tarp out the front doors.

"This morning, the body of nineties rock legend Drake Deadly was found in the hotel's swimming pool, the star having apparently drowned sometime during the night."

I sucked in a breath.

My client was dead.

CHAPTER FOUR

————

Forty-five minutes later, I was pushing through the crowd of reporters, security guards, and curious lookie-loos in front of the Beverly Hotel, scanning the faces of the law enforcement crawling all over the grounds for any familiar enough to gain me access past the yellow crime scene tape being strung up to keep the public at bay.

I spotted an older guy, portly with not a whole lot of hair covering his round head.

"Gomez!" I called, trying to get his attention.

His head swiveled my way, recognition lighting his weathered features a moment later. "Hey, Bond." He nodded toward the security guard nearest to me. "She's okay."

The guard lifted the tape so I could duck beneath.

"How's the old man?" Gomez asked as I approached.

"He's good," I said. "Does a lot of fishing."

"Lucky retired bastard," Gomez said. "I got three more years."

"I'm sure they'll go by in a flash." Having dispensed with the pleasantries, I nodded to the open doors of the hotel lobby. "So what happened here?"

"Drowning. Some celebrity. Musician."

I nodded. "Yeah, I saw on the news. Drake Deadly. They're saying he was found in the swimming pool?"

Gomez nodded. "Hotel lifeguard found him this morning when he went to open it up."

"Is Aiden Prince here?" I asked, glancing past him toward the interior of the hotel. While I knew Aiden didn't personally visit every crime scene in LA—he'd have to have the magic of Santa Claus to spread himself that thin—a high-profile death like a celebrity was usually the type of thing the DA's office liked to get ahead of before the media painted their own picture.

Gomez nodded. "Sure is. Out back by the pool." He inclined his head toward the lobby doors.

"Thanks," I told him, heading in the direction he'd indicated.

"Sure thing. Say hi to your old man for me," he said with a wave as he turned his attention back to crowd control.

The glass front doors of the hotel gave way to a sleek marble floor, large crystal chandeliers, and lots of polished dark woods that were meant to evoke the feel of old Hollywood. Art deco paintings hung on the walls trailing down a short hallway that led to another pair of double doors and a courtyard beyond. I stepped through them, taking in the lush greenery, birds of paradise, and towering palm trees. Just beyond that sat a sparkling blue swimming pool that on any other day would be the picture of Southern California paradise.

Only today, it was the picture of tragedy as guys in CSI T-shirts skimmed the pool with nets, scoured the bushes for miniscule fibers, and took pictures of just about every chaise, shade umbrella, and faux rock in the pool's cascading waterfall for evidence of what had occurred there.

Near a sign warning that diving was prohibited stood Aiden Prince, shielding his eyes against the harsh morning sunlight bouncing off the waters as he surveyed the scene with a stoic expression. He looked up as I approached him, raising an eyebrow in question. "Hey." He leaned down and gave my cheek a quick peck.

It was a small gesture, but it surged warmth into my cheeks. "Hey, yourself."

"What are you doing here?" he asked.

"I saw the news." I glanced toward the pool. "Drake Deadly drowned in there?"

Aiden nodded. "Looks that way." He cocked his head at me. "You know him?"

I paused. Usually client confidentiality was priority number one in our line of work. But considering my client couldn't very well object now, I nodded. "I was actually working a case for him."

"So you know him *well*."

"I wouldn't say well," I backtracked. "He only hired me yesterday. Any idea how he ended up in there?" I asked, gesturing to the pool.

"Not entirely sure yet. But from what the ME said, it looked like he'd been dead at least a few hours. Probably went into the water sometime last night. Pool's closed from ten to six a.m., so no one found him until the lifeguard went to open it this morning."

I shivered, trying not to think about how cold the water would have been last night. Even though we were in sunny LA, midwinter temps still were not usually conducive to midnight swims. "Did he just fall in or what?" I asked.

"It's possible." Aiden frowned. "We'll know more after a toxicology report, but the ME thinks it's likely alcohol or some other substance was in play. Something that rendered him incapacitated in the water."

"You mean, he was drunk or high and passed out." I had to admit, that didn't seem out of the realm of possibility, given the impression he'd left me with the day before. "Any idea what he'd be doing here? I mean, by the pool. You said it was closed?"

"Here specifically? No. But Drake was registered as a guest at the hotel. Checked in a few days ago. Apparently he and his wife were having some marital issues."

That much I knew, but I just nodded as Aiden went on.

"Hotel bar is over there." He pointed across the courtyard toward the buildings at the back of the property. I could see more law enforcement inside, through a bank of glass windows. "Hotel staff reported he had tequila sent up to his room earlier in the evening. It's possible Drake was drowning his marital sorrows, had a little too much to drink, wandered out for a walk, and…"

"And just fell in and drowned," I finished. I pursed my lips, thinking of the guy who'd been in my office just the day before. He hadn't struck me as particularly sorrowful about this marriage breaking up. He hadn't seemed particularly emotional about it all. More…calculating.

"What?"

"Hmm?" I looked up to find Aiden watching me.

"You look deep in thought."

I blinked, trying to put on a neutral face. "Nothing. I just…well, I was just wondering if you are sure this was an accident?"

"We're not sure of anything yet." He paused, his deep brown eyes scanning my face, scrutinizing me. "What sort of job did you say Drake hired you for?"

I hadn't said. Though, at this point there wasn't much reason not to be forthcoming. "He wanted us to follow his wife. Jenna James. They had a prenup, and if she was unfaithful, she got nothing. We were supposed to find proof of infidelity that he could take to his lawyer."

"And did you?"

I shook my head. "No. But like I said, he only hired us yesterday."

"Did his wife know he was hiring a PI?" Aiden asked.

"I don't know. I don't think so." I paused. "But she's just avoided a messy divorce, hasn't she?"

"You think the wife might have had something to do with this?" Aiden asked.

I hesitated. While Jenna James had struck me as the quintessential trophy wife, she'd seemed harmless enough the night before. In fact, she'd even struck me as kind of sweet, the way she'd been with Danny at the meeting. I didn't want to think she'd be capable of drowning her husband.

Especially since he'd hired me to keep an eye on her.

"I don't know," I said honestly. "I know she was at home at ten last night. She turned out all the lights in her house, and we assumed she was going to bed."

"We?"

I bit my lip. "I, uh, had someone doing surveillance with me." I hesitated to tell him it had been Danny. The last time we'd talked about Danny, Aiden had promised me he was ready to fight for my affections. It was too early in the morning to think about that kind of combat yet. Especially since I wasn't sure whom I'd be rooting for. "Anyway, I assumed she was in for the night, but I suppose it's possible she could have left later and driven here."

"Where does the wife live?"

"They have a place in Brentwood." I nodded in the general direction. "About twenty minutes that way."

"Well, with the water and the overnight lows, it's not likely we'll be able to pinpoint an exact time of death. After ten, when the pool closed, and at least three hours before he was found."

Which was sometime between ten and three a.m. Which was a big window. One the wife easily could have walked through if she really was worried about Drake finding proof that would end her salons and Rodeo boutiques lifestyle. Let's face it, she was a lot better off financially today as his widow than she would have been as his ex-wife.

"I was supposed to meet with Drake this morning to go over his wife's movements yesterday," I told Aiden. "I can have Maya email you the report we had ready for him if you think it would be helpful."

"It might be." Aiden's eyes went to the sparkling blue water again. "I'll look into the wife," he promised.

I had no doubt he would, and if there was anything to find, he'd find it. As much as I kind of didn't want the wife to be involved, I'd done my civic duty in telling Aiden everything I knew. This was no longer my case. My client was dead.

A fact that was not going to be good for business.

* * *

I left with a promise from Aiden that he'd let me know if they found anything.

I'd just slid into the driver's seat of my car when a text pinged in on my phone. I looked down at the readout to see Danny's name.

Just heard about Drake Deadly. You ok?

Okay was a relative word, but I was doing a whole lot better than Drake was at the moment. So I shot off an *I'm good. Out a client, but good.*

You don't think the wife did it, do you?

I hope not, I told him honestly.

A beat later his response came in. *Call me if you need anything.*

I felt myself grin at the offer. Danny could be a flirt at times and tease me, but he'd always had my back when I'd needed him.

Thanks, I told him. *But I'm putting on my big girl panties today.*

He sent a laughing emoji before I put my phone away and headed back toward the Bond Agency.

Apparently Maya and Caleigh had called Sam with the news about Drake, because as soon as I got back to the office, they were all waiting for me in reception. Caleigh popped up off the sofa first.

"Is it true? Is he really dead? Did the wife kill him?"

That seemed to be the consensus. But I held up two hands in a halting motion. "Who said anything about him being killed?"

"No one," Sam said, shooting Caleigh a look. "In fact, the media is reporting very few details at all. So, fill us in. What happened?"

"I don't really know." I set my purse down on Maya's desk and quickly gave them the gist of the conversation I'd had with Aiden. "It sounds like he didn't simply go for a midnight swim," I ended with. "But whether he got drunk and fell in or was pushed and held under are still yet to be determined."

"Come on, it has to be the wife," Caleigh said.

"That feels like a leap," I said. Even though I'd voiced the very same theory to Aiden.

"It would be quite a coincidence if it wasn't," Maya pointed out. "I mean, he hires us to follow her one day, and he's dead the next."

I cringed, not enjoying the idea that we'd had any hand in being the catalyst for a man's death. "Coincidences happen all the time. I mean, it's not like we found anything on the wife."

"Yet," Caleigh said. "Maybe she realized her husband was trying to shaft her in the divorce and she killed him before we could give him the ammo."

I shook my head. "Jenna James is barely five feet tall and a hundred pounds soaking wet. I can't see her dragging her husband down to the pool against his will."

"Maybe she got him drunk first, like Aiden said," Sam pointed out. "Or she drugged him."

"And Drake wasn't exactly burly himself," Caleigh said. "It wouldn't take much to hold him under the water."

I bit my lip, hating how plausible it all sounded. "It still seems extreme," I hedged. "I mean, even *if* Jenna was being unfaithful and *if* she knew her husband had hired us."

"If she knew she was being followed," Maya said.

We all turned to Sam.

She blinked. "I-I don't know if she saw me! I mean, she didn't show any indication of noticing me. I thought I was being careful."

I shook my head. "Look, it doesn't matter now anyway. Not our case. Drake's dead, and that's the end of our involvement with it."

The girls gave me three identical dubious looks.

I put my hands up in a surrender motion. "Aiden is extremely capable of finding out the truth. He's got the entire LAPD at his disposal. I'm sure if there was any foul play involved, he'll figure it out."

No one looked particularly convinced, but since I was the boss, I plowed ahead. "So, let's focus on the cases we do have, huh?"

"Case. Singular," Maya informed me.

I frowned. "What do you mean, singular?"

"With the Plotnikovs tied up and Drake gone, Kendall Manchester is our only active client."

"That can't be right," I said. "What happened to Mrs. Archer?"

Maya scrunched up her nose. "She called this morning and said she decided to take her husband back."

"But he cheated on her with the nanny."

Maya shrugged. "She forgave him, and they hired a male nanny to watch the kids from now on."

I closed my eyes, trying not to be mad at the happily reconciled couple. "Okay, fine." I opened my eyes back up and trained them on my office manager. "Maya, let's work on drumming up some more business. Maybe some ads, some social media campaigns. Anything to get bodies in the door."

Maya nodded. "I'll see what I can put together this morning."

"Good. In the meantime, we'll just focus on Manchester." I turned to Caleigh. "Any luck with financials for Alejandro the cheapskate?"

Caleigh straightened up. "Still working on banking records, but I did find out that his last three girlfriends have been older, wealthy widows."

"That," I said, stabbing a finger her way, "feels like a pattern to me."

"Or he has a type," Sam said.

"Still no luck finding the blonde?" I asked Caleigh.

She shook her head. "No, but there's a potluck social this afternoon at Sunset Acres. If our blonde lives at the Acres, there's a good chance she'll be there."

I nodded. "Well, then I think *Mary's granddaughters* should be there too."

CHAPTER FIVE

———

While my mind was admittedly still on Drake Deadly and his untimely death, my bank account was running on empty, so I tried to focus as I parked my car in the Sunset Acres visitor lot next to Sam's, and she, Caleigh, and I walked onto the grounds. Which, as it turned out, was nothing like the retirement home I'd been picturing. I'd had in mind bingo, shuffleboard, and the scents of disinfectant and Bengay, but Sunset Acres was more like a small resort set in the middle of Culver City. A golf course sprawled to our right, the hiss of sprinklers hitting the grass in the distance mingling with the thwack of golfers taking their aim. Several townhouses lined the course, as well as a maze of three-story condo buildings winding through the main complex. We passed a sparkling swimming pool—full of the over-sixty set doing laps and relaxing on chaises in the late afternoon sunshine—a fitness center full of state-of-the-art equipment, and a lounge with a full bar.

"Geez, I wanna live here," Sam said, glancing into the gym. "This place is way better than my apartment complex."

"Probably way pricier too," I noted. "You need Manchester kind of money to live here."

"Well, forget Junior's college fund. I'm saving up for this place from now on."

"The potluck is in the Azalea Room," Caleigh said, nodding down a paved path to our right as she shifted our offering in her arms—a cold spinach quiche we'd picked up from Whole Foods on the way over.

Sam and I followed as we approached a complex of community rooms, all sporting names of flowering foliage. I noticed several other people converging on the pathway with casserole dishes in hand. The dress attire looked to be Sunday best, and I noted a couple of women even wearing ornate hats adorned with flowers and feathers.

"I'm suddenly feeling underdressed," Sam mumbled, nodding toward a lady with peacock plumage trailing down her back.

"Bea said they do this social every month. It's the event to be at," Caleigh informed us.

"Let's just hope our blonde thinks so too," I told her as we entered a large, noisy room marked *Azalea*.

Hardwood floors and warm throw rugs made me think of an oversized family room, with several groupings of sofas, armchairs, and low tables situated around the space. A tall stone fireplace sat at the far end of the room, ablaze with an inviting fire, where several men in slacks and sport coats had converged. Long tables in cloth coverings lined the sides of the room, laden with everything from tuna salad to berry cobbler to Crock-Pots bubbling with meatballs and stews. The mingling scents made my stomach growl as Caleigh set our quiche down on the nearest table, shifting a couple plates of cookies around to make room.

"Is Gammy Manchester here?" I asked Caleigh, realizing I wasn't exactly sure what the woman looked like.

Caleigh nodded. "That's her. By the Tiffany lamp." Caleigh gestured toward a tall, slim woman with ramrod straight posture and coiffed grey hair. She was dressed in white slacks and a loose silk blouse in a light blue that complimented her pale, rosy skin. Her makeup was tasteful, her jewelry minimal but I could tell expensive even from across the room, and her smile pleasant as she nodded to the woman next to her, chatting up a storm. Everything about her exuded a poise and confidence that only years of never having to do without created.

"That's Janet she's talking to," Caleigh said, indicating Gammy's companion. "She's the one who organizes the social events."

"Not a lot of blondes here," Sam noted, eyes scanning the room. She was right. Salt-and-pepper seemed to be the predominant hair color, heavy on the salt. I spotted a few dye jobs among the crowd—some more tastefully done than others—

but no one stood out as reading "skanky" like Kendall had described Alejandro's alleged affair.

"Maybe we should split up," Caleigh suggested, grabbing a finger sandwich and taking a bite. Then she scrunched up her nose and groaned.

"What?" Sam asked.

"It's liverwurst."

I shuddered as Caleigh forced herself to swallow the bite and discreetly wrapped the remaining sandwich in a paper napkin.

"I'd like to talk to Manchester." I nodded toward the older woman. "Maybe you two can scour the room for the blonde?"

"On it," Sam agreed. Caleigh nodded then followed Sam as she slowly made her way down the food table, scrutinizing every woman she passed.

I left them to it and approached Ms. Manchester, who was still engaged in conversation with Janet the Planner.

"Uh…Eleanor?" I asked, remembering the name in our files and stopping myself from calling the woman *Gammy* just in time.

She nodded a goodbye to Janet and turned a pair of pale blue eyes my way, an expectant gaze in them. "Yes?"

"Hi, I'm Jamie." I gave a little wave. "Mary's granddaughter."

"Nice to meet you, Jamie. And please call me Ellie." Her sparse eyebrows formed a small frown as she foraged for recognition. "Mary. She lives in the Rose Garden complex?"

"That's right." I gave her a bright smile. "I hope I'm not interrupting?" I asked, eyes going to Janet's retreating form.

"Oh, no, not at all. I was just telling Janet that she's outdone herself this month. Quite a turnout." She smiled, nodding around the room.

"Agreed. I hadn't expected so many people."

"Is your grandmother here?" Ellie asked, eyes going behind me to scan the room.

"No. Her hip is bothering her," I lied. But given the audience, I figured it was a pretty plausible one.

"Ah. Poor thing," Ellie said.

"But I figured I'd come down and fix a plate for her." I gestured to the table.

"Very nice of you," Ellie agreed. "I can't imagine my granddaughter braving the potluck."

Neither could I. Kendall Manchester and liverwurst went together like a Kardashian and Arby's. But I just smiled. "Well, I live nearby."

"I see. How nice for Mary." I could see her gaze roving the room again, signaling I was losing my audience's attention.

"Are you here alone?" I asked.

"Hmm?" Her eyes snapped back to meet mine.

"Uh, just wondering if your husband was with you or…" I trailed off, hoping she would pick up the thread.

"Oh, no. I'm a widow. Have been for, gosh, well on twenty years now." She got a far-off look in her eyes, as if remembering another lifetime.

"I'm sorry," I told her automatically.

But she just smiled again and shook her head. "That's quite alright. I lost Gavin a long time ago, and I moved on with my life."

And there was my opening. "Moved on?" I asked, giving her a sly smile. "Does that mean there's a new man in your life?"

She laughed, her cheeks tinting pink. "As a matter of fact there is."

"Well, do tell, Ellie," I prompted.

"Oh, there's nothing much to tell really," she hedged. "Nothing as exciting as the fellows my granddaughter brings home."

Again, I could well imagine. Kendall had a bit of a wild streak and the common sense of a sheltered 90210-raised child. The product of which had resulted in the kidnapping debacle where I'd originally met her.

I was about to assure Ellie that her new relationship absolutely *was* of interest to me, when a man in a navy polo shirt and dark slacks approached us, wrapping one arm around Ellie's shoulders. "Hello, ladies," he said in a thick Spanish accent.

Ellie turned, and immediately her face lit up, taking ten years off her age. "Hello, darling." She turned her cheek so he could deposit a quick kiss on it. "We were just talking about you."

"Oh?" the man said, raising a pair of dark eyebrows. "All good, I hope?" he joked.

"Always. This is Jamie, Mary's granddaughter," Ellie said, making the introductions. "And this is Alejandro."

"Nice to meet you," I told him.

"Likewise, Jamie," he said, giving me a smile that showed off about a hundred gleaming white teeth. His skin was a rich tan, laugh lines creasing at the corners of his eyes and mouth that put his age at least in his sixties, though I doubted it was quite as high a number as Ellie's. His thick hair was combed back from his forehead, still dark though there were streaks of grey edging their way in at the temples. He reminded me of an older Antonio Banderas, his eyes saying all kinds of sexy things even if his mouth was idle.

"I was just telling Jamie what a lovely turnout we've had here today," Ellie said. "It's a shame Mary couldn't be here."

"Is she ill?" Alejandro asked, dark eyebrows drawing down in concern. Clearly he seemed to know Mary too. I had to tread lightly here.

"Hip," I said quickly. "Do you live here at Sunset Acres as well?" I asked, changing the subject away from my little white lie.

Alejandro chuckled and shook his head. "Too rich for my blood, I'm afraid." He gave me a wink.

"Oh, don't be silly." Ellie gave him a swat on the chest. "He's being modest."

That, I doubted. "How did you two meet, then?" I asked.

"At a social mixer Janet put together this past fall," Ellie answered.

"Oh?" I turned to Alejandro. "Then you must have other friends at Sunset Acres?" I asked, thinking of one blonde friend in particular.

"I like to be involved in the local community."

That was as vague as could be.

"We've been together ever since," Ellie added. "It's going on, what, four months now?" She turned to Alejandro for confirmation.

He nodded. "At least. Though, it feels like I've known her all my life."

Ellie giggled and blushed, suddenly seeming more like a tween than a grandmother. Though, the look wasn't altogether terrible on her. I could only hope I could still giggle and blush so happily at her age.

"That's a lovely accent," I told Alejandro. "Where are you from originally?"

"He's Spanish," Ellie said. "From Spain."

"Oh? Which part?" I pressed.

"*Lugar de pasión y amor*." He leaned in, kissing Ellie on the cheek again.

"And that means?" Even though I'd grown up in Southern California, I'll admit, my Spanish was a little rusty.

"The land of passion and love. *Amor!*"

Ellie did more giggling. I'd swear her age was decreasing by the minute. She was clearly smitten. And by the way Alejandro was looking at her, all smoldering eyes, he appeared to be the same.

Though, as I well knew, appearances could be deceiving. And he'd once again dodged my question.

"That's a lovely watch," I said, gesturing to the Rolex on Alejandro's left wrist.

For a brief second his charming smile faltered, and he had the good graces to look sheepish. "A gift. She is too good to me." He shot Ellie another heated look.

"Nonsense," Ellie shot back. "I'm only as good as you deserve."

"Ellie!" a woman in a long dress with ample hips called from across the room.

"Ah. That's Margo. I told her I'd help her slice the carrot cake. If you'll excuse me." She gave me a polite nod. "I hope Mary feels better."

"Thanks," I told her, feeling a little guilty. And hoping some Mary in the Rose Garden complex didn't get a slew of sympathy cards.

I watched her—and Alejandro, who seemed permanently attached to her side—walk away, not sure I'd made any headway at all. It was quite possible they were a happy couple—Ellie enjoying giving Alejandro some of the finer things in life. Or it was possible Alejandro just enjoyed those finer things much more than he enjoyed Ellie. As I made my way toward where Caleigh and Sam stood near the fireplace, I wondered if his blonde at the Acres was as generous with gifts.

"I saw you met Alejandro," Caleigh noted as I approached the pair. "What did you think?"

"Jury's still out," I answered. "But," I added, "he's laying the *amor* stuff on pretty thick with Gammy."

"You think he's just trying to seduce Gammy?" Sam asked.

I shrugged. "Some women are a sucker for a Latin lover."

"Don't I know it," Sam mumbled, rolling her eyes.

"How *was* bowling with Julio the other night, anyway?" Caleigh asked, a grin on her face.

Sam waved her off. "It was a *family* night. Trust me, I'm not falling for those big brown eyes again."

"Uh-huh." Caleigh sounded about as convinced of that as I was.

"You two have any luck finding our mystery blonde?" I asked.

Caleigh shook her head. "If she lives in the village, it looks like she didn't show."

"Maybe she knew Alejandro would be here with Gammy," Sam said, nodding toward the pair at the cake table. "Maybe she didn't want to make a scene."

"Or maybe Kendall was mistaken in the first place," Caleigh offered. "I mean, maybe she misread the situation between Alejandro and the blonde? Maybe she's just a friend? Or relative?"

"Maybe." I watched Alejandro lean down and whisper something in Ellie's ear that had her giggling again. "But maybe we should keep an eye on Alejandro."

"You mean tail him?" Caleigh asked.

"I'll do it," Sam offered. "Julio's taking Junior to a ball game tonight anyway."

"Wow, bowling and a ball game all in the same week?" I raised an eyebrow at her. "You really are working this, aren't you?"

"You better believe it," she said. "I'm getting a spa day on Saturday too."

"Julio sounds like he's really taking care of you," Caleigh noted, getting that mischievous grin on her face again.

Sam shrugged. "For now. Until some hot little thing comes along and takes his attention again."

Caleigh frowned. "Don't you think it's possible he's just wanting to spend time with you? Make up for the last few years?"

"Well, let's put it this way—I'm not wearing a Rolex." She had a point.

* * *

By the time we'd left Sam at Sunset Acres to keep an eye on Alejandro and I dropped Caleigh back off at the office and locked up, I was famished—not having actually partaken of any of the potluck offerings. On the off chance Aiden was free, I sent him a quick text.

Dinner in the cards tonight?

I didn't have to wait long before his reply pinged in.

Rain check? Looks like a late night here.

I tried to tamp down the flutter of disappointment and shot back an *Understand. Don't work too hard. :)*

His reply was almost immediate this time. *You know me better than that.*

I grinned. I did. Aiden's work ethic was almost as strong as his faith in the legal system. Even if I only shared one of those things with him.

Since Aiden was otherwise occupied, I scrolled through my contacts until I got to Danny's name. I hesitated a moment, wondering if it was a good idea to ask him to dinner. Then I felt silly for hesitating. Danny was my friend. I'd considered him my best friend, even, at times in my life. A friend could have dinner with a friend without it being weird.

I quickly shot off a text. *I'm starving. Wanna get dinner?*

I had to wait a couple minutes longer than I had with Aiden before a reply came in.

Sorry. Plans. Another day?

Plans. I hated that my mind immediately went to the wineglass bearing lipstick marks that I'd seen in his apartment the day before. Which was totally none of my business. Friends did not care if other friends had other friends who wore sexy lipstick.

I sent off what I hoped sounded like a nonchalant answer from a non-caring friend.

Sure. Another day.

Shot down twice in a row, I decided to soothe my ego's wounds with comfort food. I stopped at Panera for a quick clam chowder in a bread bowl and topped it off with a couple of chocolate-dipped cookies. I was feeling warm, full, and satisfied from the inside out by the time I finally pointed my Roadster toward home.

I slipped it into my designated spot in the underground parking then rode the elevator up to the twelfth floor where my loft apartment had a stunning view of downtown. I vaguely had the depressing thought that if business didn't pick up soon, I might have to downsize to something a little less view-centric and a little more budget-friendly. God forbid, maybe even in the Valley.

That last thought had my chowder gurgling in my stomach as I exited the elevator and stepped out into the hall.

Then froze.

Four doors down, a woman was standing outside my apartment door, banging her fists on it in a way that didn't seem like she was there for a friendly social call. Only as she turned away from the door and kicked it with the sole of her silver stiletto did I get a good look at her face and realized I knew the woman.

Jenna James.

CHAPTER SIX

———

My instinct was to just turn and get back into the elevator. But it was too late. Jenna had already spotted me.

"You!" She pointed a manicured fingernail at me. Hot pink with lots of sparkles.

"Me?" I asked, glancing over both shoulders as if I were an innocent bystander and surely she must be referring to someone else behind me.

"Yes, you." She crossed her arms over her ample bosom, encased in a top that was also hot pink and super sparkly. Then she shot me a narrowed-eyed look. "Unless there's some other private investigator my husband hired to follow me around."

Huh. Maybe Jenna wasn't such a ditz after all. "What makes you say that?" I asked, still trying to play at innocent.

"Please." She rolled her eyes. "Even my housekeeper noticed the car parked outside the house this morning."

Ouch. I tried not to let my ego take a hit at the fact we'd been far less stealthy than I'd hoped. Clearly we'd underestimated Jenna.

"Okay, yes. I am a private investigator."

"Duh."

"And your husband did come see me yesterday."

"Double duh. How do you think I found you?"

I paused. "Wait—Drake *told you* that he hired me?"

"Well, he couldn't very well deny it when I confronted him! I mean, first that brunette tags along everywhere I go all day, and then that Danny guy crashes my AAA meeting. It was pretty obvious what my husband was doing."

I glanced down the hallway, hoping none of my neighbors were listening at their keyholes. "Maybe you should come inside."

"Gladly," Jenna huffed as I unlocked my door.

I set my purse down on the side table and gestured toward the living room. "Have a seat?"

"I prefer to stand." She hiked her Birkin up on her shoulder and crossed her arms over her chest again in a combative stance.

"Okay," I told her as I assessed her. If she was grieving her husband's death, there was no sign of it. No tears, no red puffy eyes. Clearly no subdued mourning attire. Nothing to indicate that she'd lost a man she loved that day.

Then again, if she and her husband had been preparing for a messy divorce, maybe there hadn't been any love lost at all.

"So, what exactly can I do for you, Mrs. James?" I asked, trying to put on my best professional voice.

"You can tell your ADA friend to back the heck off!" she yelled. "I did not kill my husband!"

"Did he accuse you of that?" I asked, thinking back to my conversation with Aiden. He'd seemed interested in the wife but not particularly ready to jump to conclusions.

"I'm not stupid. I know what he was getting at with all these questions about where I was last night and what kind of 'terms' Drake and I were on. I mean, come on. We were separated—what kind of terms did he think we were on!?"

While I was honestly curious at the answers she might have given him to those questions, I shook my head. "Hang on. What makes you think I know the ADA?"

She did more eye narrowing, her false lashes kissing. "He told me 'someone' said my husband had hired a PI and that 'someone' saw me go home at ten o'clock. It didn't take a genius to figure out who that 'someone' was." She shot me a pointed look.

Okay, I'd give her that one. "You said you confronted Drake yesterday," I said, shifting gears. "Was this at his hotel?"

"What?" She shook her head. "No. I called him. On the phone."

"When?"

"After I got home last night. While you and Boy Toy were sitting across the street playing Peeping Tom."

Note to self: up your surveillance game. If Derek found out about this, he'd never let me live it down.

"So you called Drake. What did he say when you accused him of hiring me?"

"The idiot tried to deny it. But come on, how stupid do I look?"

I decided it best not to answer that question. Since I had, apparently like her husband, judged that incorrectly. "So he gave you my name?"

"After a few threats about what my lawyer was going to do to him in court, yeah. He did."

Threats. Interesting word. "I can't help but notice that you don't seem very broken up about losing your husband," I noted.

She narrowed her eyes at me again, highlighting the black eyeliner wings at the corners. "Soon to be *ex*-husband. We weren't exactly chummy. We hadn't been for a while, truth be told." She sighed, some of the fight softening out of her. "I guess I just thought being the wife of a rock star would be different, you know? More fun. More exciting."

I thought of the aging Halloween mask with legs that I'd met in my conference room the day before. I could see how the attraction might have worn off quickly.

"Anyway, " Jenna went on, "it's hard to drum up too much grief for a guy who hired PIs to follow you around."

Fair enough. "So, you figured out your husband had hired us to follow you, you threatened Drake on the phone. And then what?"

"And then nothing!" she said emphatically. "I told him to back off and hung up."

"And you didn't, say, continue the conversation in person at his hotel?"

"No, I did not!" The fight was back with a vengeance, her entire body tense as if she might lunge all five feet of her at me at any second. "I was nowhere near that pool, and I have no idea how my husband ended up in it!"

"Where were you last night, then?"

"At home! You saw me there!" She stabbed that long pink nail at me again.

"What did you do when we left your house?"

"I was tired. I went to bed."

"And you didn't leave the house again that night?"

She paused for a fraction of a second before slowly shaking her head in the negative. "Nope."

Not the most believable denial ever. A sentiment that must have shown on my face, as she continued.

"Look, I don't care what you think, but I did not kill my husband! And I told that DA Prince the same thing."

"Assistant DA," I corrected automatically. "And what exactly did you tell him?"

She frowned at me. "Nothing. I mean, there's nothing to tell. My stupid husband got drunk and fell in a hotel pool. End of story."

"Did Drake sound drunk when you talked to him on the phone?"

"What?" Her eyebrows pulled together.

"When you confronted him about being followed."

"Oh. Well, I-I don't know. I guess so. Drake always sounded kinda out of it."

From my one interaction with him, I had to agree with that assessment. "Jenna, I have to ask—are you the beneficiary of Drake's estate?"

She sucked in the side of her cheek, popping a hip out as she seemed to contemplate how much to share with me. But, considering it would be public knowledge soon anyway, she finally relented. "Yes, I am. I'm his wife, after all. There's nothing weird about a wife inheriting her husband's money."

"Inheriting *all* of his money sure beats *possibly* getting *some* alimony."

"That," she said, the sparkly pink nail getting precariously close to my nose this time, "is a slanderous accusation!"

"I didn't accuse you of anything," I pointed out.

"What's it to you, anyway? Drake's gone, so you're out of a job." She smirked.

It was getting easier and easier to not like her. "And you've avoided a divorce," I countered.

"I didn't kill him!" she protested again. "Look, if you really want to know who had it in for Drake, talk to his bandmates."

While it was, as she'd pointed out, none of my business now who'd had it in for Drake, I couldn't help curiosity getting the better of me. "His bandmates?" I asked.

Jenna nodded. "The Deadly Devils."

"Are they still together?' I asked, trying to think of the last time I'd heard of them having a new release.

Jenna shook her head. "No. They stopped touring and recording years ago. But a couple of months ago, Drake brought a lawsuit against the other band members."

"Oh?" I felt my right eyebrow raise. "What was he suing the band about?" I asked.

Jenna averted her eyes. "I didn't get involved in that. Something about rights and royalties."

Again I got the feeling I wasn't getting the full truth, but she continued before I had a chance to delve into it.

"But I do know that the other band members weren't too happy about it. Especially the drummer, Bash," she said.

"This Bash have a last name?" I asked.

She shook her head. "Nope. Just Bash."

"Okay, so you think Bash might have been unhappy enough to hurt Drake?"

"Oh yeah." Jenna nodded. "Bash has always had a temper. And a violent streak. When he found out Drake had filed the suit, he showed up at our place yelling threats at Drake until he had to call the cops."

I wasn't sure if she really felt Bash was a threat or if she was just deflecting guilt away from herself. "Did you tell all of this to ADA Prince?" I asked her.

"I did." She nodded again. "So, go bother someone who really had it in for my husband and just…leave me alone, okay?"

I put my hands up in a surrender motion. "You won't see me again."

"And tell your ADA friend to back off too!"

That, I couldn't promise. But I just nodded. "I'm sure he'll get to the truth of the matter."

Which was why I was leaving it in his hands. Not my case. Not my murder.

At least that's the mantra I mentally chanted to myself as I watched Jenna James walk down the hallway to the elevator and I shut my door on what I hoped was the end of the matter.

* * *

The next morning, I awoke to the California sunshine streaming through the curtains in my bedroom, the scent of breakfast burritos wafting up to my loft from the food truck across the street, and a car alarm going off in the adjacent parking garage. Good morning, LA.

I yawned, rolling over to grab my phone from the bedside table, and checked the time. Just past seven. I lay back on my pillow, inhaling the scents of chorizo and onions. The car alarm finally subsided with a couple chirps from someone's key fob. I contemplated going back to sleep, but it was too late. I was wide awake. I reluctantly dragged myself out of bed and into a long, hot shower.

Since I was short on work and long on bills, I decided overcompensation in the wardrobe department was in order that day. After taking my time digging through my closet, I opted for a long sleeved wrap dress in a deep purple color that hit just below the knee. The three-inch heels that capped off the outfit ensured that I'd have at least a few inches over the average guy, a position that shifted the power dynamic in my favor more often than you'd think. I went extra on the mascara, light on the lips— doing a pale nude matte—and upped the bronzer as a concession to the sparse winter sunlight.

I booted up my coffeemaker, scrolling through my email on my phone as I waited for a cup. Sadly, it didn't take long, as there were precious few messages. While I'd tried to put on a hopeful face for the girls about business picking up soon, this was the leanest things had been in a long time. Probably since I'd taken over the reins.

I shoved that anxiety-producing thought aside as an email from Maya popped into my inbox. I opened it, scanning the contents as I poured a cup of coffee, heavy on the flavored creamer. She'd sent over a few images that she said she'd used in some social media ads that were live that morning. Okay, so things were lean, but my girls were on it!

I sipped as I clicked open the first one, my heart full of hope that it would generate some real leads.

It was a photo of a man in a dog suit, the caption reading: "Is your husband in the doghouse?" I frowned. Cute, I guess. Not a lot of content. Didn't quite highlight our experience and professionalism. I scrolled to the next one.

A man in a bunny suit was being hit over the head by a female bunny wielding a carrot. The caption: "Has your husband been making like a bunny with someone else?"

I cringed, daring to scroll to one more.

A fluffy cat with a scowl on its face sat above the caption: "Why is this cat grumpy? His wife hired the Bond Agency!"

I was just contemplating a change of career when my phone rang in my hands.

Like a rookie, I swiped it on without checking the readout first. "Bond."

"Hey, kid," Derek's voice boomed in my ear.

I took a deep, cleansing breath. I wasn't sure I could deal with my father on only one cup of coffee. Not that I didn't love my dad—I did. I just loved him best in small doses at well-spaced intervals. "Hey," I said, finding my voice. "What's up?"

"Just calling to check on my favorite daughter."

"I'm your only daughter."

"That's my story, and I'm sticking to it." He chuckled at his own joke. While Derek had had a steady girlfriend for the last couple of years, she was the only steady girlfriend I'd ever remembered him having. The chances of little Dereks running around all over LA were not insignificant. "So, how's business?" he asked.

I narrowed my eyes at the phone. "Did you say you wanted to check on me or check *up* on me?"

He was laughing again on the other end, and I heard a hissing sound in the background like the top of a beer cap popping. "Hey, I know it's not your fault adulterers are germaphobes right now. I'm sure business will pick up. It always does. Why, I bet all this forced togetherness is gonna bring about a boom of cheaters soon."

I blew out a breath. "Yeah, from your lips to horny husbands' ears."

I heard Derek take a noisy slurp of beer. "Hey, you hear about that dead rock star?"

I nodded, even though I knew he couldn't see me. "Yeah. Drowned. Tragedy." I paused, hesitating to tell him the truth. But I figured he'd nose it out at some point anyway. He was, after all, a retired PI. "He was actually a client."

"No kidding? Wow. Then it really is a tragedy. You get payment up front?"

I rolled my eyes. "I'm not cashing his retainer check now." Though, the thought had crossed my mind. Briefly. What can I say—my morals weren't quite as unflappable as Aiden's.

"The Deadly Devils," Derek continued. "You remember we used to listen to their music all the time?"

"*You* used to listen to it," I corrected him.

But he didn't seem to notice. "Man, those were the days when music was music. Real instruments. None of this synthesizers and beats stuff. Guitars. Drums. Raw vocals."

"Yep, good stuff, Derek," I said, grabbing my keys and purse.

"Remember when we saw them live at the Bowl? I won us tickets off the radio and got those awesome front-row seats?"

"That was Barb."

"What?"

"You were dating Barb then. You took her to the concert. Not me."

"You sure?"

"Positive, Derek," I said, grabbing a light jacket and making for the door.

"Barb, Barb…" Derek chanted, clearly trying to place the name.

"The redhead who had a thing for neon spandex and Aqua Net."

Derek chuckled as recognition set in. "Right! Barb. How could I forget her? Man, was she limber. She had this way of twisting her—"

"Okay, cool, well, this has been a good chat," I said, cutting him off before I heard way more about his former lover than I wanted to know. "I gotta go. I'm late for work."

"I thought you didn't have any work?"

"Bye, Derek." I didn't wait for an answer before stabbing the phone off.

CHAPTER SEVEN

———

Maya was alone in reception when I pushed through the frosted glass doors of the agency, embellished with the single word *Bond* in bold black letters. As soon as she spotted me, she popped up eagerly from her desk. "Hey, did you get my email with the ads?"

I nodded. "I did."

"And?" Her eyes shone with anticipation. "They're super cute, right?"

"They are...cute," I agreed. Ish. "I don't know if we're sending the right message though. I mean, maybe we want to project a more professional image?"

"Oh, no. This is totally on trend," she assured me. "According to Connor, animals are the most shared images on the internet. Followed closely by wine jokes and videos of babies with grumpy faces. And Kylie assured me that this is the font most responded to by the Boomers. Though I did tell her that technically most of our clientele are Gen Xers and not Boomers, but she said that Boomer is a state of mind. Anyway, both Misha and Braxton agreed that these had all the elements to go viral, especially if we did a TBT version with like some vintage stuff."

I blinked, my only-had-one-cup-of-coffee brain trying hard to follow her. "Wait—who are Connor and Misha and... Who else did you say?"

"Kylie and Braxton. They're my social media consultants."

"I didn't authorize any consultants," I said, feeling sudden panic take hold. The last thing I needed was to increase overhead. I already had three employees and only one client, and that math did not add up well.

But Maya just smiled and shook her head. "Don't worry. They were happy to consult for free. Especially since they're all mainly still doing digital school."

I paused. "School? So, they're still college students?"

"Well..." Maya shrugged. "Not exactly. I mean, I'm sure they will be someday, but they're kinda still in high school right now."

"High school. Teenagers." I felt my right eye start to twitch. I needed more coffee. Stat.

"Trust me, they are like the foremost authorities on the internet! I mean, who better to know what sells there, right? Misha practically lives on social media."

"Because she's probably too young to drive," I muttered.

"Only for another three months," Maya assured me.

"Caffeine. I need caffeine."

I must have looked scary, as Maya took a step back. "I'll go for a Starbucks run."

I took a deep breath. "Thank you."

"Uh, but first, there's actually someone waiting for you in the conference room." She pointed down the short hallway to the closed door.

"Someone?" I asked, giving her a questioning look.

Maya nodded, her ponytail bobbing behind her. "Said he needed to see you urgently. Gave his name as Bash." She shrugged.

I felt my stomach clench with a bad feeling. I knew that name. Jenna had said he was the drummer of Deadly Devils. She'd also said he was violent and could have killed her husband.

And now he was in my conference room.

"Did he say what he wanted?" I asked, trying to keep the sudden nerves out of my voice.

Maya shook her head. "He didn't say. But he wouldn't take no for an answer. I told him you were out and he could make an appointment for later, but he insisted on waiting here."

Fabulous. I took a deep breath. "Okay. I'll go talk to him."

I took a moment to set my purse down in my office and gather up some courage before crossing to the conference room and pulling the door open.

The tall, broad-shouldered guy taking in the view out my windows was nothing like the previous aging rock star I'd had in my offices. His build looked more like a bouncer than a drummer. He was at least a foot taller than I was and possibly weighed twice as much. And while I could tell his age was close to Drake's, this guy was built like a bull—thick and sturdy. His head was shaved, his biceps strained against his black T-shirt, and when he spun around at the sound of my entrance, a pair of dark, calculating eyes met mine above a pointed goatee that reminded me of the devil.

"Are you Bond?" he demanded in a British accent that was anything but upper-crust. Thick arms crossed over his chest. Legs encased in dark denim were set in a wide stance. A snarl sat on his lips like he was ready to snap.

I swallowed and slowly nodded. "I am. Jamie Bond." I offered a hand his way, but he just looked at it.

"You're the PI Drake hired?" he asked.

Apparently everyone knew the dead man's business. I licked my lips, reluctant to admit to much until I knew why the drummer was here. "I did meet with Drake."

"What did that tosser tell you?"

I shook my head, slowly sitting at the conference table and clasping my hands in front of me. "I'm sorry. I can't tell you that."

"Oh, you can't, can you?" Bash took a menacing step forward, and I had to mentally remind myself that he wasn't likely to resort to actual physical violence in the offices of a PI where there were witnesses. At least, I hoped Maya had held off on the Starbucks run and was around to witness.

"No," I said, holding my ground with more bravery than I felt. "Client confidentiality prevents me from divulging the contents of any discussion we might have had."

"So Drake *was* your client?"

I nodded slowly. "Yes."

Bash put both hands on the table, leaning down so close to me that I could smell his morning eggs on his breath. "What did he hire you to do?"

I matched his hard look with one of my own. "Like I said, I can't tell you that."

He worked his jaw back and forth, chewing on that for a moment. "Alright, fine." He straightened up, walking back toward the windows again. "Just tell me this: is it about hot waitress?"

I felt a frown pull my brows together. "A hot waitress?" No one had mentioned Jenna waiting tables.

"Not *a* hot waitress. 'Hot Waitress.' The song."

My blank look must have told him I still had no idea what he was talking about, as he added, "Our song."

"This was a Deadly Devils song?" I surmised.

Bash nodded. "Not just any song. A *hit*. A bloody mega hit."

I tried to conjure up the lyrics to any of their tunes, but nothing came to mind. "Why do you think Drake came to me about one of your songs?" I asked, still not connecting the dots.

Bash paced back over toward the table and pulled out a chair, sinking into it with a sigh. "Look, I'm sure Drake told you about the lawsuit."

"I've heard of it," I said, even if it hadn't been from Drake himself but Jenna. "Although, I'm not clear on all the details," I admitted. "Why don't you fill me in on what this lawsuit is about?"

"It's about bullcrap!" Bash said emphatically. "Drake's suing the band for rights to the song. He says he wrote it, but that's total bullocks."

"Oh? Who did write it?"

"I did!" He puffed his chest out. "And I defy anyone to say differently."

That was interesting wording. "Okay, so why do you think Drake was claiming *he* wrote it?"

"Because he's a greedy tosser!" He paused. "Or was," he amended, seemingly remembering the need for past tense. "Look, 'Hot Waitress' came out over thirty years ago. It was a B side to one of our singles. Never even got any airplay to speak of."

Which didn't sound like a mega-hit to me, but I just nodded for him to continue.

"If Drake had wanted to claim some right to it, he should have done it then."

"So, why was he claiming it now?"

Bash snorted. "Because now it's making money."

"Oh?" I asked.

"Yeah, and lots of it." Bash nodded. "Last year Apple used the song in one of their iPhone commercials, and the thing blew up. It was downloaded thousands of times in under a minute. Suddenly it's on the charts, hitting higher than it ever had. Went platinum."

"Wow."

"Yeah, well, wow was right when we started seeing the royalty checks. I ain't seen cash like that in years."

"So, when the cash started coming in, Drake suddenly alleged that the song belonged to him?" I asked, starting to get a clearer picture.

Bash's features went dark again, his jaw clenching. "That's right. Trying to shaft us like that was not cool. Us! His bandmates."

"He was suing the entire band. But you said *you* wrote the song?" I said, things not quite adding up.

Bash's eyes went to the view again. "Yeah, well, we was a band. We always collaborated. We're all credited as the songwriters. We used to have jam sessions and just pound them out. 'Hot Waitress' was no different."

"But you say you wrote it?" I asked again, wondering how much stock I put in that.

"Yeah." He puffed out his chest defiantly.

"But Drake claimed he wrote it."

"That's right."

"Did he have anything to back up his claim?"

"'Course not! 'Cause it ain't true."

"Drake's lawyer must have thought he had a legitimate argument if he agreed to take Drake on as a client," I pointed out.

Bash turned a pair of angry eyes on me, as if I'd been the one to take Drake's case. "Yeah, well his lawyer is an idiot if he believed that crap Drake was spewing." He paused. "But I'm guessing that's where you come in."

"Me?" I asked.

"Admit it—Drake hired you to find proof he wrote that song."

I blinked at him. While that had clearly *not* been why Drake had hired me, I felt like I'd already given Bash more than I'd intended. "I'm not admitting to anything," I told him. "Yes, Drake hired me. But why is between me and my client."

"Who is dead," Bash said.

Like I needed reminded.

I just gave him a palms-up shrug, indicating there was nothing I could do.

Bash narrowed his dark eyes. "Fine. You can only talk to your clients?"

I nodded.

"Then I'm hiring you."

I froze mid-nod. "What?"

"I'm your client now. I'm hiring you to find proof that *I* wrote that song. Not Drake."

I shook my head. "Wait—that's not what I said. I can't take you on as a client. That's a conflict of interest."

"Whose interest?" Bash spread his hands wide. "Drake's dead," he pointed out unnecessarily again.

"Look, I'm not even sure what sort of proof there could be."

"Tapes. Recordings of our jam sessions. They'll show you who really came up with the idea for the song. Because I know it wasn't Drake."

I tapped the toe of my stiletto on the ground, my mind churning this over. According to Jenna James, Bash was potentially a murderer. And I wasn't sure I bought his convenient claim to "Hot Waitress." I could see just by the way he paced my office that the guy was tightly wound, and he had more than enough brawn to be able to toss Drake into the Beverly Hotel pool without breaking a sweat. Or even a nail. My better judgment said to pass hard on this one.

"As you pointed out, Drake's gone. Why does the author of the song matter now?" I asked, stalling.

"Because my lawyer says the lawsuit is still pending. If the court rules in Drake's favor, the royalties go to his estate."

His estate. Meaning Jenna. I had a fleeting thought that maybe her pointing a finger at Bash as her husband's murderer was more self-serving than I'd originally thought.

"Before I even consider taking on your request, I have to ask you one thing," I said, choosing my words carefully. "Where were you last night?"

Bash frowned. "Me? Why?"

"Because it's possible Drake didn't just fall into a pool and drown. It's possible he was pushed."

His eyes narrowed again, a flash of anger in their dark depths. "And you think I pushed him?"

"I think I'd like to know where you were."

"I was at the gym." He gave me his defiant look again, as if challenging me to dispute it.

Not the most convincing alibi. And I wasn't getting the most forthcoming vibes from the guy either. In fact, the vibes I was getting were all waving little red flags that, if we'd had more than one client on our roster at the moment, I'd have paid attention to immediately.

"So, you in or not?" Bash demanded, making it sound like more of a threat than a question. "'Cause I got cash." Then he reached a hand into his back pocket and pulled out a wad of hundreds.

Hundreds. Not twenties. I tried not to drool as he counted a few of them out on the table.

"Cash works for me," I said before my better judgment could stop me.

CHAPTER EIGHT

———

"I thought you said this was not our case?" Sam said, giving me a knowing look an hour later as she, Caleigh, and Maya sat in reception with fresh coffee in hands, Maya having made good on her Starbucks promise.

"You're right," I told her. "Drake's death is not our case. Our case is now the song."

"'Hot Waitress,'" Caleigh said.

"You know it?" I asked, turning to her as I sipped my drink. It was hot, sweet, and giving me both a sugar and caffeine high. Heaven.

Caleigh nodded. "Next to 'Being Rick-rolled,' it's the most shared song online right now. It's hecka popular."

"And apparently hecka lucrative," I said, sharing with them the story Bash had told me. "If Drake had been able to prove he wrote the song and owned the rights, it would mean a lot of money lost to the rest of the band."

"Which sounds like it could make the band angry enough to commit murder," Maya jumped in.

I shot her a look. "We're not investigating a murder."

She shrugged. "Just saying."

I frowned. "Yeah, the wife *just said* too." I quickly filled them in on my visit the night before with Jenna.

"You think she was telling you the truth about not leaving the house after you and Danny left?" Sam asked.

I pursed my lips. "I'm not sure. If I had to guess, she was hiding something. What? I don't know."

"It could be she didn't *leave* but her boyfriend *did* come over later?" Caleigh offered. "After killing Drake."

"Or possibly she was actually pointing you in the right direction with Bash. If Drake had found proof he wrote the song, Bash might want to get rid of him before he could show his lawyer," Sam said.

"But then why come here and hire us to find the proof that *Bash* wrote it?" Maya asked.

Sam shrugged. "Maybe he killed Drake but wants to make sure the proof isn't still out there?"

"Maybe it's a red herring?" Caleigh said. "A misdirect to make him look innocent?"

"*Maybe* we should focus on the case we have and not the murder," I suggested.

Caleigh pouted.

"Killjoy," Sam said.

I shook my head. "Look, we're just looking for some old cassette tapes or videos or notes. No killers. Just a song."

Maya sighed, clearly as disappointed as the others. "Okay, where do you want to start?"

I turned to Caleigh. "I'd like to know if the studio where the band made their original recordings kept any masters."

After Bash had left, I'd gone to my trusty friend Google and found out everything I could about the history of the Deadly Devils. They had, as I'd already heard, been moderately popular for a couple of years during the hair metal days in the nineties. Enough that there'd been the expected amount of touring, groupies, drugs, and debauchery that qualified one for rock star status. The band had consisted of Drake, the lead singer, Bash, the drummer, and three other members—a guitarist, a bass player, and a keyboard player who'd left the group after their second album. The band was managed by a guy named Alvin Carmichael, who kept an office in North Hollywood, and the last time any of them had played together professionally had been over a decade ago.

According to the Wikipedia page I'd found, the band's first two albums—including the one featuring "Hot Waitress"—had been recorded at a place called Dragonfly Studios in Inglewood. After that, the keyboard player had left and the rest of the band had done one more studio album, recorded somewhere in Mexico, where apparently studio time was cheap.

The band's popularity had already started to fizzle at that point, and the gigs stopped coming shortly afterward.

I gave Caleigh the address of Dragonfly Studios. "It's possible the studio kept masters of some of the raw early tracks or the jam sessions Bash mentioned that might give us a clue to who wrote the song."

Caleigh nodded. "I'm on it."

I turned to Maya. "In the meantime, maybe you can track down some current contact info for the other band members?"

Maya nodded.

"And," I continued, "I'm going to pay a visit to the group's manager, Mr. Carmichael, and see what his take on the lawsuit is."

"I'm guessing that leaves me on Gammy Manchester again?" Sam said from her spot on the sofa.

I nodded. "How did it go with Alejandro last night?"

Sam shrugged. "After the potluck, they both went back to Gammy's place, watched a little TV, then went to bed."

I shrugged. "I guess older people go to sleep early."

"Oh, I didn't say they went to *sleep*. They were awake for quite some time. And very vocal." Sam's face took on a pained expression at the memory.

Maya did a snort-slash-giggle thing.

"Please tell me you didn't watch?" Caleigh said, clearly trying hard to contain laughter.

"No way. It was traumatic enough to have to listen. But even from a bench in the adjacent garden, I couldn't help hearing them. Over and over," she emphasized.

"Wow." Apparently Alejandro wasn't just smoldering *looks*. "Well, good for her," I decided. "At least someone is getting some."

All four of us single girls contemplated that thought for a moment.

"Well, I'm off to North Hollywood," I said with about as much enthusiasm as anyone about to enter the Valley could muster. "Wish me luck."

* * *

Alvin Carmichael's offices were in a large, nondescript building off Vanowen that looked like every other grey, stucco office building on the block. Four stories high, square, and dingy from years of smog exposure, it was far from the high rises of Wilshire. Then again, Deadly Devils were far from A-listers also.

I parked my Roadster beneath a tall palm tree in the lot at the rear of the building and made my way inside, where a directory near the back door told me Carmichael Management was on the third floor. The elevator smelled like stale cigarette smoke and groaned as it struggled up the two flights. I let out a sigh of relief when the doors finally opened on the third floor and made a mental note to take the stairs on the way down.

Carmichael's office was located at the end of the hallway, indicated by a brass sign on the door covered in fingerprints and a layer of grime of indeterminate origin. I gave a quick knock on the door before pushing inside to find myself in a small reception room.

"May I help you?" a dark-haired woman asked from behind an oak desk. She looked about as nondescript and grey as the building itself, her expression one of neutral boredom.

"Hi, I'm Jamie Bond, and I'm here to see Mr. Carmichael," I told her, giving her what I hoped was a pleasant smile.

"Do you have an appointment?" she asked.

I shook my head. "No, but one of the talent he manages is a client of mine."

"One moment," she said in a monotone that told me she really didn't care who I was or why I was there.

She rose from the desk and traveled the three steps down a short hallway to a closed door. She gave a sharp rap before opening it and sticking her head in, the rest of her body hanging back in the hallway as she talked in muffled tones to someone inside. After a moment, she popped back out and addressed me. "What did you say your name was again?"

"Bond. Jamie Bond of the Bond Agency." I purposely neglected to tell her what kind of agency it was. I'd learned that in entertainment circles, it helped get a foot in the door if people labored under the misconception that I was the kind of agent that could book you on a film set rather than the kind that would catch you doing naughty deeds and report it to your spouse.

The receptionist turned back to the doorway, relaying the info to the person in the other room. Who apparently deemed me worthy of his time, as she finally stepped back and gestured toward the door. "Mr. Carmichael will see you now."

"Thanks," I told her, giving her a bright smile as I passed her.

That she completely ignored.

The inner office was just a shade bigger than a closet and gave off a distinct vibe of claustrophobia with the amount of clutter packed into it. Large file cabinets stood in the two back corners, both topped with stacks of folders and loose papers threatening to topple over. A desk sat in the middle of the room, the top littered with more papers and various electronics. It was flanked by two leather chairs showing wear on the arms. One small window sat on the back wall, though most of the light in the room came from buzzing fluorescents overhead.

Behind the desk stood a slight man with thinning brown hair, a pale complexion, and a dark suit that seemed to hang on his thin frame. A dark mustache twitched above his lip, and his eyebrows seemed pinched together in a slightly pained expression.

"Alvin Carmichael." He stepped from behind the desk to greet me.

"Nice to meet you," I told him.

"My, uh, receptionist said we have a client in common?" Carmichael gestured to one of the worn leather chairs as an invitation to sit.

Which I did, feeling a sort of sticky film on it. "Yes. I was hoping to ask you some questions about the band Deadly Devils."

Carmichael's pained expression deepened, and he opened a desk drawer, extracting a bottle of antacids. "I feared you were. Press has been unrelenting."

"I'm sorry for your loss," I told him.

He popped one of the pills into his mouth and crunched down loudly. "Thank you. It's been a...shock." He paused. "What sort of agency did you say you ran?"

I shifted in my seat. "I'm a private investigator," I told him, coming clean.

Carmichael's skin paled even further, looking an almost sickly grey beneath the fluorescent lights. "A private investigator..." He trailed off, sinking slowly back down into his desk chair, which groaned with a creak. He shook his head. "I've been fielding calls all day from the press and the police. And now a private investigator."

"Were you and Drake close?" I asked, trying to sound sympathetic, lest the guy pass out on me.

"Well, I don't know about close. But, I've been managing the band since they started. Almost thirty years now."

"That's a long time. You must have gotten to know the band well."

He let out a short, humorless laugh, but I was glad to see his color returning some. "Well, it's not as if we're best friends. Most of that time I've been on damage control."

"Damage control?" I clarified.

"Trying to keep the more, shall we say, distasteful antics of the band out of the media." He shook his head. "You don't get a reputation like the Devils did by being angels."

"Any recent antics come to mind?" I asked, trying to get a better picture of the dynamics of the band.

"Oh, the usual." Carmichael blew out a breath. "Last year Bash threatened a paparazzi member who took an unflattering picture of him at the beach. And there was a DUI from Keith, some woman claiming to be carrying Harry's baby, and as soon as Drake discovered Twitter, he had to be monitored constantly to make sure he didn't say anything libelous."

"Sounds like babysitting the band is a full-time job."

"It is. I tell you, I'm on high blood pressure medication, antianxiety medication, and my doctor thinks I'm developing an ulcer. All thanks to the Devils!"

"And now Drake's death."

The pained expression was back, his eyebrows pulling together. "Yes. Terrible tragedy."

"I understand there was some tension lately between Drake and the other band members?" I asked.

Carmichael didn't answer right away, grabbing his bottle of antacids and extracting another one. "Who did you say your client was?"

I cleared my throat. As twitchy as the guy seemed, he was careful. Then again, he'd just admitted that the better part of his life had been spent cleaning up the Devils' messes. He had reason to be.

"I'm afraid client confidentially prevents me from saying." I paused. "But I did meet with Drake Deadly the day before he died."

Carmichael popped the pill into his mouth and chewed. "I see."

"I understand Drake was suing the rest of the band. Over rights to a song called 'Hot Waitress,'" I said, coming to the actual point of my visit.

"That's right." He blew out a breath. "But I'm sure the guys would have worked it out. I mean, it's not like the song was worth killing over."

I gave him a questioning look. No one had said anything about killing.

Yet.

"You think Drake was intentionally drowned?" I asked, watching his reaction carefully.

"Well, I…I mean, that's what I assumed from the way the ADA was talking," he sputtered, backtracking.

"ADA Aiden Prince?" I asked. "He was here to see you?"

Carmichael nodded slowly, as if unsure he should admit to anything. "Yes. Earlier this morning. He wanted to know about the meeting."

I frowned. "What meeting?"

Carmichael licked his lips. "The meeting Drake called the night he died."

This was news to me. And it must have shown on my face, as Carmichael added, "That's why we were all at the hotel that night. Drake said he needed to talk to us."

"Who is *all*?" I asked. "You and…"

"And the band." Carmichael shook his head. "But I told you, none of them would have harmed Drake. They were like family."

Family who sued each other. But I set that aside, focusing on something else he'd said. "The entire band was at the Beverly Hotel the night that Drake died. All the members?"

"W-well, yeah. I mean, Keith was a little late, but he was there. Harry too. We were all at the bar. Waiting for Drake."

"And Bash? Was he there too?"

Carmichael nodded. "Yes. Everyone. Why?"

Because my client had told me he'd been at the gym. Those waving red flags started chanting *I told you so*, and I had a sinking feeling the wad of cash sitting in my desk drawer at the agency was going to have to be returned.

"No reason," I said, trying to ignore the dread collecting in the pit of my stomach. "So, you said Drake called a band meeting. Why?"

Carmichael sucked in more air, as if he were having a hard time getting enough. "Drake said he had something he wanted to show everyone."

"Must have been something important for everyone to show up," I said, immediately thinking of the proof of song ownership that I'd been hired to find. "What was it?"

"I don't know," Carmichael answered. "Drake never made it. I mean, we all waited a good hour, but when Drake never appeared, we all assumed he'd changed his mind or had one too many and passed out somewhere. We never imagined he was…" He trailed off, swallowing hard, his eyes bouncing around the room as if struggling for something to look at that didn't make him envision how Drake had been found.

"What time was this meeting supposed to take place?" I asked.

"Uh, eleven."

Which was right in the window Aiden had given me for Drake's time of death. "That's a little late for a business meeting," I noted.

Carmichael shrugged. "Not for rock stars. These guys didn't usually get out of bed until afternoon."

"You mentioned Keith and Harry. I think I read that they played guitar and bass for the band, correct?"

Carmichael nodded.

"Didn't the band have a keyboard player there too?"

"Uh, yeah. Tosh. Tosh Thomas."

"Was he at the hotel that night as well?"

"No. No, he left the group years ago. I haven't seen him in forever. I think he moved back East or something," Carmichael added. "Why?"

"Just trying to get a clear picture of what happened that night."

He shrugged and sighed. "I'm not sure we'll ever have that. I mean, it's not like Drake can tell us what happened." He sighed, looking positively ill again.

"Mr. Carmichael, what can you tell me about 'Hot Waitress'?" I asked him, changing gears.

"Uh, well, what do you want to know?" He clasped his hands on the desk in front of him, looking grateful for the change of subject.

"Drake was claiming he wrote the song originally. But I understand some of the band members didn't agree with that?"

"Right, yeah. Drake even had a lawyer. Served the other guys notice of a civil suit."

"Did you know about this beforehand? That Drake was planning to sue?"

"Me?" Carmichael squeaked out. "No. No, I would have strongly advised against it."

"And why is that? Did you think Drake's claims were false?"

He shook his head. "Honestly? I don't know. I never had a hand in the creative side of things. As long as the record company was happy, what the band wrote was up to the band."

"So you don't know who wrote the song?" I clarified. "Or if, say, someone else in the band might have written it?"

"Like Bash?" Carmichael asked. "Yeah, I've heard his claim too."

"And you don't believe it?"

Carmichael shrugged his slim shoulders. "Who knows? Maybe he did."

"What about the other band members? Keith and Harry? What did they think?"

"I can't imagine they were happy about the lawsuit, but you'd have to ask them."

"They ever say who they thought had written the song?"

Carmichael shook his head. "But they wouldn't now, would they? I mean, the band splits royalties five ways right now. If *either* Drake or Bash proved in court that they should own the rights, the rest of the band would be out of luck."

"Can I ask what sort of royalties we're talking about?"

Carmichael gave me a dubious look, like that was pushing it.

"My client mentioned that the song had a resurgence in popularity recently," I added.

"It did. Thanks to that commercial." He sighed, relenting. "I-I don't have exact numbers in front of me, but royalties were in the high six figures last quarter."

Whoa. "High six figures just last quarter?"

Carmichael nodded. "Each."

I took a moment to drag my tongue off the floor. "That's one hot waitress."

"You're telling me," he agreed.

"And a lot on the line if Drake's claim had any merit."

Carmichael licked his lips again. "That band…they were like brothers. None of them ever would have harmed Drake. I mean, they've known each other for decades." He gave me a pleading look, like he hoped I was buying his reasoning.

"Did Drake ever tell you if he had anything to back up his ownership claims?"

"No." The manager shook his head.

"Do you think it's possible he found something and was going to show that proof to the band the night he died?"

He paused before answering, his chest rising and falling quickly, as if he'd definitely had the same thought. And it was giving him minor heart palpitations.

"I don't know why Drake called the meeting," he said, repeating his earlier line. "And at this point, I doubt we ever will."

I sincerely hoped he was wrong. Because if it had anything to do with the song rights, I was possibly working for a murderer.

* * *

I left Carmichael with my business card and took the stairs down the two flights to the parking lot. The bright sunlight was a welcome relief from the artificial lights of his office, and I sucked in cool, crisp air along with it.

My mind churned over what Carmichael had told me as I unlocked my car and slipped inside. Drake calling an important meeting right before his death put a whole new spin on things. Especially since he'd never had the chance to tell anyone *why* he'd called it. Clearly he hadn't been on good terms with his bandmates, so it must have been important for him to reach out. And they must have thought it important to show up.

Even my client, who'd said he'd been elsewhere at the time.

Bash had come to my office assuming Drake had hired me to find proof that Drake had written "Hot Waitress." But just because Bash was still looking for that proof now, that didn't mean he hadn't killed Drake first to prevent him from telling the rest of the band about it.

Of course, the other band members had just as much to lose as Bash, if that was the reason Drake had called them all to the hotel. And at least the guitar and bass players had just as much opportunity to stop him, too. Any one of them could have shown up a little early for the meeting and killed Drake first.

But if that was what Drake had been planning the night he died, where was that proof now? Had the killer taken it? Destroyed it? Or was it still out there?

I picked up my phone and called Aiden's number. Four rings in, it went to voicemail.

"Hey, Aiden, it's me," I started. "Listen, I was wondering if you guys have found something among Drake's possessions at the hotel. Something relating to an old song he may have written. Like maybe cassette tapes or recordings." I knew it was a long shot, but if Drake had been about to present proof of his ownership to the band, it's possible he'd had a copy of it on hand. "Specifically relating to a song called 'Hot Waitress.' It's possible it had something to do with his death and why the band was at the hotel. Anyway, call me back when you get a chance. Thanks."

I hung up, feeling a little like I was chasing down a poodle when there was an elephant running loose. Who wrote a song thirty years ago was certainly going to seem secondary to Aiden while he was trying to figure out how a celebrity had died.

But, I reminded myself, as long as I wanted to deposit Bash's cash, the poodle was my case. While I was feeling a little unsettled over the fact my client had given me a false alibi, I wasn't 100% ready to write him off as a murderer. At least not yet. There was no way I would take a murderer's money. A mostly innocent guy who just lied about his gym dedication…that was possibly another story.

I picked my phone up again and called the office number.

"Bond Agency," Maya answered, her voice the perfect blend of perk and professionalism.

"Hey, it's me," I told her.

"Hey, boss. Did you meet with the band's manager?" she asked.

"I did." I quickly relayed the gist of our conversation to her. "I'd like to talk to the other band members who were there that night. Have you been able to get their contact info yet?"

"The guys who were at the hotel that night—yes." I heard rustling as Maya shifted papers at her desk. "I haven't been able to find anything on the old keyboard player yet. It's like he disappeared after he left the band. But I did track down the guitarist and bass player."

"I'm assuming they're local?"

"They are," Maya confirmed. "Keith Kane and Harry Star. They're roommates, sharing a house in Tujunga, just over the canyon. They do a podcast from there every week about the current hair metal scene."

"There is one?"

"Apparently the genre is hard to kill," Maya said. "I'll text you the address."

"Thanks," I told her before hanging up.

A moment later my phone buzzed with the info she'd sent over, and I pulled out of the parking lot, heading toward the 5.

CHAPTER NINE

The city of Tujunga was nestled at the north end of the LA Basin, the last outpost of civilization before the outer hinterlands that existed beyond the city. Or so I'm told. No self-respecting Angelino ever traveled east of the 210.

The address Maya had given me for Keith and Harry was a turn of the millennium style McMansion, set on a small plot of land in a row of several other almost identical McMansions, all with small squares of lawn, spindly trees struggling to compete with the towering two-story homes, and three-car garages set close to the street. Keith and Harry's place was done in a pale peach colored stucco with a red tile roof that I assumed was supposed to evoke visions of Spanish haciendas, but in reality the high archways and rounded windows just reminded me how terrible mass-produced architecture could be.

The small yard was tidy, if lacking the personal touches of a gardening enthusiast, and as I stepped from my car, I could hear the wail of a guitar from somewhere inside the home. I beeped my Roadster locked and made my way up a stone pathway to the front door. I rang the doorbell beside the solid wood door inlaid with wrought iron touches, listening to it chime on the other side. No answer. I gave it a twenty-count, and when no one had appeared, I tried again. This time the guitar screeching stopped, and a few seconds later, I heard footsteps approaching on the other side.

"Yeah?" The door opened to reveal a tall, skinny guy. He had a hooked nose with a pair of blue tinted glasses perched on it, and he was dressed in bell-bottomed jeans and a loose tunic style shirt. His long dark hair was liberally shot with grey as it hung over his shoulders.

"Hi, I'm looking for Keith Kane and Harry Star?"

The guy shifted, and I could see an electric guitar slung over his back. "I'm Keith." He glanced behind me, as if looking for a clue to my identity. "Can I help you?"

"I hope so. My name's Jamie Bond. I'm a private investigator. I was hoping I could ask you a few questions."

"Whoa." Keith tilted his head down to squint at me over the top of his glasses. "A PI, like, for real?"

"Yep. For real." I gave him a wide smile.

"Who is it?" a male voice called out from deeper in the house.

"Cops, man!" Keith yelled over his shoulder. "Lady cops!"

"Uh, actually, I'm a *private* investigator. I'm not affiliated with law enforcement—"

"Dude, that's hot!" the male voice said, coming into view. In contrast to Keith, this guy was shorter and rounder, with deep wrinkles around a pair of eyes that looked like they were set in a perpetual squint. He was dressed in a pair of black leather pants that clung unflatteringly to his ample hips and a black T-shirt that was small enough I could see a sliver of pale belly sticking out beneath it. His shaggy hair was jet black, showing grey roots where his dye job was in need of a touch-up. "Hey, lady cop." He gave me a little wave.

I raised my hand in greeting. "Jamie," I supplied. "And I'm actually a PI."

"Still hot." The second guy waggled his eyebrows at me, and the distinct scent of marijuana wafted toward me from his direction.

I looked down and spotted a vape pen in the guy's hand. He must have seen me looking at it, as he immediately put his hand behind his back. Even though the rising plume of smoke was a dead giveaway that it hadn't disappeared.

"This is Harry." Keith nodded toward the guy in leather.

"Nice to meet you," I told him, trying to take in shallow breaths to avoid a contact high.

"You said you want to ask us some questions?" Keith said.

"Yes. About Drake Deadly."

Both men's expressions immediately turned somber at the mention of their deceased bandmate.

"Dude. Drake's dead," Harry told me.

"I know." I turned to Keith, who seemed to be the more sober of the two. "I understand you both were at the Beverly Hotel on the night he died?"

The two men shared a look, but between Keith's tinted glasses and Harry's barely open eyes, I couldn't be sure exactly what it meant.

"Uh, maybe you better come in," Keith decided, standing back to allow me entry to the house.

I did, stepping into a small foyer and following Keith into a living room to our right.

The outside of the house might have looked like every other home on the street, but the décor inside was less well-off suburbanite and more teen dorm room. Posters of rock bands— including several of the Deadly Devils—were hung by thumbtacks on the walls, the furniture seemed to be a mish-mash of garage sale specials, and bags of chips, Cheetos, and Oreos littered the surface of the low glass coffee table in the center of the room.

While the room lacked an interior decorator's touch, it was clear someone had sunk some money into the entertainment center, as a ginormous television set took up almost the entire length of the back wall. Beside it sat a bunch of shiny black boxes housing all manner of media components and video game consoles.

"I'm sorry for your loss," I told the pair as I took a seat on an armchair.

Keith and Harry both sat on a low black leather sofa. Harry's pants squeaked as the leather hit the leather, and Keith pulled his guitar around to rest on his lap.

"Thanks," Keith said. "You know, the police have already been here. We've already talked to them."

"About the night Drake died?"

The two shared that look again, and this time I did catch a whiff of the emotion behind it. If I had to guess, it looked a lot like fear.

"There wasn't much to tell," Keith said carefully. "We never even saw Drake that night."

"He was a no-show, dude," Harry added.

"I understand he asked you all to meet him at the hotel bar. How long did you wait for him before you decided he wasn't coming?"

Harry shrugged. "Maybe an hour?"

I raised an eyebrow his direction. "That's a long time."

"Drake wasn't always known to be punctual," Keith said. "I mean, sometimes he kinda lost track of time, you know?" He idly started plucking at his guitar strings, producing a low, tinny sound.

"Did any of you try getting in touch with him? Calling him?"

"Bash did," Harry offered. "Said it just went to voicemail."

Which meant Drake was likely already dead by then.

"What time was this?" I asked.

Harry shrugged. "I dunno." He looked to Keith, but the guitarist just did a repeat of the shrug.

"I guess you'd have to ask Bash," Keith offered.

I made a mental note to do that. Right after I asked him about the false alibi he'd given me.

"Did Drake tell either of you why he wanted to meet?"

Harry shook his head and looked to Keith.

"Drake didn't say," Keith answered. "He just sent me a text saying it was important that we all be there. That he had something to show us that he knew we'd want to see."

"And he didn't say what it was?" I pressed.

More head shaking.

"Do you think it could have been about the lawsuit?" I asked.

Harry opened his mouth to speak, but Keith jumped in first.

"What do you know about a lawsuit?" Keith said, silencing Harry with a sharp look.

Harry shut his mouth quickly.

Interesting…

"I know that Drake was suing the band for sole ownership to the song 'Hot Waitress.'" I paused, watching their reactions. "And I would imagine you weren't very happy about that."

Harry snorted. "That's an understatement."

Keith shot him a warning look again, and Harry bit his lower lip.

"It's understandable," I said. "I mean, it sounds like there was a lot of money on the line. And I'm sure you must have felt a little betrayed by your friend as well."

"It's been a long time since I've called Drake a friend," Keith said.

"Oh?" I asked. "Why is that?"

"Nothing," Keith mumbled, suddenly seeming to think better of speaking ill of the dead. "We just…the band hasn't played together in a long time. We've all moved on."

I glanced around the room filled with memorabilia from their heyday. Maybe *some* of the band had moved on, but it looked like these two had yet to make that leap.

"Back to the lawsuit," I said. "Do you think it's possible that's why Drake called you all to the hotel? That he had some proof to show you that he'd written 'Hot Waitress'?"

"No way!" Harry piped up. He shook his head so hard I feared his brains would start rolling around in there. "No chance. Drake did not write that song."

"Oh? Who did? Bash?"

Harry looked to Keith. "No. I mean, I don't think so."

"We all collaborated," Keith jumped in. "Look, we just jammed back then, man. The music flowed out, and we recorded it. Added a couple lyrics to it. We didn't pay attention to who wrote what parts or came up with which lines."

Which was certainly a convenient arrangement to claim now that the song was worth millions.

"Right," Harry agreed. "I mean, who can remember who wrote what now? That was like thirty years ago now, dude. And we were all stoned off our butts back then, right?" He laughed, which turned into a hacking thing.

I refrained from asking just how stoned off his butt he might be at present.

"If that's true, then why do you think Drake was claiming it was his song?" I asked.

"Because the guy got greedy," Harry said, an angry edge creeping into his voice for the first time.

"So you think Drake had nothing to back up his claim? That he was just making a grab for the rights?" I clarified.

"Drake had a habit to keep up," Harry said. "He needed the money."

"Habit?" I asked, wondering if he meant drugs.

"Yeah. Her name was Jenna." Harry giggled at his own joke.

"Come on, the kid's not that bad," Keith said, his eyebrows drawing down toward his blue glasses.

"She's what they call high maintenance," Harry explained.

"Did you get the impression that Drake was in financial trouble because of it?" I asked.

But Keith shook his head. "No. Drake was doing fine. I mean, look at where he lives. Brentwood ain't cheap."

I nodded my agreement. However, just because he had a home in a pricey neighborhood, that did not mean it wasn't mortgaged to the hilt. I made a note to ask Maya to look into Drake's finances. Not, mind you, that his death was any of my business, but if he was in trouble, he might have been motivated to bring the lawsuit against his bandmates whether he had real proof or not.

"Yeah, well, *I* still wouldn't put up with my old lady running through my dough like that girl does," Harry added. "I mean, she's hot and all, but she ain't worth that much."

"Do you know Jenna well?" I asked, trying not to wonder if they might have thought her capable of killing her husband.

Harry shrugged. "Met her a few times. We were at the wedding."

I glanced to Keith, who shrugged. "She seemed like a sweet girl."

"Did you know they were getting divorced?" I asked.

"Ha!" Harry let out a blast of air. "Figures. That old turd couldn't hold on to a hot young thing like her forever."

I glanced to Keith, but if he had thoughts on the subject, he kept them to himself, his eyes on his guitar strings again.

"You mentioned that you recorded your jam sessions," I said, steering the conversation back to the song. "Do you know where those recordings could be now?"

"I'm sure they're long gone," Keith said.

"Probably destroyed," Harry added.

"I mean, why hang on to them, you know?" Keith added. "Who even has a tape player anymore, right?"

"What about notes, original sheet music, anything like that?" I grasped.

But they both shook their heads again. "Carmichael handles all the paperwork for the band," Harry offered.

I nodded. "Yeah, I've already been to see him. He said he didn't have anything to do with the creative side of things."

Keith nodded. "He's just the money guy. He probably has a record of every penny we ever earned, but the actual art…totally eludes that guy."

"Do you think there's any chance Drake could have kept those kinds of things? Recordings or notes?" I asked, watching their reactions. "Maybe that's what he was going to show you the night he died?"

"There's no way of knowing now," Keith said. I could have sworn I detected a note of a threat in there, but he looked down, running his fingers over his strings again before I could read more into it.

"What about your keyboard player?" I asked, feeling like I was about at the end of their attention span. "Tosh Thomas?"

"Oh, man, it's been a long time since I heard that name," Harry said, his eyes glazing over with nostalgia. Or maybe just with weed.

"What about him?" Keith asked, frowning.

"Well, for starters, do you have any idea where I could find him?"

Both Keith and Harry shook their heads.

"I haven't heard from that guy in, what, like twenty years?" Harry said, glancing to Keith for confirmation.

"At least," Keith said. "Not since he quit the band."

"You didn't keep in touch at all?"

"We didn't really part on keeping-in-touch terms," Harry answered.

"Oh?" I said. "He was unhappy with you when he left, I take it?"

"Not with us—with Drake," Harry said.

Keith shot him that look again. The one that made Harry shut his mouth with a click and me perk up with interest.

"What happened between him and Drake?" I pressed.

"It was nothing," Keith tried to cover. "Tosh had anger issues back then. He blew it out of proportion."

"Back then. You're sure he doesn't have any issues now?"

"I-I don't know. I told you, I haven't seen the guy since he stormed out on us!" Keith said, looking distinctly cornered.

"Why did he storm out?" I asked.

Keith licked his lips. "It was over the hot waitress."

I frowned. "Was there a dispute over the song rights even back then?"

"No, dude." Harry laughed. "Not 'Hot Waitress' the song, hot waitress the actual hot waitress."

I shook my head. "I'm lost."

"There was this diner across the street from where we used to record," Keith explained. "We'd go there all the time after sessions, and there was this waitress who worked the graveyard shift." Keith turned to Harry. "What was her name?"

Harry looked to the ceiling as if the answer might be there. "Mandy? Maci?" He shook his head. "I dunno. I always just called her Jugs." He giggled.

"Anyway," I prompted, turning back to Keith. "I'm guessing she was the inspiration for the song?"

"Yeah," Keith confirmed. "We were *all* into her, you know. But then she and Tosh ended up kinda getting a thing going."

"Until Drake messed it up," Harry cut in. "Totally snaked her out from under him."

"Drake hooked up with Tosh's waitress?" I clarified.

Keith nodded. "We all thought she was hot. It wasn't that big of a deal."

"Sounds like it was big enough that Tosh quit the band," I noted. "Do you know if Tosh had any contact with Drake afterward?"

Harry shook his head. "Why would he?"

Revenge came to mind. Especially if, say, the song about the woman Drake had stolen from him was suddenly getting enough airplay to make the band millions. Maybe an old wound had been opened, enough time had passed that it festered, and Tosh had decided to get even.

Or, that's what I would have been thinking, if Drake's death was my case. Which it was not. I gave myself a stern mental talking to and tried to refocus.

"You said Tosh and the waitress had a thing. Any chance that *Tosh* might have been the one to originally write the song about her?" I asked.

"I told you, man, we all collaborated." Keith gave me a hard look, and I could tell that was his story and he was sticking to it.

"Let's go back to the night Drake died," I said, feeling like I was on borrowed time at this point. "What time did you arrive at the hotel for Drake's meeting?"

"Maybe eleven. Eleven fifteen," Keith said.

"Try eleven thirty," Harry corrected. He turned to me. "Keith was running late."

I raised an eyebrow at Keith. "Any particular reason?" Like you were busy murdering your bandmate…?

But Keith grinned, showing off a row of crooked teeth. "Yeah, a really good one. A really cute, stacked one." He waggled his eyebrows up and down.

Harry giggled again.

"You're saying you were with a woman?" I had a hard time picturing the type of groupies the band might still attract. Scratch that—I didn't *want* to picture the type.

Keith nodded. "A real *live* one, if you know what I mean."

"What was her name?" I asked, wondering if Aiden had checked out this alibi yet.

"Sorry. Didn't get a name." Keith leaned his head back on the sofa cushion and gave a sly smile, as if being on a no-name basis showed off just how desirable he still was to his fan base.

Or possibly just how clever he thought he was to invent this alibi.

"What about everyone else?" I asked.

"I got there early," Harry said. "I wasn't sure what Drake was going to say and thought I should probably have a drink before. You know, to take the edge off."

"What time did you arrive?"

"Like, ten thirty? Forty-five, maybe?"

"And you were there alone?"

Harry nodded.

Which wasn't much of an alibi either. "What about the rest of the group?" I asked.

"Carmichael came in next," Harry said. "Right on time. As usual, the bean counter."

"And Bash?" I asked. "He was there as well, right?"

"Yeah, he came in a couple minutes after Carmichael. Said he'd just come from the gym or something."

I bit my lip. Okay, so maybe my client wasn't a total liar. He *had* been at the gym that night. He'd just left out the part where he'd also been at the scene of a murder.

"And I was last to arrive," Keith said. "Eleven thirty, right?"

Harry nodded. "Then we all waited until, I don't know, at least midnight, but Drake never showed up."

Because he'd already been dead by then.

Which meant that any one of the band could have easily arrived at the hotel early, gone up to Drake's room, and somehow convinced the aging rock star to go down to the hotel pool where they'd drowned him before making a cool appearance in the hotel bar to pretend to show up for the dead man's mystery meeting.

CHAPTER TEN

_____

I left Keith and Harry's place with several more theories about who might have killed Drake than I'd had when I'd arrived and absolutely no more clue about where to look for Bash's proof that he'd written the band's hit song. If, in fact, that story was true. The more I learned about the Deadly Devils, the more I thought Drake might very well have been the original songwriter. And it might have gotten him killed.

Then again, there was still the wife, who, according to Harry at least, was running through Drake's earnings and possibly about to be cut off. It was still entirely possible the lawsuit about the song and the band had had nothing to do with Drake's death at all.

I was just getting into my car when my phone pinged with an incoming text. I pulled it out of my purse and glanced at the readout to see Aiden's name.

Got your message. Any chance of cashing in on that dinner rain check tonight?

I glanced at the dash clock on my car. Almost six. Hardly enough time to race home and change into something a little more dinner date worthy. On the other hand, I was starving, and I did have to eat.

Very good chance. Currently in Tujunga.

I could feel him calculating traffic times on his end before his reply came in. *How about La Pastoria? 7?*

La Pastoria was a little Italian place that was conveniently located equa-distance between my apartment and Aiden's. The atmosphere was casual, the food authentic, and the location perfect for whatever might happen after dessert.

I'll be there, I told him.

I put the car in gear and was just pulling away from the curb as his response pinged in.

Looking forward to it.

My stomach did a little flip at the words, which had nothing to do with the fact I'd skipped lunch that day and a huge plate of homemade pasta sounded heavenly.

Unfortunately, La Pastoria was in Mid-town, and I was north of the Valley, and the 5 looked like a parking lot at that time of day. I merged onto the freeway, slogging down the onramp at a pace just slightly faster than a tortoise on Valium. I finally slid in between a couple of semitrucks that immediately filled the interior of my car with the scent of exhaust. I flipped on the AC to clear the air and the radio to clear the theories swirling in my head.

After over an hour of pop songs, upbeat DJs, and bumper-to-bumper commuters, I finally pulled up to the restaurant only ten minutes late. Amazingly I found a metered spot at the curb just three spaces down and paused only for a quick makeup check in my rearview before locking my car and heading inside.

La Pastoria was a family run place that was what some might affectionately refer to as a hole in the wall. It featured dim lighting, lots of small tables with red and white checkered tablecloths, and cheesy dripping candles stuck in Chianti bottles to set the mood. While the vibe was more seventies cliché than romantic chic, the food was as close to homemade by Nonna as was possible to get this side of Sicily. As soon as I walked through the doors, the scents of oregano, garlic, and tomato sauce that had been simmering all day greeted me, instantly giving me a homey feel.

I blinked as my eyes adjusted to the dim lighting, and I spotted Aiden at a table for two near the back, already perusing the menu. He'd clearly come straight from the office, still in his usual uniform of a pressed dark suit with a pale grey dress shirt and navy tie. His sandy hair was neatly combed back from his face, and his clean-shaven cheeks had yet to show any sign of five o'clock stubble. While I felt like I'd just spent a lifetime in traffic, he looked as clean and fresh as if he'd just woken up.

He looked up as I approached, and the smile he sent me was enough to make a lesser woman weak in the knees. Luckily, I was a tough chick, and mine only wobbled a little as I let him pull my chair out.

"You look nice," he said, his mouth close to my ear.

I shivered at the sensation of his breath on my skin.

"I look like I've been sitting in traffic for an hour," I joked, trying not to let his compliment make me blush.

Aiden grinned. "Sorry. The 5 is thick this time of day, huh?"

I nodded. "Two accidents. I thought at one point we were driving backward."

A waiter appeared almost instantly, taking our drink order. I went with a glass of merlot, and Aiden did the same, adding a platter of fried calamari to go along with it.

"So Tujunga," Aiden said once the waiter had left the table. "You wouldn't happen to have been visiting a couple of Deadly Devils there, would you?"

I shrugged. But I couldn't help the playful grin that tugged the corners of my mouth. "Maybe."

"Come on now, Bond. I showed you quite a bit of mine at the hotel yesterday. Surely you can show me yours." The crooked smile he sent me was accompanied by just enough heat in his eyes to let me know he meant every bit of the double entendre.

"Okay," I relented. "Yes. I was there talking to Keith Kane and Harry Star. But, I doubt I found out anything you didn't. They said the police had already been to question them."

Aiden nodded as he grabbed a breadstick from the basket on the table and broke off a piece. "We found out that Drake's bandmates were all at the scene the night he died." He paused. "I'm guessing you know that as well."

I nodded. "According to Harry, they all arrived after Drake was presumably dead." I paused. "Or at least I'm guessing that's why he didn't show for the meeting."

Aiden nodded. "We're going on that theory as well. Which narrows the time of death considerably."

"You said you got my message," I prompted. "Did you get a chance to look through Drake's effects?"

Aiden nodded. "Forensics is going through everything still, but to answer your question, we haven't found anything about a waitress song." He paused. "Want to tell me what that's about?"

"'Hot Waitress,'" I said. "It's a Deadly Devils song. Have you heard it?"

He shrugged. Aiden's taste in music ran more along the lines of my own. "Can't say I have. Why?"

I quickly filled him in on its commercial surge to popularity again, the impending lawsuit against the band, my latest client, and the thought that Drake might have called the band meeting to present proof that he had originally penned the song. By the time I was done, we were both sipping our wine and nibbling on calamari. "I think it's possible he'd found some proof and was going to drop it on the band that night," I said.

"And someone killed him before he had the chance?" Aiden finished for me.

I nodded. "None of them have super solid alibis." I paused. "As I'm sure you know."

Aiden nodded. "Yeah, I caught that too. We're still checking them, but I saw a lot of holes."

"So any one of them could have easily arrived earlier, killed Drake, then sauntered in as if they'd just gotten there."

"But, if the lawsuit is going ahead anyway, what's the point of killing Drake?"

"Maybe to destroy the proof. Take it from him before he could show everyone? I mean, at this point the ownership is a dead man's word against the rest of the band's."

Aiden sipped his wine, looking deep in thought.

"What?" I asked.

"Hmm?" His eyes met mine.

"You know something I don't," I surmised, scrutinizing his face.

His features broke into a wide smile. "I know a lot of things you don't, Bond," he teased.

I picked up my own wineglass. "Come on, now. I thought we were laying it all on the table."

Aiden cleared his throat, leaning forward. "Okay. Forensics did find something in Drake's room."

"Oh?" I gave him an expectant look.

"Not related to your song," he quickly covered. "But it looked like Drake had a drink with someone before he went downstairs."

"So he *was* drunk when he hit the pool?"

"More than drunk. Preliminary tox showed oxycodone in his system," Aiden replied.

"Recreational, you think?" I asked.

Aiden shrugged. "It's possible. It's not a difficult opiate to get. But there was a large amount in his system. Enough that he would have been nearly comatose by the time he hit the water."

"Which is why he drowned instead of swimming to safety." I shivered, thinking about it.

Aiden nodded. "With the mix of the oxy and alcohol in his system, it's hard to imagine he could even walk to the pool on his own. It's possible he wasn't even conscious when he went in."

Part of me hoped he hadn't been. I could only imagine the horror of feeling yourself drowning and not being able to do anything about it.

"If he was that out of it, someone else must have helped him from his room and downstairs to the pool," I said, following Aiden's train of thought. "Security cameras in the hotel pick up anything?"

He sighed. "Not enough. One by the elevators showed Drake going down to the main lobby around ten thirty. But if there was anyone with him, they were off camera. No security by the pool."

"You think the killer knew that?"

"Or got lucky," Aiden said.

"You said he was having a drink *with* someone. I'm guessing you found two glasses?"

Aiden nodded again. And again I could feel him holding something back.

"What?" I asked. "Were you able to pull fingerprints from it? DNA?"

"Not yet," Aiden said. He blew out a breath. "It was wiped pretty clean. But forensics found evidence of lipstick on it."

"Lipstick..." I trailed off, thinking that bill fit only one person in this story. "You mean the wife?"

Aiden picked up his wineglass. "Like I said, Trace is still working on it. Without a positive DNA match, I'm not ready to say definitively."

"But you can speculate."

"I'd rather not."

I was about to press more when I felt my phone buzz with a text. I was tempted to ignore it, but the waiter arrived then to take our orders, an interruption Aiden seemed grateful to jump at. As he ordered the pasta pomodoro, I pulled my phone out, giving the screen a quick glance.

It was one word from my latest client, Bash.

Update

Rather a demanding way of asking how the case was going, but consistent with the personality I'd witnessed at our one meeting.

"And for you, ma'am?"

I looked up to find the waiter's pen hovering over his order pad.

"Uh, I'll have the seafood fettuccini," I said, handing him my menu.

"Work?" Aiden asked, gesturing to the phone with a breadstick as the waiter walked away.

I nodded. "My latest client looking for an update."

I shot back a quick text to Bash. *Nothing to report yet. Will call tomorrow.*

Which was mostly true. I was honestly no closer to finding what he'd hired me to find. However, I had gotten plenty of motive, a busted alibi, and everyone I'd talked to that day saying how much Bash had hated Drake. The case against my client as a murderer was mounting, but the case he was paying me to follow was coming up empty.

* * *

An hour later, the pasta was a thing of the past, my belly was full, and the dim lighting and mellow wine were making the man sitting across from me look almost more temping than a tiramisu.

"What?" Aiden asked, swirling the last of his merlot in his glass as the waiter cleared our plates.

"What, what?" I asked.

"What's the goofy grin on your face all about?"

I let out a laugh. "Nothing. I was just wondering about dessert."

Aiden raised one eyebrow up into his hairline. "Shall I ask for a dessert menu?"

I slowly swallowed my last sip of wine and shook my head. "Actually, I know exactly what I want." Where that confident, bold voice came from, I'll never know. I had a suspicion it might have had to do with the second glass of merlot I'd ordered.

"Oh really?" Aiden asked, his coy smile telling me he knew exactly what I was thinking—and it had nothing to do with what the restaurant had to offer. "Shall I get the waiter?"

I shook my head slowly, giving him my best come-hither smile. Which, granted, might have been closer to a goofy grin in the moment, but I didn't care. And from the heat radiating from Aiden's gaze as his dark eyes seared into mine, I didn't think he did much either.

"How about," I suggested, "we just get the check."

* * *

The ride to my apartment in Aiden's SUV was a complete blur, and luckily it was a short one. By the time I unlocked the front door, the heat between us had spilled over into a frenzy of jackets shedding, keys dropping, and shoes being kicked off into far corners of my apartment. Aiden walked me backward toward the sofa in the center of the living room, his hands at my waist.

His lips moved toward mine, and all rational thought went out the window. Suddenly I was no longer a strong, independent woman but a bundle of hormones whose sole focus was the soft, hot, and oh so tasty feel of Aiden's mouth pressing against mine. My arms wrapped around his neck all on their own, my body moving on pure instinct and the need to touch him. I felt the warm sear of his palm against my hip as his hands explored lower, pulling me tightly against him. As his other hand went into my hair, creating a tingling sensation along my scalp, my entire body started to vibrate with the need to be near him.

"Your phone," he mumbled against my lips.

"Hmm?" I'll admit, my mind was in a fog, completely overtaken by lust.

"Your phone is vibrating."

Aiden pulled back just enough to let me up for air, and I realized he was right. My phone, still in my pocket, was buzzing insistently. I blinked, trying to get some blood back to my brain as I slipped my hand into my pocket to silence the offending object.

I might have just chucked it out the window at that point, but Aiden had stepped back, putting enough distance between us that the moment was stilled whether I answered or not. I glanced down at the readout. A number I didn't recognize flashed across the screen with the incoming call. I swore, if this was a telemarketer...

"Yes?" I answered with maybe a bit more irritation in my voice than the situation called for.

"Jamie?" The voice was female, but I didn't recognize it.

"Who is this?" I asked.

"It's Jenna. Jenna James. Drake's wife."

I glanced at Aiden, still wearing my lipstick on his face. I gave him a one-finger wait signal and turned my back to him before replying. "Listen, I told you I'd leave you alone—"

But before I got any further, she cut me off.

"I need your help!"

The note of urgency in her voice was unmistakable, and it immediately sent my spidey senses tingling. "Help with what? Are you okay?"

"No. I mean, yes, but I...something happened. I-I didn't know who else to call."

She sounded flustered and scared. Not at all like the woman who had been on the attack in my apartment just the night before. "What happened?" I asked, trying to keep my voice low enough that Aiden didn't hear the concern in it.

"Someone broke into my house. I-I need your help."

"Are you okay? Where are you?"

"I'm at home. Outside. I-I ran to my car. I think they're gone now, but I don't know."

"Hang up and call the police," I instructed her. I glanced behind me at the seductively sexy man standing in my living room and, with a deep sense of regret, told her, "Stay where you are. I'll be right there."

CHAPTER ELEVEN

———

I made it to Brentwood in just under fifteen minutes, which was a small miracle in itself and probably would have earned me at least a speeding ticket and possibly a sobriety test had any CHP been hanging out on my route. Luckily, if Jenna's call hadn't sufficiently sobered me, the halfway-true halfway-skirting-the-details story I'd had to give Aiden about a client in distress did. I'd hated withholding info from him. But I knew Jenna was his number one suspect in Drake's murder. Truth be told, she wasn't off my list either. Not that I had a list. Which I didn't. Not my case.

But, I was pretty sure Aiden wouldn't be a fan of me taking off in the night to meet Jenna alone at her deserted Brentwood estate where a robbery had just occurred. Luckily, even though I was pretty sure he could feel me holding something back, he didn't pry. Instead, he'd driven me back to my Roadster, still parked at La Pastoria—reluctantly, I'd like to think—with a promise from me to call him later and another rain check added to our growing list.

I pulled up to Jenna's street to find the house looking largely abandoned. I'd hoped that a patrol car would have beaten me there, but apparently they—unlike myself—were obeying posted speed limits on their way.

Or the wife hadn't called them yet.

I pulled off the main road and onto a winding driveway that cut through the trees to the large colonial style home. Jenna's mint green Jaguar was parked at the head of the driveway. The outdoor lighting nestled in the artful landscaping provided enough illumination that I could see Jenna hunkered down inside the vehicle, her phone in her hands as she furiously texted someone. At the sound of my tires approaching, she looked up, relief unmistakable on her face.

I parked next to her car, and we both got out at the same time, Jenna tucking her phone into the back pocket of her skinny jeans. "Finally you're here," she said, her voice still holding a shaky edge to it.

"I came as soon as I could," I told her, trying to sound reassuring. I looked up at the house, where I could see a couple of lights on in the downstairs rooms. "Have you gone inside?"

She shook her head back and forth. "No. I-I've just been waiting here. Like you said." She bit her lip, glancing up.

"Tell me what happened," I said, coming around my vehicle to stand next to her.

She licked her lips. "Well, I was just coming home from a book signing. Dave was doing a reading in Century City."

Dave. The guy who wrote alien porn. "Go on," I prompted.

"Well, when I went inside the house, I heard something."

"What kind of something?" I asked.

"Like, noises upstairs. Like someone moving around up there. Only no one else was home but me. I mean, no one should have been there. I'm the only one living here now." Her voice broke on the last word, and I wasn't sure if she was finally experiencing grief that her husband was dead or just fear at being abandoned in the wilds of the upper-middle-class neighborhood.

"So, you heard sounds upstairs." I glanced up at the dark second story. "What did you do?"

"Well, I-I ran. I kinda just freaked out, you know? Like, an intruder was in my house!" Her speech was halting, as if her brain couldn't quite keep up with the nervous pace of her mouth.

"Then what?"

"Then I called you." She bit her lower lip, pink lipstick transferring to her white veneers. "I wasn't sure who else to call."

"You said on the phone you thought they were gone," I said, eyes scanning the yard. Everything looked serenely still and quiet.

She nodded. "When I went into the house, I think I scared them. As I was going back to my car, I saw someone running across the yard." She pointed to the side of the house, where an expanse of lawn gave way to tall cyprus trees creating a border between Jenna's home and the neighboring property. "They must have run out the back door."

"Are the police on their way?" I asked.

Jenna squared her jaw, her eyes going to the ground.

"Jenna?" I prompted. "You did call the police like I told you to, didn't you?"

"No, I didn't." She lifted her eyes to meet mine, a defiance replacing her earlier fear. "The *police* think I'm a killer. You really think I want to invite them into my home?"

"If someone broke into your house, you need to call—"

"I called you, okay?" She let out a shaky breath, as if that one moment of moxie had taken everything out of her. "I-I just don't want to go in there alone."

I assessed her wide, innocent-looking eyes, trying to decide what to make of her. If I had to guess, the fear she was projecting now was real. Of course, just because she was afraid of an intruder *now,* that didn't mean she hadn't killed her husband before. Or it was just as possible she was innocent and trying to put on a brave face while she'd had to endure both the death of her husband and someone breaking into her home all in the same week.

"Okay," I finally relented. "Let's go take a look inside together." What else could I do? I couldn't force her to call the police, and if there really was a threat of danger, I couldn't very well just abandon her. Not if I wanted to sleep that night.

I paused only long enough to grab my Glock 27 from my glove box before following Jenna to the front door.

Which, as she turned the knob, I noticed she'd left unlocked in her haste to get away from the intruder. She stood back, letting me enter the house first, which I did with a two-fisted grip on my gun. Just because Jenna thought she'd seen the guy leave the house, that didn't mean he couldn't still have a buddy inside.

"Hello?" I called out, listening for any sign of life above us. Only silence greeted me. I took a few tentative steps into a large foyer. The ceiling was two stories high, adorned with a sparkling glass chandelier the size of a small car. Its light shone off a tile floor, done in large black and white stone checkers that led toward a curved grand staircase. My heels echoed with each step as I peeked into the two rooms flanking the entry—a dark formal living room on the left and a small den on the right. Neither showed any signs of life.

"I heard him upstairs," Jenna whispered behind me. She pointed a pink nail toward the stairs.

I glanced up toward the second-story landing, where I could see several closed doors.

I took the first few stairs slowly, feeling Jenna at my back. Adrenaline flowed through me, making me tense and antsy at the same time. I tried to modulate my breathing as I neared the top of the staircase, gun first.

"Wait here," I told Jenna, slowly moving toward the first closed door. I took a deep breath, turned the knob, and pushed it open, ready for anything that might jump out at me.

But all I found was an empty guest bedroom. No intruder. No sign of life.

I sucked in air, slowly exhaling, before I turned back and did a repeat of the process at the next closed door. This one revealed a room full of gym equipment and a treadmill. The next two were bedrooms and a bathroom. All empty. By the time I'd gone through the master bedroom and bath at the end of the hall, I'd done a full tour of the upstairs, and it appeared we were alone in the house.

"Is it safe?" Jenna asked, coming up behind me as I finished checking the master closet. (Which was impressively large and packed full of designer items. I had a serious case of envy brewing.)

"I think so," I told her, holstering my gun and letting the fight-or-flight sensation slowly drain from my limbs. I glanced around the bedroom. A four-poster bed sat in the center, flanked by two dark wood nightstands—one of which was overturned. A couple of chests of drawers stood along the far wall, their drawers open, contents strewn across the floor. A smattering of jewelry was splayed across the top of the vanity.

Jenna walked to the table, picking up a necklace. "He was in my room." Her voice was very small and childlike.

"I'm guessing you didn't leave this mess?"

She shook her head, her wide eyes filling with tears. "He went through my things." Her gaze pinged from one surface to another.

"Can you tell if anything is missing?" I asked.

She blinked back the moisture in her eyes, focusing them on the jewelry in front of her. "I-I don't know." She picked up a couple of pieces, setting them into a wooden jewelry box to her right. "I don't think so. I mean, the bigger pieces are still here." She licked her lips. "Maybe I caught him in the act?"

"Maybe." As far as the upstairs rooms went, the master had appeared to be the only room rifled through. Then again, if I were a thief looking to grab some easily offloaded items, that would be the place I'd start. "You said he went out the back door?"

Jenna nodded. "I think so. I mean, I saw the shadow run from the back of the house."

"Show me the door," I said.

I followed her back down the stairs and through a large kitchen full of marble, stainless steel appliances, and tons of cooking gadgets that I'd bet money Jenna had never touched. Beyond the kitchen sat a breakfast nook and a sunken family room, where a pair of French doors led to a backyard that was illuminated with the same tasteful uplights as the front of the property. A swimming pool and an outdoor kitchen were visible through the doors.

One of which had been left open.

Jenna and I shared a look before she bit down hard on her lower lip.

I moved in closer and saw the wood at the lock had been splintered, the door forced open. If I had to guess, a crowbar or large screwdriver had done the trick. Not terribly sophisticated but highly effective.

"Looks like this is how he got in." I turned to Jenna. "You don't have a security system?"

Jenna's eyes were wide and threatening to spill tears again. "I-I don't know. I mean, Drake always took care of that stuff. Maybe we do. But I don't really know how to work it."

"You should find out," I told her, stating the obvious. "And you should call the police."

"No." Jenna sniffed loudly, getting her emotions under control. "No. I-I don't think anything has been taken. There's no need to get the police involved."

"Are you sure?" I asked, looking around the family room. Nothing appeared to be disturbed. "I'd suggest doing a thorough inventory of your valuables." I glanced down the hallway. "I saw a desk in your den. Maybe we should make sure he didn't get any of your personal information—"

"No!" Jenna shook her head, her voice more forceful this time. "I interrupted them. They took off. I can tell nothing important is missing."

"You're sure?" I asked her. "Don't you think we should at least check to make sure?"

"Look, no one is here," Jenna protested with defiance that would put any two-year-old to shame. "It's safe. I'm tired. It's been a long day, okay? You can go now."

"I'm not sure I feel right leaving you alone," I told her. Though, honestly, in that moment, she looked as capable as anyone of taking care of herself. Her shoulders were squared, arms crossed over her chest, eyes hard. The fight was back in her, and any sign of fear I'd seen earlier was fading fast.

"I'm fine," she said. "Really. Thank you for coming, but I can take it from here."

I glanced at the broken back door. "You should call someone to get that fixed. Soon."

Jenna nodded. "I will." Then she gestured toward the front of the house, indicating my exit.

As much as I didn't want to leave her alone, there wasn't much I could do. It was her house, her call to bring the police in or not. And while a busted back door that anyone could waltz in through and a security system beyond her capabilities to navigate didn't exude safety, if she really *had* caught a burglar in the act, the chances were slim he'd come back. He was probably feeling lucky to have gotten away at that moment.

"I'll check on you in the morning," I promised her as I complied with her silent request, making my way back through the house to the tiled foyer.

Jenna shook her head. "No need. I told you, I'm fine now." She paused at the front door as I stepped out into the chilly air. "But thanks for your concern."

And with that, she shut the door on me.

I stood there a moment, looking up at the impressive home as the cool night air seeped into my skin.

If I didn't know better, I'd say Jenna James had been trying to get rid of me.

I thought back to what Aiden had told me earlier about lipstick stains on the second wineglass in Drake's hotel room, and I suddenly wondered if this was a random break-in…or if Jenna knew more than she was willing to admit.

* * *

"Morning, boss," Maya said, rising from her desk the next day to hand me a paper coffee cup.

"You are a goddess," I told her, taking the cup from her and sipping deeply. Caramel macchiato with extra whip. Perfect.

After I'd finally gotten home the previous night before from Jenna's, I'd first texted Aiden another apology at having to take off so suddenly, and then I'd taken a long hot shower before falling into bed exhausted. Unfortunately, as tired as my body had been, my mind had still been wide awake, tumbling over possible reasons why someone would break into Drake and Jenna's home. And what, if anything, it had to do with Drake's death. And who had killed the rock star. So far, everyone in Drake's life seemed to have a reason to hate him and no one had been totally straight with me.

Including my own client.

That last fact had me mulling over my moral dilemma into the wee hours of the morning, wondering if I should just walk away from the whole mess and let the authorities sort it out. I'd finally fallen into a fitful sleep somewhere just before dawn, only to be awakened by the sound of my neighbor's car alarm going off again. I swore, if that guy didn't get his alarm fixed, his car was liable to mysteriously disappear.

"What's on the agenda today?" I asked, taking another sip of sweet, sweet life-giving caffeine as Caleigh and Sam came into reception from the back rooms.

"Well," Maya said, grabbing her phone and scrolling through the calendar entries. "You've got Kendall Manchester this afternoon for an update on Gammy."

I glanced at Sam. "Do we *have* an update on Gammy?"

Sam nodded, a gleeful look in her eyes. "Oh, boy, do we. Or, more accurately, on Alejandro."

"Oh?" I sat on the sofa, crossing one skinny jean clad leg over the other. "Do tell."

"Well, as I was just telling Caleigh," Sam said, gesturing to her, "I spent most of yesterday following Alejandro around, in hopes he'd decide to look in on his mystery blonde."

"And did he?" I asked, sipping my coffee.

"Nope." She paused for dramatic effect. "But he *did* go see a redhead."

I nearly choked on my drink. "Wait—he's seeing *two* other women?"

"Apparently," Sam said. "He met up with her at happy hour in a dive bar near Sunset Acres. Bought her a drink, then they left together in her car."

"Where did they go?" Maya asked, clearly invested in the drama.

"Back to the Acres."

"So the redhead lives at the same retirement village too?" Caleigh asked.

Sam shrugged. "Looks like it. I lost them when I had to detour to visitor parking, so I don't know which building. But I saw them pull into the resident lot, so she must live there."

"Risky." Maya clicked her tongue. "I mean, does he really think word won't get back to Ellie?"

Sam shrugged. "Maybe he's counting on his ladies to be discreet."

"Well, if the residents of the Acres gossip anything like my mom and her friends, there's no such thing as discreet enough," Maya said.

"I don't suppose you got a name for the redhead?" I asked.

Sam shook her head. "Unfortunately, no. Alejandro never called her by name."

"Did you recognize her from the potluck?" Caleigh asked.

She shook her head again. "No, I don't remember seeing her there. But I never got a really good look at her face. She had her back to me most of the time at the bar."

"And you're sure this was more than just a friendly drink and a lift to the Acres?" I pressed.

"Oh yeah." Sam nodded. "The reason her back was to me is that most of time her lips were attached to Alejandro's. And I can tell you she was *not* dressed for a friendly drink. Thigh-high boots, minidress, leather jacket. She basically had sex oozing from her outfit."

"I don't suppose you got photos?" I asked.

Sam grinned at me. "Now, how would I be able to live with myself if I didn't at least get photos?"

Had I mentioned how much I loved my girls?

"I was just about to go print them off," she added.

"At least I can count on one happy client today." That settled, I turned back to Maya. "Anything else?"

"Yes." She scrolled through her calendar again. "A message from Bash. He wants to meet to go over what you've found so far."

So far what I'd found was nothing. No one seemed to remember who had come up with the idea for the song, and no one seemed to have saved anything from that era. Except maybe Drake, but if he had, it was MIA.

Or in the hands of his killer.

"I don't suppose you found anything at the Deadly Devils' studio yesterday?" I asked Caleigh.

She shook her head. "Sorry. Anything from before they went digital is gone. They said anything the band didn't want, they destroyed."

"Should I schedule an appointment for him?" Maya asked, stylus hovering over her phone.

I nodded. "Yeah, but make it at the end of the day. Late end of day." We needed all the time we could get to have something—anything—to present to him. "I don't suppose we have any new business?"

Maya shook her head. "Sorry. But the social media campaign is in full swing, and Connor said we've gotten retweeted by two influencers already."

"What kind of influencers?" I asked, narrowing my eyes.

"One does Easter memes, and the other owns a petting zoo."

I thought I heard Sam snort behind me.

"Fabulous. If a goat cheats on his wife, we'll be their go-to firm."

"It's all about visibility," Maya assured me. "Don't worry. Connor knows what he's doing."

At least Connor wasn't being paid. "Keep me updated," I told Maya as I turned to go into my office. "And in the meantime, see if you can get me some info on Drake's financial situation."

She made a note on her phone. "You think it was shaky?"

"Not sure. His bandmates seemed to think his wife was running through his money too quickly."

"And you think maybe she killed him to get her hands on what was left?"

"I think *maybe* it has some bearing on his decision to sue the band. You know. Our real case."

Maya rolled her eyes but grinned. "Sure. I'm on it."

As soon as I'd settled at my desk, I pulled out my phone and called Jenna's number, checking in on her as promised. Even though two rings in, it went to voicemail. A sure sign I was being screened. Still, I left her a message telling her to call me if she needed anything and once again urging her to file a police report. A plea I feared would fall on deaf ears.

I hung up and forced myself to focus on my paying client's case.

I jiggled my mouse to bring my computer to life and pulled up all the files Maya had sent me on the Deadly Devils' history. I was pretty sure the bass player and guitarist were dead ends as far as remembering who had originally penned "Hot Waitress." Even if their brains hadn't been laboring under decades of sex, drugs, and rock 'n' roll, it was clearly better for their financial situations if no one ever remembered who wrote the song and they all kept splitting the proceeds. And it wasn't as if Drake could tell me anything now. Which left me with one other band member who might have some recollection of the event: the keyboard player, Tosh Thomas.

Unfortunately, Maya's research on him had turned up precious little. After splitting with the band, he seemed to disappear completely from the music scene, not even putting in an appearance at the Global Music Awards that year when the band had been up for best rock single.

I clicked on a link that pulled up the song in question and listened to what everyone was fighting about. I had to admit, the chorus was catchy and did sound vaguely familiar, as if I'd heard it on TV during a commercial break. The lyrics weren't exactly on par with classic poetry—citing that the "hot waitress" was going to "make my brain insane with pain" if she didn't kiss the singer soon. After which he went on to describe her many physical attributes that made her such a "hot" waitress.

As I listened, I pulled up a promo photo of the group from their first world tour. I could easily recognize both Keith and Harry. Their styles hadn't changed much over the years, even if time had added a few wrinkles, a little grey, and, in Harry's case, a lot of belly. But I could almost swear Keith was wearing the same bell bottoms in the old picture as he had been the day before. Bash was also easy to spot, looking like a younger, slightly less hardened version of the man I'd met recently.

Drake Deadly, on the other hand, was harder to recognize. I had no idea what he had been doing for the last thirty years, but whatever it was had aged him about fifty. In fact, in his youth, he'd actually been a pretty good-looking guy. If you could see past the pound of makeup and lewd tongue wagging he was doing in the photo.

To his right stood a tall, slim guy with spiky black hair that defied gravity. Presumably Tosh Thomas. His face was contorted in a snarl, and he was flexing one bicep with a tattoo of a devil on it in a menacing threat for the camera. It was hard to know if the look was all part of the persona or if the keyboard player really did have a natural violent streak.

He'd been a part of the band back when they'd recorded their hit song. Which meant he had to be getting paid a portion of the royalties for it as well. While that gave him just as much motive to want Drake's lawsuit silenced as the rest of the band, it also might provide a clue to where I could find him.

I picked up my phone, keying in Alvin Carmichael's number. I heard it ring on the other end and tapped my pen cap against the wooden top of my desk. Finally, four rings in, a woman's voice answered.

"Carmichael Management, how may I help you?" came a bored monotone I knew belonged to the bland receptionist.

"May I speak with Alvin Carmichael, please?" I asked.

"And who may I ask is calling?"

"This is Jamie Bond. I was in yesterday," I said, trying to jog her memory.

"One moment," she said in the same monotone voice that left me wondering if she'd remembered me at all.

I listened to some jazzy Muzak for a few moments, did some more pen tapping, and finally the line picked up again.

"Hello, this is Alvin Carmichael."

"Hi, Jamie Bond. We met yesterday," I told him.

There as a pause on his end. Then, "I remember. How may I help you?"

"I wanted to ask you about Tosh Thomas. The keyboard player for the Deadly Devils."

"Tosh?" he asked, confusion clear in his voice. "What about him?"

"I'd like to talk to him."

"I-I can't imagine why?" Carmichael said, his voice going up at the end as if it were a question.

"Do you know how I could get ahold of him?"

"No. I told you, I haven't spoken to him in years."

"But he receives royalty checks from you, correct?" I pressed.

There was another pregnant pause. "Well, yes, of course. I mean, all of the band do. I handle all of the financials. We send them out every quarter." I heard a pill bottle rattling on the other end and pictured him popping an antacid.

"Where do you send them?"

"W-what?" he asked.

"I was just curious where you send Tosh Thomas's royalty checks. You do mail them out, correct?"

"Of course. I just told you we send them to all of the band."

"So where does Tosh receive his?"

"Well, I don't have that information in front of me right now," Carmichael said, and I detected a note of irritation creeping into his voice.

"I can wait while you look it up," I told him pleasantly. "I'm in no rush."

I heard a sigh and some rustling, like a phone being shifted. "Alright. Fine. Just…just give me a minute."

I could hear the phone being set down on a hard surface and the sound of fingers clacking on a computer keyboard. A few minutes in, I was thinking I preferred the Muzak. Finally, Carmichael came back on the line.

"Alright, it looks like all of Tosh's earnings go to his accounting firm. A place in New Jersey."

I felt my shoulders sag. "An accounting firm? In Jersey."

"Yeah. Weissman and Associates. Did you want their address?"

"If it's handy," I said, trying not to let the disappointment show in my voice.

Carmichael rattled it off, and I jotted it down on a piece of paper. "Anything else I can help you with?" Carmichael asked when he was done, sounding not at all like he wanted to help me with anything else.

"No. Thanks," I told him.

"In that case, have a nice day, Ms. Bond." And then he hung up on me.

I set my pen down and googled Weissman and Associates, coming up with a phone number that went with the address Carmichael had given me. I tapped it into my phone, mentally crossing my fingers this paper trail would lead me somewhere other than in circles.

"Weissman and Associates, how may I direct your call?" a perky receptionist answered, her chipper attitude the polar opposite to Carmichael's receptionist.

"Hi, I'm Jamie Bond, from the Bond Agency," I told her. "I'm hoping you can help me with some information."

"I'd be happy to try," she told me, and I honestly believed her.

"Great. I'm looking for contact info for a Tosh Thomas. I believe he's a client of yours."

"Oh." Some of the perk slipped from her voice. "Oh, I'm sorry, but I can't give out any personal information about our clients."

Rats. "Is there any way you can put me in touch with him? Possibly pass along *my* contact info to him? It's important."

"I suppose I could do that," she said slowly, as if mentally going through her employee handbook to make sure it was permitted. "Let me see if I can find his files and give a message to the CPA attached to his account."

"Thanks," I told her, though I had less and less hope of this panning out, the more people this message had to pass through.

"Thomas, Thomas," she chanted, and I heard clacking in the background. "Huh."

"What is it?" I asked.

"Well, I'm actually not finding a client file under the name Tosh Thomas."

I frowned. "That's odd. His manager said he sent Tosh's checks to you. Royalty checks for a song he recorded with the Deadly Devils."

"Okay, yes! I do know who you're talking about now. It's Mr. Baskin's account." I heard more clicking. "Sorry, the files are under the client's new stage name."

"*New* stage name?" I perked up myself, almost matching her sunniness. "So Tosh Thomas was just a stage name?"

"Yeah, they all do that. We get a lot of performers here," she explained.

No wonder he had seemed to disappear. If he'd left the name behind and adopted a new persona, "Tosh Thomas" would have ceased to exist.

"What's his real name, then?" I asked.

"Oh. Yeah, I probably shouldn't say. You know, personal information and all."

"Right." I chewed my lower lip. "How about this—can you tell me the stage name he performs under now?"

"Well, I guess I can tell you that much. I mean, that's public, right?"

"Absolutely," I agreed.

"Our files are listed under Tad Windhorse."

"Tad Windhorse," I repeated, writing the name down. "That's a mouthful."

"Yeah, well, what do I know about Hollywood, right?" She laughed.

"Thanks," I told her. "You've been a big help."

"Did you still want to leave your info?" she asked.

I nodded, giving her my name and number, even as my fingers were busy typing his new pen name into a Google search.

By the time I hung up with Perky Receptionist, I had a page of hits for Tad Windhorse—who appeared to be some sort of new age musician based out of upstate New York, performing in a duo with a woman called Sierra Lightfoot.

And, coincidentally, was playing at a venue right here in LA this week.

Or, possibly not so coincidentally. It looked like he'd arrived in town just a couple of days before Drake was killed. Possibly his gig in LA had been just the opportunity he'd been looking for to be in the same city as his old rival, and he'd acted on it.

I picked my phone back up and called the number listed for the club where Tad was playing.

"Blue Moon Lounge?" came a man's voice.

"Hi there, I'm looking for Tad Windhorse. I believe he's performing at your venue?"

"Yeah, he'll be here through the 14th. Tickets are seventeen-fifty apiece through our website, and there's a two drink minimum."

"Uh, that's great, but I was hoping I could speak to him," I said quickly before the guy hung up. "Is he there right now by any chance?"

"He is," the guy said, a note of uncertainty in his voice. "But he's in the middle of a rehearsal right now. I can have him call you back?"

"Uh, no. Thanks. That's fine. I'll call again later."

I thanked the guy and hung up. But now that I'd tracked down the elusive keyboard player, I wasn't going to let him go that easily. Especially when I knew exactly where he was right then. I grabbed my purse and headed out the door toward the Blue Moon Lounge.

CHAPTER TWELVE

———

The Blue Moon Lounge was located just off Sunset, in the touristy section of Hollywood. Parking spots were few and far between, and I ended up stashing my Roadster in a pay lot several doors down. I passed by street performers and several couples posing for selfies in front of iconic storefronts before I finally found the club, housed in a small dark building with posters on the walls touting several different acts who would be appearing there in the near future.

While a sign on the door said they didn't open until 3p.m., the door wasn't locked and swung open easily as I pushed inside.

At the far end of the room sat a stage where a woman in a long white dress wearing turquoise tribal beads was stroking a harp. Beside her stood a slim guy wearing a checked cardigan and a beret, playing a flute. The combination of the two instruments was calm and serene, and I could hear the accompanying sound of wind being piped in through speakers.

A long bar ran through the center of the room, breaking up several groupings of small tables and booths, all positioned to view the stage. A guy in a black T-shirt with a logo of a blue moon holding a beer stood behind the bar slicing up lemons and limes.

"May I help you?" he asked as I approached.

"I'm looking for Tad Windhorse," I told him.

He inclined his head toward the guy in the beret on the stage. "That's him. He should be almost done with the sound check."

"That's Tad?" I glanced back at the subdued man with the flute. I had a hard time reconciling the man in the beret with the snarling rocker I'd seen in the Deadly Devils' promotional materials. Granted, some time had passed, but while the other Devils had merged into faded versions of their young selves, Tad/Tosh had seemed to reinvent himself into a compete opposite.

"That's him. He and his partner, Sierra, are the Wind Dancers."

"Thanks," I told the bartender as he turned back to his lemons.

I took a stool at the end of the bar closest to the stage and watched the pair finish their rehearsal. The music had a rhythmic feel to it that, along with the woman's occasional chanting, had an almost hypnotic feel. It reminded me of what you'd hear at a spa or a yoga class, and the relaxing effect had me feeling every minute of my sleepless night. I stifled a yawn as they finished their song.

The woman, presumably Sierra, gave a few notes to someone mixing the sound, and I slipped off my stool and approached the man who was twisting his flute apart, setting the pieces reverently down in a velvet-lined case.

"Mr. Windhorse?" I asked.

"Yes?" He turned a pair of warm brown eyes my way. A serene smile sat on his face, as if playing music had been a meditative experience for him.

"Hi. My name is Jamie Bond. I was hoping I could ask you a few questions."

"About?"

"Drake Deadly."

The serene smile died an instant death. His features sagged, his eyes flitting away from mine. "Yes, I heard about his transition to the other side. Terrible. Tragic."

"Very," I agreed. "You knew him well?"

"No," he said quickly. Maybe too quickly.

"You were in a band with him, though," I pressed. "The Deadly Devils."

"That was a long time ago," he said, his eyebrow still drawn down in a frown. "I don't do that type of music anymore."

"I can tell." I nodded toward the flute. "That was beautiful."

"Thank you," he said, attempting the smile again, but it didn't quite reach his eyes. "Who did you say you were again?"

"Jamie Bond," I repeated, not giving him much more to go on than the first time. "When was the last time you saw Drake?"

"Are you a reporter?" He narrowed his eyes at me.

"I'm actually a private investigator," I confessed.

He scoffed. "I suppose Drake hired you?"

I hesitated. He had, but not for this job. "Why do you say that?"

"Well, he was suing us all, now wasn't he?" he said, an edge to his voice as he closed his instrument case.

"So you knew about the lawsuit?"

"Of course. He had me served in the middle of a set in Portland." The snarl I'd seen from his youth made an appearance again, this time punctuated by a network of fine lines around his mouth.

"That sounds like it didn't go over well."

His eyes snapped up to meet mine. "I wasn't happy about it, if that's what you mean." He took a deep breath in through his nostrils and out again slowly. "But what I cannot change, I must let go and let fate guide the way."

"Even if Drake was looking to take the rights to 'Hot Waitress' away from you?"

"Away from the *band*. This lawsuit wasn't about *me* personally."

"But you did have your *personal* differences with Drake in the past," I pointed out.

"That was a long time ago." He glanced at the woman in white, now chatting with the bartender, as if looking for an escape route.

"Mr. Windhorse, do you know who wrote the song 'Hot Waitress'?" I asked, getting down to the real point of my visit.

He sucked in another long breath, pursed his lips, and thought about that a beat. A beat too long, if you asked me. Either he knew or he didn't. I wasn't sure what there was to think about. I felt like he was weighing his options for answering in his mind before speaking. Finally he must have decided he didn't like any of them, as he settled on a repeat of, "That was all a long time ago."

"So it would seem, but someone had to have written the song. Was it Drake?"

He scoffed again. "Drake didn't have the soul to write a grocery list, let alone a song."

I might have argued that "insane pain brain" about her "legs up to here" and "double Ds that bring me to my knees" were hardly the most heartfelt lyrics I'd ever heard. But I let it go.

"So who did write it? Bash?"

He frowned. "Is that what Bash is claiming?"

"I'd like to know what *you* remember," I said, skirting the question.

He shrugged. "I honestly don't know. Look, we all used to go to this diner. There was this waitress..." He trailed off, emotion flitting across his face momentarily before he cleared his throat. "Anyway, we all thought she was attractive."

Hot, even. But I just nodded for him to go on.

"One day we were jamming, and the song kind of wrote itself."

"But surely someone must have come up with the initial idea. Written down the lyrics? Come up with the bridge?" I reasoned.

But he just shrugged again, his gaze going to his flute case. "Sorry. It was a long time ago."

While that statement may have been true, the way he was avoiding my eyes made me think that time hadn't completely robbed him of his memory.

"This waitress. I understand you were dating her at the time?"

Again that hint of emotion flashed behind his eyes. "Yeah. So?"

"So I also understand you weren't very happy when you found out Drake had started seeing her behind your back."

"No," he said. He shook his head. "No, I was not. And whoever told you this story probably told you we had it out too, huh?"

I nodded. "I'm told it's why you walked out on the band."

He did more deep breathing. In. Out. "I was a hothead back then. Very hot. But, look, that was a lifetime ago. Things are different now."

"Are they?"

"Yes," he said emphatically. "I've had a lot of anger management since then. And yoga. I meditate. I'm a different person."

I'll admit, I'd certainly noticed his physical appearance was much different than the punk look he'd sported during his Devil days. But if all the near-hyperventilation-like breathing he'd been doing was any indication, there appeared to still be an undercurrent of anger running through him that he was attempting to manage. And the emotion behind his eyes felt less like serenity and more like resentment bubbling just below the new age surface.

"So you had forgiven Drake for stealing your hot waitress?" I asked, watching his eyes.

He nodded. "Yes. Look, Drake and I had our differences in the past. But that was in the *past*," he said, drawing the word out for emphasis. "In fact, Drake came to see me here, and we let the ghosts of our previous quarrels dissipate like mist upon the mesa."

"He came to see you here?" I asked, ignoring the poetry. "At the Blue Moon?"

He nodded.

"When was this?"

"The day before he died."

That was interesting timing. The look on my face must have said as much, as he frowned and shook his head.

"Now, wait a minute." He held both hands up in a halting motion. "His seeing me had nothing to do with his tragic death. It was just fortuitous timing."

"Fortuitous?" I repeated.

"Yes. That we had a chance to set aside old differences before his passing to the new light."

"I find it interesting that you don't see each other for twenty years, then you chat, and he dies the next day."

"Karma is a mysterious animal."

So was murder, but I set that thought aside.

"What did you two talk about?" I asked.

He fiddled with the latch on his flute case. "Old times."

"That's it? He just came by to chat about the good old days?"

He lifted his chin defiantly. "Yes."

"You didn't discuss the lawsuit?"

"No."

"Or the song?"

"No."

"Did he tell you he'd called a band meeting for the following night?"

His eyes went back to his instrument case. "No."

"Where were *you* the following night?"

His head snapped up. "What?"

"The night Drake died. Were you here?"

He glanced over at the bartender, as if calculating his merit as an alibi. "N-no, the lounge is closed on Mondays."

"Then where—"

"I was with Sierra. Rehearsing," he said quickly. "Now if you'll excuse me, I have somewhere to be." He didn't wait for an answer as he picked up his flute case and brushed past me.

I'd bet money he was lying to me.

I watched his retreating back and wondered just what Drake had really come to see him about. Possibly the same thing he'd planned to meet with the rest of the band about. If Windhorse had gotten a preview, maybe he hadn't liked it at all…and killed Drake before he could share it with anyone else.

* * *

"So you think Keyboards might be our killer?" Caleigh asked an hour later as I filled her in over a couple of tacos from the food truck outside our building.

I shrugged as I chewed and swallowed, standing in the parking lot under the shade of a scrawny palm tree. "Possibly. But," I said, pointing my taco at her, "he's not *our* killer. Not our case, remember?"

"Right." Caleigh winked at me as she sipped lemonade through a straw.

"What's with the wink?"

"Oh, come on, Jamie. You really think that this song and the murder are unrelated?"

I set my taco down on my paper plate. "Okay. No, I think they're totally related."

"And if one is tied up with the other, the answer to one is most likely going to lead to the other, right?"

"Maybe."

"So, quit trying to pretend a murder lands in your lap and you don't care who the killer is."

I couldn't stifle my grin. "Geez, am I that easy to read?"

"Like a cheap paperback," she answered before shoving carne asada into her mouth.

"Okay," I conceded. "Yes, I care who killed Drake. I mean, he *was* our client."

"See!"

"But," I added, "I don't know that our *current* client is going to be happy if we don't make headway on his issue."

Caleigh shrugged. "Fair." She paused to swallow her bite of taco. "But I don't buy for a second that Drake just visited Windhorse out of the blue to apologize, coincidentally the day before he was killed."

"Me neither," I agreed.

"So what do you think he really went to see Windhorse about?"

"Best guess? I think he showed him the proof that Drake wrote 'Hot Waitress,'" I decided. "The same proof he was going to show the rest of the band the following night."

"Why show Windhorse a day early?"

"Maybe Windhorse refused to come to the band meeting? Or maybe Drake had to track him down like I did?"

"So, you think Windhorse killed Drake and took the proof before he could share it in order to keep receiving his cut of royalties?"

"Maybe." I took another bite, chewing thoughtfully. "But the wife is still bothering me."

"How so?" Caleigh asked, crumpling up her empty wrapper and tossing it into a nearby trash can.

"Well, if we're talking about coincidences, it's a whopper of one that her house was broken into right after her husband was killed."

"Agreed. You think it has to do with Drake's death?"

I nodded. "Aiden said they didn't find anything in Drake's personal effects that had anything to do with the song. So, it's possible Drake didn't even have it with him at the hotel."

"And it was in his house for safekeeping," Caleigh finished for me. "You think that's what the intruder was looking for?"

"I think it's one possibility. Jenna said nothing had been taken, but she didn't look very thoroughly."

"So maybe she interrupted them before they could find it," Caleigh said, her eyes shining with eagerness. "Which means maybe it's still there! Do you think Jenna would let us look for it?"

I laughed. "Fat chance of that. She practically threw me out."

"Well…" Caleigh said, undeterred. "In that case…do you think there's any chance her back door is still busted?"

CHAPTER THIRTEEN

"Wish I'd dressed for the occasion," Caleigh said, looking down at her white jeans, baby blue sweater, and nude heels an hour and a half later.

"You look fine," I told her, slowly easing my car down Jenna's street.

"I feel a little too pastel for breaking and entering."

"We're not breaking and entering," I corrected her quickly. "Someone else already did the breaking. We're just..." I trailed off, looking for the right word.

"Entering?" Caleigh supplied with a smile.

I shrugged. "Having a little more thorough look around than I got last night."

"Right. I'm sure Aiden will totally see it that way." Caleigh was still grinning.

I shot her a look. "I wish you wouldn't bring up the ADA when we're about to—"

"Enter?"

I shot her a *stronger* look. "And wipe that grin off your face."

"Anything you say, boss," she said, not even trying to comply. "You're sure Jenna won't be home?" She glanced up at the colonial looming through the trees ahead of us as I flipped a U-turn in front of Jenna's place.

"She shouldn't be. According to the sheet Drake initially gave me, she sees her personal trainer every Tuesday and Thursday at two." I parked at the curb two houses down and opened my glove box. Which, in this particular case, actually did contain gloves. A box of latex ones that were super handy when encountering gross stuff or when doing things where one might not want to leave fingerprints behind. I grabbed a pair and handed another to Caleigh.

"How long do you think she'll be?" Caleigh asked, slipping her gloves on with a satisfying thwack.

I shrugged. "I'm hoping at least an hour. Depends on traffic I guess."

"So you're saying we need to work quickly."

"Speed would be optimal," I told her, getting out of the car and locking it.

While Jenna and Drake's house was on a fairly quiet residential street, I still felt adrenaline building in my stomach as we backtracked to their place. I looked over both shoulders before slipping behind a line of trees and hugging the property line as we quickly jogged through the front yard. I felt Caleigh a step behind me, but I kept my eyes firmly on the house, watching for any signs of life. Jenna's Jag was gone. No other cars in the curved driveway. No movement behind any of the windows.

My heels sank into the lawn as we reached a side gate that led toward the back of the property. As we slipped through it and into the backyard, I felt a little less exposed.

"This yard is huge," Caleigh said, eyes going to the swimming pool.

She was right, but the sight of the sparkling blue water only made me think of Drake and his last moments. I suppressed a shudder in the crisp air.

"There," I said softly to Caleigh, pointing to the French doors leading off the back patio. "That's the door with the broken lock." I glanced up at the house, scanning the back windows for any movement. But as far as I could tell, the place was empty.

I licked my lips, hoping my luck held out as I motioned for Caleigh to follow me and crossed the patio to the French doors. I put one gloved hand on the knob and easily pushed it open.

"Wow, nice place," Caleigh whispered as we stepped inside the family room. Her eyes roved the neighboring kitchen with clear envy. While I had to agree it rivaled anything I'd seen on HGTV, I was too far from an accomplished home chef to properly appreciate it. My culinary talents ran more toward microwaveable and takeout.

"So, where do we want to start?" she asked.

"I noticed a computer in the den."

"The den it is," Caleigh agreed.

I led the way down the short hallway toward the front of the house, taking a left once we got to the foyer, into the den near the front door. We stepped inside, and in the bright light of day, I could clearly see Drake's hand in the décor. The walls were adorned with posters similar to those I'd seen in his bandmate's house—though these were displayed in large frames under glass that gave them more of an illusion of artwork than the thumbtacks at Keith and Harry's had. A couple gold records sat near a bookshelf and some built-ins, and several guitars were hung on the back wall, looking more for display than play. In front of them sat a large wood desk holding a computer monitor and an old-fashioned landline.

Caleigh instinctively moved toward the computer, stepping around the desk. "Computer's still here. I guess the police haven't taken it yet."

"Or they've already been through it," I mused as Caleigh powered it on, pulling out a leather chair behind the desk and settling in.

Since she was in her element, I left her to it, browsing the contents of the bookshelves. Which held very few books. Instead, more memorabilia sat on display—bobbleheads of the band, framed photos with other musicians, a couple of awards, and some pins and other collectibles from their world tours. Unfortunately, no old cassette tapes labeled *Hot Waitress* or any items that screamed "songwriter."

I opened a couple of cupboards in the built-in wall unit, finding printer paper, envelopes, and a half-empty bottle of tequila.

"I need a password to get in," Caleigh called from the desk.

"Any chance you can bypass it?" I asked, coming to stand behind her.

She shook her head. "Maybe. But not quickly." She typed some numbers into the password field and hit enter, earning her a screen that told her she was incorrect.

"What did you type in?" I asked, watching her fingers try again.

"Birthday. Anniversary. And..." She paused, trying again. "The date on his first gold album." She frowned. "All wrong."

"Maybe he's more of a word guy than numbers?" I offered.

"Maybe." She opened the top drawer of the desk. "Think he might have it written down anywhere?"

I shrugged. "It depends on how paranoid he was about privacy."

I watched Caleigh rummage through the top drawers. Pens, Post-its, a calculator, and some rubber bands. Nothing terribly useful to us.

As she moved on to the next one, my eyes scanned the room for any clue to what might have struck Drake as a secure word. "Did you try *Hot Waitress*?"

Caleigh shook her head and went back to the keyboard, typing it in. A second later she shook her head. "No go."

"*Rock star*?" I offered. "*Groupie*? *Deadly Devils*?"

Caleigh tried them all, adding various numbers and symbols along with them, still coming up short.

"What about his wife?" I offered. "Maybe he made a password when they were in happier times?"

"Okay, let's try *Jenna*," she said, typing it in. Only, Drake was not that simplistic, and we were not that lucky. Caleigh began typing in variations on her name, birthday, some cutesy monikers.

"Got it!" she finally yelled triumphantly.

"What was it?" I asked, leaning to look at the screen. "*JennasJugs*."

The man was a true romantic. "So we're in?"

Caleigh nodded, and I tried not to celebrate too heartily yet as I glanced down at the time. We'd been in the house for almost twenty minutes already.

"Okay, what are we looking for?" Caleigh mumbled, almost more to herself than me, her eyes scanning lists of files.

"Anything that looks like it could be about the song." I paused. "Or possibly anything Jenna didn't want us to see."

Caleigh swiveled in her seat, giving me a questioning look.

"She got defensive when I mentioned checking out the den last night," I said, remembering how quickly she'd wanted me gone.

"Right. In that case, I'd say let's start with financials," Caleigh said, flicking open an accounting program. A few moments later we were looking at an array of spreadsheets, showing lots of columns of amounts and dates.

"Looks like royalties?" I asked, squinting at the first column. While I didn't consider myself a dummy, math had never been my strong suit.

Caleigh nodded. "Detailed account of them, too. Sale price, net, fees, commissions. Look, you can see here the number of downloads and physical media sold each day and average costs." She scrolled to the right, bringing up more columns. "He's even got currency conversion in here for foreign sales."

I frowned. "This looks a lot more detailed than any royalty statement I've ever seen before," I noted. Not that I'd seen many, but I had grown up in LA, where half the town made their living off royalties of one kind or another.

"Oh, it is. Way more detailed." She turned to face me. "If I had to guess, this was a system Drake was using to keep track on his own. Maybe trying to estimate revenue on his next check."

I nodded. "His manager said something about being paid quarterly. I could see wanting to have an idea of how much was coming each period."

"Especially with numbers like these." Caleigh pointed to a line of zeroes.

"This is a lot more organized than I would have given Drake credit for," I said, scanning over the document. "I wonder if looking at these balance sheets was the catalyst to Drake claiming rights to the song," I mused.

"Well, he definitely had a lot on the line if he was the rightful owner," Caleigh noted.

"And the band had a lot on the line as well," I said.

Caleigh pulled a thumb drive from her jeans pocket and plugged it into Drake's computer.

"You just walk around with a thumb drive in your pocket, just in case?"

"Yeah." She blinked at me. "Doesn't everyone?"

I grinned. "They should," I told her as she copied the files. I glanced at the time. 2:52. I had no idea how long Jenna's personal training session were, but we had to be cutting it close. "Are there any recordings on that thing?" I gestured to the monitor.

"Like songs?" Caleigh asked, switching screens.

I nodded. "I mean, I know we're looking for some old jam session cassettes, but maybe he made a digital copy of them or something?"

Caleigh flicked through several folders. "I'm not seeing anything that's clearly labeled, but if he were trying to hide it, he might not."

"Maybe in the 'my music' section?" I suggested, wondering if that was too obvious.

Caleigh clicked there, bringing up dozens of playlists and hundreds of little album icons. She did a search for "Hot Waitress," but the only thing that came back to us was the official recording. No jam sessions. No homemade copies. No images of handwritten lyrics neatly signed *by Drake*.

"It could take a while to go through everything on his hard drive," Caleigh said, glancing at the time.

I sighed, straightening back up and focusing my gaze around the room. "So, maybe we focus what little time we have left on an analog search. The intruder seemed to focus his search on the master bedroom." I moved into the foyer, where staircase curved to the second floor. "Maybe we should too."

Caleigh nodded, slipping her thumb drive back into her pocket and powering the computer back down. "How much longer until the wife comes home?"

"Not much," I said, leading the way to the stairs. I took them two at a time, hearing Caleigh's heels clack up behind me.

I noticed the door to the master was open at the end of the hallway. We stepped inside and saw largely the same scene I'd found last night. Jenna had righted the nightstand and put the bulk of jewelry back in her case, but the clothes were still in piles of disarray on the floor.

I went to the dresser, checking the drawers for anything the intruder might not have gone over, while Caleigh took the closet. We worked systematically for a few moments in silence, each of us moving our hands over Jenna's possessions as quickly and unobtrusively as possible. Though, considering the state they were already in, I doubted she'd notice them being moved a second time. I still felt the slightest bit guilty about the intrusion.

"Did you see the collection of Louboutins this woman owns?" Caleigh asked, stepping from the walk-in closet.

"I did. I'm pea green."

She shook her head. "Almost makes me want to go find my own fading rock star."

I laughed. "Yeah, well, it couldn't have been that great of a deal if she was divorcing him."

Caleigh shrugged. "Still. She gets to keep the shoes." She crossed the room to the doorway of the master bath. "Did you look in the bathroom yet?"

I shook my head. "No, but I'm coming up empty here." I closed the last drawer of the dresser, feeling more and more like we were just trespassing and not getting any closer to finding anything.

I followed Caleigh into the bathroom, where she crouched down and started pulling open cupboards and drawers. "Wow, her collection of beauty products almost rivals her shoes."

"Being a trophy wife is a tough job. Or so I'm told."

"Anti-acne cream, anti-wrinkle cream, hair removal cream. Antifungal." She scrunched up her nose. "She's got a cream to get rid of everything."

"No anti-husband creams?" I joked.

"No." Caleigh opened the next drawer and froze. "But she does have anti-baby measures here."

I grinned as I crossed the room to look in the drawer. "Anti-baby?"

Caleigh pointed down at a box of condoms in the bottom of the drawer.

I blinked, the meaning of the find sinking in. "Didn't Drake Deadly tell us he was sterile?"

Caleigh's eyes went big and round. "Ohmigosh, that's right! So, if he was shooting blanks, then the only reason the wife would have these is—"

"—is if she really *was* sleeping with someone else."

"Dang." Caleigh shook her head. "And here we close Drake's case too late for anyone to care about it."

Which didn't mean it wasn't still relevant. I took out my phone, popping off a couple pictures of the incriminating evidence. My mind was suddenly buzzing, thinking this put everything with Jenna in a whole new light. If Jenna really was cheating after all, and she figured out Drake had hired us to tail her, she knew she stood to lose everything if we found out her secret. Had his death been about his unfaithful wife all along, and the song had nothing to do with it? If Jenna had been home all evening like she claimed, it's possible she'd enticed her lover to off Drake. Maybe the two of them had decided that living off a widow's inheritance was a much better way to start their life together than risking a busted prenup and no alimony. Or possibly—

"Jamie!"

I snapped out of my thoughts, realizing Caleigh had been calling my name. "What?"

"I said, 'Did you hear that?'" Her mouth was tense, her eyebrows drawn down in concern.

"Hear what?"

"I thought it sounded like a—"

A key being turned in the lock downstairs. I knew because I heard it too. The sound freezing Caleigh's thought on her lips and sending a surge of panic through my limbs.

Someone was home.

CHAPTER FOURTEEN

"What do we do?" Caleigh whispered, the same panic I felt racing through me evident in her voice.

"I don't know," I whispered back. I dove behind the master bedroom door, peeking around it to see a vacuum cleaner edge its way through the front door.

"Hola, Señora James," a woman's voice called. A beat later I saw a portly Hispanic woman walk into the foyer carrying a bag of cleaning supplies. "Anyone home?" she called again.

"Who is it?" Caleigh's breath came close to my ear.

"Cleaning lady," I hissed back.

"What do we do?" she repeated.

I pursed my lips together. "Wait until she moves to the back of the house. Then we'll slip out."

Caleigh looked down at her watch. "Isn't the wife supposed to arrive home now?"

"Pray she hits traffic," I whispered back, turning my eyes to the doorway again.

I could see the housekeeper slowly moving all her supplies inside the house, taking off her shoes and putting on a pair of blue paper booties, pulling her hair back into a no-nonsense ponytail. She started humming, and I could tell she was in no hurry. She slowly went through her bag, pulling bottles and brushes out and arranging them in a bucket.

I closed my eyes, willing her to get a move on to that big, beautiful kitchen full of lots of shiny appliances to wipe down. I heard Caleigh shifting nervously from foot to foot beside me.

"Come on, come on," Caleigh chanted.

I opened my eyes and peeked around the doorframe again. The woman seemed satisfied with her choice of cleaning products and picked up her bucket, finally moving down the hallway and out of sight.

"Let's go," I whispered, keeping my back to the wall as I slid out the bedroom door and onto the exposed second-floor landing. If the wife came home now, we were sitting ducks. I quickly walked across the thankfully carpeted floor, slipping my shoes off once we hit the wooden stairs. Caleigh did the same, and we softly padded our way down, cringing with every creak of wood beneath our feet.

I was halfway down when the housekeeper's humming got louder, her footsteps returning.

I froze, feeling Caleigh bump into me from behind. We were too far from the top of the stairs to beat a hasty retreat and too far from the door to make an escape. I ducked down below the banister, pulling Caleigh with me but knowing full well that if the housekeeper turned toward the stairs, the slim spindles would be useless to hide us.

My breath came slow and shallow as I watched the housekeeper come into view again, still blissfully singing to herself, and grab her vacuum. When she spun around to go to the far end of the house, my heart stopped beating for a second. All she'd have to do was look up, and she'd see us both.

The next three seconds felt like they took a lifetime as the housekeeper slowly pushed the vacuum toward the back of the house...her eyes on the floor.

I heard Caleigh let out a long shaky breath behind me as the housekeeper moved out of view.

"I thought we were sunk for sure," she whispered.

"Come on. We're not home free yet," I whispered back, quickly racing down the rest of the stairs and practically sprinting barefoot to the door.

I gingerly turned the knob, hearing a loud click as it shifted in my hands but not breaking my quick stride for anything. We slipped out, shut the door softly behind us, and again sprinted down the driveway as fast as our bare feet could take us. It wasn't until we'd crossed the lawn to the tree line that I dared to breathe again, pausing to put on my heels.

By the time we got back to my car, my breathing was almost back to normal, but my legs felt like jelly and I had wet grass between my toes.

"That was close," Caleigh said, slipping into the passenger seat and automatically checking her makeup in the visor mirror.

"Too close. I thought her housekeeper came in the mornings," I mumbled, slipping my shoe off again to wipe the earth off my feet. We both sat there for a couple moments, getting our breath under control, our heart rates out of sprinter range, and our composure back to calm, cool, collected PI levels.

Then I nearly jumped a mile when my phone's ringtone filled the interior of my car. Caleigh put a hand to her heart beside me, signaling she was still on the jumpy side as well.

I looked down to see Maya's face and stabbed the *On* button.

"Hey," I answered. "What's up?"

"Uh, Derek is here," came Maya's voice.

"Hey, James!" I heard my father call in the background.

Oh boy. As if my blood pressure hadn't suffered enough today.

"What does he want?" I asked.

But it wasn't Maya's voice that answered me. "*He* wants to see his daughter!" Derek yelled.

I heard rustling, then Maya's voice close to the phone receiver, muffled as if she were trying to cover it. "Sorry. I told him you were out, but he insisted I call you."

"It's fine," I reassured her, slipping my seat belt on. "We were just heading back anyway."

"Oh good." The relief in Maya's voice was unmistakable. Then again, Derek usually referred to her as "the Playboy Bunny one," so I could see why.

"Be there in fifteen minutes," I told her before hanging up and pulling away from the curb.

Just as Jenna's mint green Jaguar came speeding down the street.

Caleigh swiveled in her seat, watching it pull up Jenna's driveway. "*Way* too close."

* * *

"I thought you said you'd be here twenty minutes ago," Derek said, rising from the sofa in reception as Caleigh and I pushed through the frosted glass doors.

"Hi, Derek. Nice to see you too," I said, heavy on the sarcasm in response to his welcoming greeting.

"Don't play cute with me, kid. I thought you were standing me up."

If only.

"There was traffic," I told him honestly as I pushed past him to my office. Which was true. Apparently our praying earlier to stall Jenna on her way home had not fallen on deaf ears. It just had backfired on us, resulting in a near parking lot on the 405.

"I didn't hit any on the way over from the marina," he said, trailing after me.

I dropped my purse down on my desk. "Maya said you wanted something?"

Derek grinned at me, creating a dimple in his left cheek that had about three days' worth of white scruff clinging to it. He was dressed today in a pair of jeans with holes in the knees, Birkenstocks, and a Hawaiian shirt with parrots and Corona bottles all over it. His hair was going grey and several weeks past a haircut, but the mischievous glimmer in his blue eyes gave him a perpetually youthful look.

"You're all business today, huh, kid?" he said.

"I am at work." I gestured around me to illustrate the point.

"Well, I just wanted to stop by and see how things are going with your case." He plopped himself down into one of my client chairs, putting his feet up on the desk like he owned the place.

Or, I should say, like he *still* owned the place.

"And which case would that be?" I asked, shoving his feet back down to the floor with a thud.

"Which case? Come on, James. The exciting one. The dead rock star."

I shrugged, sitting in the chair behind my desk. "There is no case. He's dead. End of our involvement."

Derek gave me the same sort of *get real* look Caleigh had given me over tacos earlier that day. "Who do you think you're talking to, kid?"

I blew out a lungful of air at the ceiling. "Al*right*. Geez, everyone around here thinks I've got some sort of nosy streak."

"Curious. Not nosy. I always thought you were a curious kid."

I wasn't sure that was a compliment, but it was the closest I'd get from Derek, so I let it go. "Sorry to burst your bubble, but I'm really not involved. Drake is not my client anymore."

Derek narrowed his eyes at me. "Don't hold out on me, kid. I know you're working for the drummer now."

"How did you know..." I trailed off, halfway thinking Derek had the place bugged as his face broke into a slow, sly smile.

"You can take the man out of the PI office, but you can't take the PI out of the man." He leaned back in his chair, looking particularly satisfied with himself.

"You badgered Maya for info, didn't you?" I surmised.

He shrugged. "You were twenty minutes late. What else was I gonna do?"

I shook my head at him. "Okay, fine. Yes, we have been retained by the Deadly Devils' drummer. Bash. But we're just looking for something for him."

"Yeah, Maya told me. Some sort of proof that he wrote 'Hot Waitress.'"

I glanced toward reception. He'd really worked over my employee, hadn't he?

"Yes, but we're just looking for some old cassette tapes. *Not*," I emphasized again, "a murderer."

"I think the guitar player did it." Derek nodded sagely. "Keith Kane."

I knew I was going to regret asking this, but... "Why do you think that?"

"That guy was always in trouble back in the day. You know he has an arrest record?"

I did not know that, but I was not going to admit that to Derek, so I just nodded.

"He always felt like the ringleader to me, you know? Always the one at the microphone for interviews, always the one in the headlines. Like the other Devils kind of followed his lead."

I'd seen some of that same dynamic when I'd visited him and Harry in Tujunga. "All very interesting, but not my case," I decided.

"Of course, they were all pretty wild back in the day," Derek went on, totally ignoring me. "Even Drake had a couple skirmishes with the law. That manager of theirs...what's his name?"

"Carmichael," I supplied automatically.

"Yeah, I remember he had to keep bailing these guys out left and right. I think the band had at least four arrests the year they won the Global Music Award. I mean, all petty stuff. But three of those were Keith Kane."

I thought of the retiree in bellbottoms I'd met the day before. He had definitely seemed like he was not only holding something back, but also keeping a tight rein on his pal Harry as well.

I shook my head. "Look, Derek, I have no idea who killed Drake—"

"I don't believe that for a minute."

"—but I'm confident that the authorities have the necessary resources to find the responsible parties."

Derek gave me that dubious look again. "You've been hanging out with that attorney fellow too much. His lawyer double talk is rubbing off on you."

"I have not been hanging out with him too much."

"Maybe just enough?" Derek waggled his eyebrows at me.

"I am *not* discussing my love life with you."

"Love? Wow, it must be getting serious."

"I have work to do, Derek." I stood and crossed the room to the door. "Was there anything else?" I asked superfluously as I opened it for him to exit.

Derek just laughed, rising slowly from his seat and purposely taking his time as he sauntered the two steps to reception. "Call me if you need a hand on this one," he told me. "You know I'm a big Devils fan."

"Will do!" I told him. Meaning it about as much as he meant he was retired.

* * *

As soon as Derek left, I picked up my phone and keyed in Jenna's number. I was tired of getting the runaround from the wife, and I wanted answers. While I doubted she was going to get me any closer to "Hot Waitress," I still felt I had some sort of obligation to the dead man to find out exactly what a box of condoms was doing in her bathroom drawer. Especially if we had played any part as catalysts to said wife murdering him.

I listened to the phone ring three times on the other end before it went to voicemail again.

But I wasn't giving up that easily this time.

I grabbed my purse and marched purposefully through reception.

"Are you leaving again?" Maya asked.

"I want to talk to Jenna James," I told her, putting on my jacket.

"I thought you were just at her place." Maya frowned.

"I was." I quickly filled her in on what Caleigh and I had found.

"So Drake was right about his wife being unfaithful," Maya mused when I was done.

"It appears that way." I hiked my purse up on my shoulder. "But I'd still like to hear it from the wife. Is Caleigh still here?"

Maya shook her head. "Just stepped out. Why?"

I shook my head. "Never mind." I was pretty sure I could take Jenna without backup on this one. "I'll be back in a couple hours."

"Hour and a half," Maya corrected. "You have Kendall Manchester at 4:30."

"Right." I nodded. "Hour and a half. I'll be here."

CHAPTER FIFTEEN

———

Fifteen minutes later I stood on Jenna's doorstep again, this time in full sight. I rang the bell, listening to the chimes echo on the other side. A minute later, the door was opened by the same Hispanic woman I'd seen earlier.

"May I help you?" she asked, her voice calm and pleasant.

"I'm here to see Jenna," I told her. "Jamie Bond."

"Is she expecting you?" she inquired.

I highly doubted it. But I didn't get a chance to answer, as I heard Jenna's voice from farther within. "Who is it, Lupe?"

"A Ms. Bond to see you," Lupe said, opening the door wider and standing back to allow her employer a look at me.

Jenna was halfway down the staircase, dressed in a pair of tight leather pants, a tight shimmery pink top, and matching pink heels. She looked like Brentwood Barbie, with her pale blonde hair puffed within an inch of its life around her like a fluffy yellow cloud.

"You again." She narrowed her eyes at me.

Not the most gracious greeting I'd ever received.

"Hi, Jenna. I was hoping we could talk."

"I really don't have anything to say to you," Jenna said, coming down the rest of the stairs to stand in the foyer.

Lupe seemed to sense the tension in the air, and wisely faded back into the house, leaving us alone.

"Well, you have two options," I told her, not backing down. "You can talk to me, or you can explain to the ADA why you have a box of condoms in your bathroom."

Her eyebrows drew down, and I could see her formulating a denial.

"There's no use lying about it. I have photos."

"How did you get those?" she shot back.

"Answer my question first. Were you cheating on your husband?"

She scoffed, her eyes still narrowed. "You can't prove anything. What sort of birth control I have in my private residence is none of yours or the ADA's business." She crossed her arms over her chest. With difficulty. Her boobs were huge.

"Your husband was sterile," I pointed out.

"How do you know that?"

"He told me himself. Which means you would have no reason to use those condoms." I paused meaningfully. "Unless he wasn't the only person you were sleeping with."

Jenna sucked in her cheeks, narrowed her eyes further, and gave me a good long stare. I wasn't sure what sort of thoughts were flitting through that bleached blonde brain of hers, but she was clearly contemplating her options. Finally she spat out one word. "Fine."

"Fine?" I clarified.

"Fine. Yes, I was having an affair. Happy?"

Kinda, yeah. Not for Drake, clearly, but it was always satisfying to finally get the truth.

"Did Drake know?"

Jenna let out a bark of laughter. "Like he would have cared. I told you, our relationship was over far before he moved into that hotel."

"I think the infidelity clause in your prenup was plenty of reason for him to care," I pointed out.

She jutted her chin out. "Drake was clueless."

"Was he? Or did he find out, and you killed him before he could cut you off?"

"That's a lie!" She stabbed a glossy pink fingernail at me.

"Or maybe it was your secret lover who drowned your husband for you."

"No!" she shouted. "No, you are way off base."

"You knew you were being followed. You called Drake and confronted him about it on the phone," I said, laying out the scenario for her. "He told you he knew about your affair and that he was going to cut you off. So, you called Lover Boy and told him he needed to get rid of Drake so you two could live happily ever after off his money."

"That is not how it happened!" Jenna said, her cheeks starting to tinge pink with anger.

"So clue me in. How did it happen, Jenna?" I challenged her.

She shook her head. "Look, you've got this all wrong. Drake didn't know I was seeing someone. He didn't *care*. Prenup or not."

I opened my mouth to refute that, but she just plowed ahead.

"Drake hired you to *follow* me."

I shut my mouth with a click. "He did," I agreed, wondering where she was going with this.

"He wanted to know where I was going, who I was seeing. Am I right?"

I nodded. "Because he wanted proof you were being unfaithful."

Jenna shook her head. "That was just the line of bull he sold you. What he wanted to know was where I was keeping the tapes."

"Tapes?" I frowned.

She nodded. "All of the band's old recordings."

"Including 'Hot Waitress.'" I felt puzzle pieces starting to slowly rearrange themselves.

Jenna glanced behind her, as if suddenly aware the housekeeper might be within earshot. Then she stepped out onto the porch, shutting the door behind us.

"Look, it wasn't supposed to pan out like this, okay? I never meant for Drake to get hurt."

"How was it supposed to pan out?"

"With a nice divorce settlement."

I glanced up at her house. She wasn't making out too badly now. "Okay, start at the beginning. How did you end up with the band's recordings?"

"Drake gave them to me. They were supposed to be some sort of wedding present. He thought the old memorabilia was 'one of a kind' and 'a piece of rock 'n' roll history.'" She rolled her eyes. "*I* was angling for a Bentley, but whatever."

"So what did you do with the tapes he gave you?"

She shrugged. "Just chucked them into storage. What else was I going to do with them?"

"I take it this was before the song hit big."

She nodded. "Once it was used in that commercial, Drake started paying close attention to the song's sales. He was obsessed with it, watching every chart, subscribing to sales tracking services, calling Carmichael all the time for updated numbers."

"And when he saw how big those numbers were, he suddenly wasn't happy splitting profits with the rest of the band," I surmised.

She nodded. "That was Drake. Always was a cheap, greedy jerk."

"Okay, so Drake brings the lawsuit, then what? He asks you for the tapes back?" I guessed.

She nodded. "He sure did. Not only does he give me the lamest wedding present ever, but then he has the nerve to ask for it back."

"But you didn't give it to him."

"Heck no! Look, he wanted something—I wanted something. I hid the tapes nice and secretly and told him if he gave me a divorce without any fuss, with a nice little alimony settlement, he could have them back."

"But instead of agreeing, he hired us." I thought back to the meeting I'd had with Drake. At the time I'd thought he'd been lying about his suspicions about his wife just to bust the prenup. But he'd actually been lying in order to get me to keep tabs on her. What had he said—tell me everywhere she goes and everyone she sees. He'd been looking for a clue as to where she'd stashed the tapes.

"You said you confronted Drake about being followed?" I asked.

Jenna nodded. "Yeah. Like I said, I called him as soon as I got home from the AAA meeting. I told him to back off. He'd never find the tapes, and the only way he was going to get his hands on them was if he gave me what I wanted."

"And then someone killed him."

She bit her lip, nodding slowly. "Now Drake's dead and someone else is after the tapes."

"The break-in last night." I glanced back up at the house. "You think that's what they were after?"

"What else would they be looking for?"

"Did they take them?" I asked.

She shook her head. "No. But that doesn't mean they won't be back." She crossed her arms over her chest again, this time in a less combative and more instinctively protective gesture.

"I have to ask: Jenna, *did* Drake actually write 'Hot Waitress'?"

She sighed. "I don't know."

"What do you mean you don't know? Haven't you listened to the tapes?"

She shook her head. "It's like hundreds of hours of stoned dudes playing guitar solos. I couldn't even get through one tape."

"Where are they now?"

She did more lip biting, and for a moment I feared she wasn't going to give them up. Finally she nodded toward the Jag. "In my trunk."

I glanced at her car. "Here?"

She nodded. "I-I didn't know what else to do with them. Drake still had keys to the house, and I was afraid that if I left them inside, Drake would find them while I was out or something. So, I just took them with me. Everywhere."

I felt my hope surging. "Jenna, can I have those tapes?" I asked slowly.

She sucked in a cheek, thinking about that. Finally she shrugged. "Fine. I guess it's not as if they're of any use to me anymore anyway."

I followed her as she walked to her car and lifted the latch to open the trunk. She pushed aside some reusable shopping bags and a yoga mat before she pulled out a shoebox and handed it to me.

I lifted the lid, peeking at the contents. Inside sat a row of at least a dozen cassette tapes, all unlabeled.

"Is the jam session where they wrote 'Hot Waitress' in here?" I asked.

She shrugged. "Like I said, I didn't listen to them. But Drake seemed to want them pretty badly, so I'm guessing it is."

I put the lid back on and turned to Jenna. "So who is he?"

"He?" Jenna asked, leaning one hip against her bumper.

"Your boyfriend." I gave her a pointed look.

She scoffed. "Not important. You have your tapes. What do you care?"

And with that, she slammed the trunk shut and stalked back into the house, shutting the door behind her with decided finality.

* * *

As soon as I got back into my car, I called Caleigh's number. She picked up on the second ring.

"Hey, boss. What's up?"

"You busy this evening?" I asked, my eyes darting back to Jenna's quiet colonial.

"Nooo…why? What did you have in mind?"

"I was hoping you could tail Jenna James again."

"Sure. You have somewhere that you think she'll be going?"

"I *hope* she'll be going to see her boyfriend."

Caleigh sucked in a breath. "So she admitted that she was seeing someone?"

"Most definitely." I quickly filled her in on my conversation with Jenna. "She says it doesn't matter now who her boyfriend is, but I'm not so sure."

"You still think he might have had something to do with Drake's death?"

"I don't know. Jenna might have been telling the truth about why Drake originally hired us. But the fact is, she's still way better off widowed than she would have been divorced."

"I'm on it!" Caleigh said, and I heard rustling in the background like she was already on the move. "Is she at home right now?"

I nodded. "Yeah, I'm just leaving Brentwood. But be careful," I cautioned, remembering how Jenna had made us in the past. "She's smarter than she looks."

"I'll be there in ten," she promised before she hung up.

That settled, I glanced at the shoebox on the passenger seat beside me. In all likelihood, it contained the proof of ownership that my client, Bash, had hired me to find. Job well done.

Only I didn't feel that sense of satisfaction at having closed a case that I should.

I still didn't know who had killed Drake or what role, if any, this little shoebox had played in his death. And I had no idea what was on these tapes—whether I would be handing over the rights to "Hot Waitress" to my client or if they contained the proof Drake's lawyer needed to win his lawsuit posthumously. In the case of the latter, I had a feeling the tapes might mysteriously disappear forever once I gave them to Bash.

Which meant as much as I wanted to close the book on the whole Deadly Devils mess and feel giddy about spending Bash's wad of cash, this still felt unresolved enough that I wasn't ready to call Bash yet and give him the good news.

I glanced at my dash clock. Half an hour before I was supposed to meet Kendall Manchester. Making a spur-of-the-moment decision, I put my car in gear and pointed it toward the marina. After all, Derek *had* offered to help. And he *was* a fan of the band. And a houseboat in Marina Del Rey seemed like as safe a place as any to stash a few tapes for a while.

* * *

"So is this guy scamming Gammy or what?" Kendall Manchester popped a wad of gum between her teeth as she jiggled her knee up and down in my office.

"Scamming? Maybe," I answered. "Cheating on? Definitely." I plopped the 8x10 glossy photos Sam had taken of Alejandro and his paramour at the dive bar the previous night down on my desk.

Kendall sucked in a breath as she leaned forward to look at them. "I knew it!"

As Sam had warned me, most of the pictures were from her vantage point behind the redhead. But they clearly displayed Alejandro, sitting on a wooden barstool beside her, leaning in close, bedroom eyes on his companion, a lazy smile playing on his lips. That is when his lips weren't on hers. And while her back was to us in most of the photos, Sam's description of the redhead had been spot-on—she was dressed one small step up from a lady of the evening. Her hair was done in a sleek bob, her skirt short, her legs encased in fishnet stockings. It was hard to tell her age from the back, but I put her near Alejandro's own from the look of the exposed skin on her arms and shoulders. Old enough to be a resident of Sunny Acres. Young enough to meet men in a dive bar and bring them home afterward.

"Who is that skank?" Kendall demanded.

"My associate didn't get a name," I confessed. "But, we know Alejandro met her for drinks last night and left the bar with her afterward."

"You mean as in they left *together* and…" she trailed off.

"One can assume."

"Ew." She did an exaggerated shudder. "So this creep is using Gammy."

I sighed, flipping to the second photo, which showed pretty much the same scene but from a slightly different angle. "From everything we could find, Alejandro's finances seem solid, but he's living well below the Sunny Acres level of means."

"In English?"

"He's not as rich as your grandmother. Or this woman." I nodded to the redhead.

"Or the blonde," Kendall noted. "The one I originally saw him with."

"Right. Assuming she lives at the Acres as well." I shook my head. "Unfortunately, we weren't able to track down the blonde. Sorry."

Kendall shrugged. "What difference does it make? When Gammy sees these, it won't matter if he was with one woman or a hundred." She paused, a look of horror going over her features. "You don't think he's been with a hundred old women, do you?"

I stifled a laugh. "No. But I do think your grandmother has cause to be concerned."

Kendall nodded. Then she paused. "Would you tell her for me?"

"What?" I asked, blinking at her.

"Please!" Kendall clasped her hands in front of her in a pleading motion. "I hate delivering bad news. It's like, all emotional and stuff, and people cry. It's so draining."

Her compassion for her grandmother was overwhelming. I suddenly felt twice as sorry for Gammy. "I don't think that's a good idea. She should hear this from family."

"But Daddy won't be home for weeks!"

"She should hear it from *you*."

Kendall made a groaning sound in the back of her throat and scoffed, slouching in her chair like she might melt into a puddle on the floor from annoyance. "It's *too* stressful. I *can't* do it alone. You *have* to come with me."

I didn't *have* to do anything. A point I was about to make when she added, "I'll pay you extra. Like, double!"

My protest died on my broke lips. "Double?"

Kendall nodded, suddenly perking up in her seat. "You take Amex?"

I'd take anything but bankruptcy at this point.

"Fine," I relented. "I'll come with you."

* * *

Fifteen minutes and one American Express black card later, Kendall was walking out the door with a promise from me to meet her at Sunny Acres the following afternoon to break the bad news to Gammy. It wasn't a meeting I was looking forward to—especially since I'd have to confess that I was not related to any Mary with a bad hip in the Rose Garden complex. But the thought that I could now pay our electric bill was slowly buoying my spirits.

I glanced up at the clock in reception. Bash was due any minute. I still wasn't sure what to tell him. But I was certainly going to start with asking him why he'd lied to me about his alibi for Drake's murder.

"You okay?" Maya asked, pulling me out of my thoughts.

My conflicted emotions must have shown on my face. "Great. Dandy. Peachy."

"You don't look peachy for a woman who just charged quadruple digits to Kendall's credit card."

I sighed. "I don't like these emotional cases. I'd just like to go back to catching low-down dirty cheaters who deserve it."

"I'm sure adulterers can't be germaphobes forever."

"I didn't think they'd be germaphobes this long. Who knew they'd fear a flu more than an STD?"

Maya grinned. "Well, I'm sure business will pick up soon. Bad Bunny is getting a ton of hits."

"Bad Bunny?"

"Oh, that's what Connor decided to name our social media campaign." She pointed at her computer screen. "People are clicking on the naughty man bunny 2 to 1 over the guy in the doghouse or the grumpy cat."

I shook my head. "Great. People are watching bunny videos. I feel saved already."

Maya ignored my sarcasm. "It's gotten like thousands of views so far."

"Thousands?" I had to admit, that sounded like a lot. I came around her desk to take a look at her screen.

"Yeah. We're up to 300k so far."

"Wow." Okay, so a real lot. "Any new calls from it yet?"

Maya frowned. "No. Not yet."

"Figures."

"But give it time. Kylie said she has a friend whose cousin is friends with the guy who made that pug in a top hat go viral, so she thinks we might have a chance at some serious visibility."

I glanced down at the screen again. I still didn't see how the cartoons were going to get us clients, but until I had a better idea, at least this was free.

"What's that on the sidebar?" I asked, gesturing to a line of thumbnails.

"Trending videos," Maya informed me. "I mean, it's a goal to be there, but I'm not sure we're up to that level of subscribers yet."

I squinted down at the row of images and noticed one of Drake Deadly. "Can you click on that?" I pointed at the icon.

"Sure." Maya clicked, and the trending video in question came up on the large player.

It was a clip of Drake Deadly getting out of a black car in front of the Beverly Hotel. The angle and background noise made it clear it had been shot on someone's phone. The guy holding it yelled to get Drake's attention, and the rock star turned, waved toward the camera, and then did some lewd tongue wagging that had the guy holding the phone screaming, "Rock 'n' roll forever!"

A caption scrolled across the screen saying the video had been taken the day Drake died.

"So sad," Maya said, shaking her head at the frozen image of Drake on the screen.

I agreed. But something in the background had caught my eye just as the video ended. "Can you play that again?"

Maya shrugged. "Sure. Why?"

"I thought I saw something. Right at the end, behind that palm tree on the left."

Maya scooted her chair in closer to the keyboard and hit a button to replay.

We both watched the screen as the scene played out again. Drake got out of the car, the phone owner hailed him, he wagged his tongue. Then, just as Drake was turning his back to the camera to go into the hotel, I spotted it again. A figure coming out from behind the palm tree at the left of the frame.

"Pause it," I said. I pointed a finger at the screen. "There."

Maya leaned forward, squinting. "Looks like some guy in a beret."

"That's not just any guy in a beret," I informed her, staring at the tall, slim, balding man in a cardigan. "That's Tad Windhorse."

The keyboard player who told me he'd been at rehearsals that evening.

And not at the scene of his former rival's murder.

CHAPTER SIXTEEN

———

I grabbed my phone and keyed in the number for the club where Tad was supposed to be playing. Three rings in, a male voice answered. "Blue Moon Lounge?"

"I'd like to speak with Tad Windhorse. Is he in?" I tapped my toe impatiently on the floor of my lobby, Maya looking on from behind her desk.

"Sorry, no. Not yet."

"But he is scheduled to be there tonight, correct?"

"Yeah. His first set starts at seven. Tickets are eighteen at the door."

"Great. Thanks," I said, hanging up and making a mental note to call back later.

"You think Tad was at the Beverly Hotel to kill Drake?" Maya asked as I hung up.

"I don't know," I said honestly, putting my phone back into my pocket. "But I know he lied to me about not being there."

"Maybe Drake invited him to the band meeting after all?" she suggested.

"Then why not say so?" I asked.

She shrugged. "It does make him look guilty."

I let out a deep sigh. "Guilty of lying to me at least. Then again, almost everyone involved in this case has committed that sin."

Maya grinned. "Including your client."

I glanced up at the clock. "Including my very *late* client."

Maya followed my gaze. "Want me to call him?"

I nodded. "Probably stuck in traffic," I decided as she looked up his number in our system and punched it into her phone. She put it on speaker, and we listened to it ring. Finally, after four rings, it went to voicemail.

"Hi, this is Maya Alexander from the Bond Agency," Maya said at the beep. "We're just checking in about our appointment that was scheduled for six. Please let us know if you're on your way or need to reschedule." She rattled off the office number and hung up.

"I'll give him a few more minutes," I decided. "You can go ahead and go home, though."

"You sure?" Maya asked, though I could see relief in her eyes. I knew she lived a good forty-five minutes away in rush hour traffic.

I nodded. "Totally sure. I can handle him on my own if he shows."

"Okay, but call me if anything comes up," she said, grabbing her purse.

As soon as she left, I went back to my office and sat at my desk. I answered a few emails. I browsed social media, bookmarking a couple beauty tutorials and recipes I knew I'd never make. I made an Amazon order for more coffee pods and some hairspray. I listened to a voicemail from Derek about how "bitchin'" the jam session tapes were and how he and his girlfriend Elaine were totally "rockin' out" to them. I was glad someone was enjoying them.

Then I checked the clock again. Bash was over an hour late. I was pretty sure I'd officially been stood up.

While I was a little annoyed he hadn't called to cancel, I wasn't totally unhappy about the idea of putting off this meeting. Maybe if Derek could rock out to enough of the tapes, I'd know exactly what I was handing over to Bash before I did the handing. Which wouldn't really tell me either way if my client was a killer or not, but at least it would put the issue of who wrote "Hot Waitress" to bed.

I called Bash's number one more time, leaving a voicemail saying I'd waited an hour, I figured he was a no-show, and I was leaving the office. He could call to reschedule tomorrow.

Then I powered down my computer and grabbed my purse, locking up the office behind me as I made my way to my Roadster.

Once I pulled out of the parking lot, instead of heading toward my apartment, I made a right at the light, in the direction of Hollywood and the Blue Moon Lounge. It was dark by the time I arrived, and I had to park a couple blocks away in a garage that charged by the minute. I threw my jacket on and hiked back toward the lounge, moving through the colorful nightlife of LA. Tourists mixed with well-dressed locals out for a night on the town. Cocktail dresses, suits, jeans, Hawaiian shirts, and one guy in a Big Bird costume. Anything goes in Hollywood. A couple crazies were yelling in front of an old art deco theater about the apocalypse coming, but as far as I was concerned, 2020 had already brought it. They were a bit late with the warning.

I tried to ignore the mingling scents of fried food, car exhaust, and stale urine wafting toward me on the cool night breeze as I approached the Blue Moon. Luckily, being that the Wind Dancers were hardly top tier celebs, there was no line outside the club. Just a bouncer sitting on a tall stool looking bored as he scrolled through his phone. He looked up as I neared.

"ID please," he said, grabbing a wristband from behind him that apparently would identify me as old enough to partake in their two drink minimum.

I fished my ID out of my purse and handed it over. He did a quick scan with his phone, then slapped the yellow bracelet on me and asked for the cover charge.

Once I'd paid, I slipped into the club, which was surprisingly full and brimming with life. The bar was packed, and most of the tables were filled. Apparently the new age scene was larger than I'd thought. On the stage, I could see the lady in white, Sierra, with her harp, but she was singing a solo. No sign of Tad.

I put my phone on vibrate in deference to the music and threaded my way through the after-work crowd, mostly dressed in blazers and jeans as they swayed to Sierra's haunting melody. I found an empty spot at the end of the bar and noticed the same guy I'd seen on my last visit was standing behind it, filling cocktail glasses with a flourish. It took me a couple of tries, but I finally caught his attention.

"What can I get for you?" he asked, setting a cocktail napkin down in front of me.

"Vodka martini," I said, hoping it didn't go to my head too fast on my empty stomach. "Hey, have you seen Tad Windhorse yet tonight?" I asked as he poured.

He shook his head. "No. He hasn't come in yet."

I frowned. "I thought he was supposed to start at seven." I glanced down at my watch. It was well past that.

"He was. Didn't show."

"Did he say why?"

The bartender shrugged as he added an olive to my drink. "As far as I know, he hasn't called in." He nodded toward the stage. "Sierra went on without him, but she said she hasn't heard from him either."

That didn't sound good.

It also didn't sound like the actions of an innocent man. As I gave the bartender a twenty, I silently wondered if Tad had skipped town. Had my previous visit made him that nervous? It was entirely possible, considering he'd been at the crime scene. And lied about it.

Then again, it was possible he was just stuck in traffic, too.

I settled in on the barstool, sipping at my martini, watching the stage. The song was soft and moody, and the harp gave it an ethereal feel. I found myself swaying along with Sierra's chanting, being lulled into an almost hypnotic state. Or maybe the vodka was just hitting me harder than I thought.

After an hour—I'd sipped my drink as slowly as humanly possible—I was starving, and the music was putting me to sleep. And there was still no sign of Tad.

I caught the bartender's attention again.

"Hey. Refill?" he asked, grabbing my empty glass.

"No, thanks. Actually, I was wondering if you could give this to Tad for me when you see him?" I slid the guy my business card. "And please ask him to call me?"

He looked at the card, nodding before he slipped it into his back pocket. "Will do."

I thanked him and slid off my stool, making my way to the door. The cool night air had a sobering effect as I walked the two blocks back to my car. I left Hollywood and hit up a drive-through Del Taco on the way home, silencing my growling stomach with a red burrito and a melty quesadilla. Fully sated with comfort food, I finally pulled into my parking garage at a quarter to nine. I rode the elevator up to my floor, dreaming of a glass of cabernet and an evening of mindlessly mushing in front of reality TV.

As soon as I got inside, I poured the cab then stripped out of my work clothes and into a pair of comfy pajamas with little rubber ducks on them before settling on the sofa. I flipped the TV on, but even as *Real Housewives* and *90 Day Fiancé* played their drama out on my screen, my mind was on Drake, Bash, and the whole Devils' drama in my real life.

I picked up my phone, scrolling through my contacts until I got to Danny's name. Usually when I was stuck on a case, I talked things out with my best friend. While he was a flirt and sometimes a tease, more often than not, he was a voice of reason when pieces just weren't fitting together right.

My finger hovered over the call button. The last thing I wanted to do was interrupt him in the middle of more *photo shoots* or *plans* with some other woman. A couple of years ago, I wouldn't have even hesitated. I hated that things had become more complicated between us now.

I was still contemplating his number when a knock sounded at my door.

I was tempted to ignore it. But as the person on the other side knocked again, I realized they were not going to give up that easily.

"Coming," I yelled, reluctantly getting up to open it.

To find Aiden standing on the other side.

"Oh. Hi." My hand immediately went to my hair, wondering what its current state was. I couldn't remember the last time I'd run a brush through it.

Aiden, on the other hand, looked as polished and fresh as always—as if he'd just stepped out of a cologne commercial and not spent a long day at the office chasing bad guys. His sandy hair was smoothed back from his head, chin clean shaven beneath a lopsided grin, brown eyes warm and inviting as they stared down at me with just the slightest hint of mischief in them that made a girl wonder what he was up to.

"Hi. Can I come in?" he asked.

"Uh, yeah. Yes. Of course." I pulled the door back to allow him entry, trying not to trip over my tongue too badly as I got over the shock of seeing him looking positively tasty on my doorstep. I smoothed down my ducky jammies, as if that might infuse them with a little dignity.

"I didn't mean to show up unannounced." He was such a gentleman, his gaze only strayed to my duckies for a second. "I tried calling, but it just went to voicemail."

"I had my ringer off," I explained, realizing I'd forgotten to turn it back on after leaving the Blue Moon. "I was at a music lounge."

He gave me a raised eyebrow coupled with a grin. "Sounds like fun."

"More work than play, really," I said as Aiden sat on my sofa, making himself at home and crossing one ankle over his knee. Something about how comfortable he looked in my apartment made my stomach kind of fluttery.

"Oh really? Anything to do with the Deadly Devils case?" he asked.

I nodded as I grabbed my wineglass and walked to the kitchen to pour Aiden one. "Actually, yes. I was there looking for Tad Windhorse."

Aiden gave me a questioning look. "Should I know that name?"

"Aka Tosh Thomas. The Deadly Devils' original keyboard player." I quickly filled him in on Tad's history with the band and the fact that he'd been in town conveniently when Drake had died. "He said Drake visited him to bury the hatchet," I finished as I sat down on the sofa beside him. "According to Tad, they met at the Blue Moon, made up, and Drake went on his way. Tad claimed he never saw him again and that Tad was at rehearsals the night Drake died."

"But he wasn't?" Aiden asked, taking a sip from his wineglass.

I shook my head. "At least not all night. Maya and I found a video taken by a Devils fan outside the Beverly Hotel the night Drake died. Tad is in it."

"I'm guessing that's why you wanted to talk to him tonight."

I nodded. "Only, he didn't show up for his set."

Aiden shook his head. "There could be lots of reasons he didn't show up."

"True," I agreed. "But he lied about his alibi."

Aiden sighed. "Well, I hate to break it to you, but no one seems to be able to account for their whereabouts when Drake was killed."

"Oh?" I tucked a foot up under me and leaned my head on the back of the sofa. "Do tell."

"Well, let's start with the wife, who claims you are her alibi."

A snort escaped me before I could stop it. "I am *not* her alibi. I followed her home, and then Danny and I left."

"What?" Aiden's wineglass froze midway to his mouth.

"I said we left."

"You said you and *Danny* left."

Oh crap. I did, didn't I?

"Yes," I said slowly. "Danny was doing surveillance with me."

"You didn't mention that before." His voice was a monotone, the emotion I'd heard a second ago carefully modulated out of it.

I took a deep breath, trying to cleanse away my guilt. I had no reason to feel guilty. Danny and I had been working together. That was it. And even if we had been flirting a little, it wasn't as if I had any commitment to Aiden. I didn't.

I'd carefully avoided that.

I shoved that last thought down, realizing he was watching me, waiting for a response. "No. I guess I didn't mention it." I tried to keep my voice as unemotional as his, but I'm not sure I was quite as successful.

We were both silent a minute. I could see thoughts swirling behind Aiden's dark eyes, but none were things he chose to voice as he stared me down, almost willing me to apologize or explain.

But if he wasn't going to actually ask, I wasn't going to offer. I matched his stare with one of my own. One that I tried to infuse with a whole lot of *strong independent woman* but I feared was closer to *guilty little secret*.

Finally Aiden was the one to break the standoff, turning his gaze to the view outside my window of the sparkling layer of lights downtown.

"Well, if you left the wife alone at home, you're not much of an alibi, are you?"

"No." I let out a mental sigh of relief to be back to more pleasant topics, like murder. "Jenna turned out her lights, and I'd assumed she was going to sleep. But I didn't stick around."

Aiden nodded, swirling his wine in the bottom of his glass. "You went home?"

"Yes." I paused. "Alone, if you're asking."

He looked up at me and had the good graces to look a little sheepish. "I was. And I'm glad."

I cleared my throat awkwardly. "What about the band members' alibis?"

"Well, the bass player, Harry Star, arrived at the bar around ten thirty." Aiden sipped from his wine, seemingly glad to change the subject too. "Bartender said he served him a Jack and Coke. However, the bartender also said Harry left the bar for a while then returned just before the other band members arrived."

"That's interesting timing. Where did he go?"

"Harry said he got a phone call and took it outside. The bar was too noisy."

"Anyone see him?"

Aiden shook his head.

"So it's possible he could have gone up to Drake's room, spiked his drink, and pushed him into the swimming pool," I said.

"It is. But the guitar player was at the hotel during that time too."

"Keith told me he was with a groupie."

"I got the same story." Aiden nodded. "One whose name he claims not to remember. In fact, he can't remember much about her other than she was 'hot.'"

I grinned. "And stacked. I got that much out of him."

"Anyway, the rest of his story checks out. He had a room at the hotel registered to his name, and one of the housekeepers says she saw a woman with him."

"Which doesn't mean he couldn't have left her early, spiked Drake's drink, and killed him before meeting with the rest of the band. He *was* late to the meeting."

"So was Bash," Aiden pointed out.

I bit my lip. "I was afraid you'd get around to him."

"He said he was at the gym."

"Was he?" I dreaded the answer.

But Aiden thankfully nodded. "Yeah. Several witnesses saw him arrive around nine, though no one can pinpoint exactly when he left."

"The meeting wasn't until eleven," I hesitated to point out.

"I know." Aiden sipped his wine. "The band's manager, Carmichael, said Bash arrived a few minutes after he did. About ten past eleven."

"Which leaves Bash with a pretty big hole in his alibi." I scrunched up my nose. "Crap."

"Sorry." Aiden gave me a sympathetic smile.

I shook my head. "He stood me up today."

"Oh?"

"Yeah. I was supposed to give him an update on the case. His request. But he didn't show."

"You call him?"

"Left a couple of messages." I suddenly wondered if he was avoiding me on purpose. Why, I wasn't sure. But guilt sprang to mind. I thought about telling Aiden I'd found the jam session tapes, but on the off chance my client was not guilty and the tapes had nothing to do with Drake's death, I wasn't sure I should share yet.

"What about the lipstick?" I asked instead. "You said there was lipstick on the second glass in Drake's hotel room. Any idea yet where it came from?"

"Forensics is still working on that." Aiden rolled his head lazily to the side to face me. "But it does indicate a woman, don't you think?"

I shrugged. "I don't know. You see some of the band's early album covers?"

Aiden laughed, setting his empty wineglass on the coffee table. "Touché."

"Anyway, just because Drake had a woman in his room, that doesn't mean she was the *only* one in his room that night. I mean, it's possible she left, someone else came in, they spiked Drake's drink and killed him. Right?"

"Anything is possible, Bond." The way his eyes went all dark and bedroomy on me with that last phrase made me wonder if we were still talking about the murder case.

"It's late," I said.

He reached a hand out and tucked a strand of hair gently behind my ear. "Is it?"

I nodded, my eyes suddenly rooted to his lips.

"Maybe I should go." He made no move to get up, his eyes intent on mine.

"Maybe." My voice sounded smaller and far away, as my focus homed in on his lips, which seemed to be moving closer to mine.

"Do you want me to?" he asked, his voice husky and low.

I knew what I should have answered. My emotions were a jumble of guilt, lust, independence, and want. And I wasn't even going to go near the subject of the dangling L-word still hovering in the air between us. The truth was, I wasn't sure of anything about Aiden. Every interaction I had with him left me feeling warm and tingling and at the same time afraid he was going to force my hand where our relationship status was concerned. And I wasn't sure what that hand would look like when he did.

So I knew what I should have said.

But it wasn't what I did say.

"Stay," I heard my voice tell him.

A wicked grin snaked across his features, his lips converging on mine. "I thought you'd never ask."

* * *

The sun was blinding as it pushed through the cracks in my curtains the next morning, assaulting my eyes with an unrelenting brightness that had me burrowing into my covers. And I might have stayed there too, if my neighbor's car alarm hadn't started blasting next. I swore, if he didn't get that thing fixed, I was gonna take a tire iron…

I cracked one eye open, checking the time. Just past eight.

I rolled over, the other side of my bed smelling woodsy and warm, like Aiden's aftershave. Unfortunately, it was also empty. I sat up, blinking the sleep out of my eyes as I looked around the room. His clothes were gone too. I picked up my phone and saw a text had come in from him about an hour earlier.

Didn't want to wake you. Had an early call. xoxo

I felt a big, goofy grin spread across my face at the little X's and O's and was totally powerless to stop it. Even as I shoved myself into a hot shower and a pair of leggings, a soft grey sweater dress, and suede ankle boots with spike heels, the grin was still lingering.

I grabbed my purse and headed to the door. Since I was already late for work, I hit a drive-through coffee stand and ordered a large vanilla latte and a cinnamon frosted scone to go with it. The caffeine, the sticky pastry, and possibly even a little tiny bit of the memory of Aiden the night before had my mood so elevated by the time I hit the Bond Agency that I was even humming as I pushed through the doors.

But that was where my good mood ended.

Sam and Maya were both huddled around her computer, matching frowns on their faces. Even before anyone spoke a word, I could feel the dark cloud hanging in the air around them.

Maya looked up as I walked in the door, her eyebrows draw down in concern. "There you are."

"Sorry I'm late." I looked from her to Sam's stoic expression. "Why? What's wrong?"

Sam tore her eyes away from the computer screen to pin me with a dark look. "You better see this."

Dread pooled in my belly, erasing any previous feelings of lightness and glee as I crossed the reception room in two quick strides, coming to stand beside Sam.

The computer screen showed a news clip that had a little *Live* icon in the righthand corner. The scene was in front of a white, two-story house that was flanked by palm trees, and a caption along the bottom told me it was in West Los Angeles. The same perky redheaded reporter I'd seen before was holding a microphone, and behind her I could see a police car and an ambulance parked in the street.

"…just moments ago," the reporter was saying. "Police have confirmed that the body is that of the Deadly Devils' drummer known simply as Bash. He was found dead in his West LA home this morning. This is the second member of the band to pass away this week. Fans have planned a vigil…"

The reporter droned on, but I tuned her out, my mind reeling as it homed in on one terrible thought.

My client was dead.

Again.

CHAPTER SEVENTEEN

———

Details were scant, though Maya, Sam, and I flipped between different news outlets trying to piece together what had happened. Bash's body had been found in his West LA home that morning by his manager, Carmichael. I thought of the naturally antsy man and had a moment of sympathy. He was probably eating antacids like Pez. Police had been called in, and at the moment it was being reported as a possible robbery gone wrong.

Which I didn't buy for a second.

As soon as we'd gleaned all we could from the media, I grabbed my purse and made for the door, quickly navigating the morning traffic toward West LA, where the street leading to Bash's house was all but blocked off by dozens of news vans, paparazzi, and law enforcement vehicles. I parked around the block and wished I'd gone with lower heels that day as I quickly made my way toward the hub of the commotion.

Bash's house was an older two-story home in a historic district on a lot that was impressively large—and probably expensive. Mature trees flanked the front of the property, and a large expanse of lawn separated the house from the street. Along with several wooden police barricades and uniformed officers, holding nosy reporters and curious passersby back at the sidewalk.

I scanned the assembled crowd, hoping to find another old pal of my dad's among the law enforcement, but my luck wasn't that good today. None of the faces looked familiar. Or friendly. I had a hunch Aiden might be inside the house, having had to respond to that "early call." I was just about to engage in that awkward morning-after moment by calling him at a crime scene, when I did finally spot someone I knew. Alvin Carmichael, the band's manager.

His brown suit was rumpled, his face pale, his few remaining hairs on his head flying at odd angles. He had one hand to his chest in an unconsciously protective gesture. A uniformed officer spoke softly to him as he led Carmichael away from the house. As they moved closer, I could see Carmichael's face and had another pang of sympathy for the man. His eyes looked like they were rimmed in dark circles, his mouth set in a grim line below his twitching mustache, and his forehead a network of worried wrinkles.

"Mr. Carmichael?" I hailed him, causing his watery eyes to turn my way. I wasn't sure the expression on his face as he spotted me could be called relief, but it at least held recognition.

"Ms. Bond," he said. Then he gave a nod of thanks to the officer and joined me on the other side of the barricade.

"I'm so sorry," I told him, meaning it. "I heard you found the—" I stopped myself just in time from calling his client a body. "You found Bash."

Carmichael sucked in a long breath and let it out slowly, as if trying to steady himself enough to talk. "I did. Earlier this morning."

"What happened?" I asked softy, putting a comforting hand on his arm.

He shook his head. "I-I was supposed to meet him this morning. Bash, that is. I knocked on the door, but when no one answered, I went in, and I just found him..." He trailed off, his skin ashen as he obviously relived the scene in his mind.

"The door was unlocked?" I asked.

He nodded. "Maybe Bash forgot to lock it?"

Or maybe his killer hadn't bothered.

"What time was this?" I asked.

Carmichael licked his lips. "About eight. A little before. I-I was early."

"Do the police have any idea what happened to him?" I asked, my eyes cutting to the officer Carmichael had been chatting with.

Carmichael reached into his jacket pocket, pulling out a prescription pill bottle and fussing with the childproof lid. "They said he was probably killed sometime yesterday evening. Blunt force trauma, I heard them say."

"Meaning he was hit over the head," I mused, more to myself than him. "Any idea what the murder weapon was?"

Carmichael visibly cringed at the word *murder*. "A Grammy."

"The award?"

Carmichael nodded. "They're really heavy."

I didn't doubt it, but I wondered if someone had been sending a message with that particular choice of weapon. Possibly a disgruntled bandmate?

"You said you were supposed to meet Bash here," I said. "What was the meeting about?"

"I don't know." Carmichael finally got the bottle open and popped a little white pill into his mouth, swallowing it dry. "Bash called me yesterday and said he needed to see me. That it was important. I agreed to meet him this morning, but when I got here…" He trailed off again, his Adam's apple bobbing up and down like the pill might have gotten stuck. Or maybe he was just trying to swallow down the bad taste in his mouth at finding a dead man.

"Bash didn't give you any indication of what he wanted to see you about?" I grasped.

But Carmichael just shook his head. "No. Just that it was important."

"What time did he call you yesterday?"

"I-I don't know. Maybe a little after five?"

I bit my lip, staring back at the house teeming with law enforcement.

Bash was supposed to have met me at six. I'd thought he'd stood me up, but now…now I wondered if he'd already been dead by then.

My mind flashed on the wife's tapes, sitting in Derek's houseboat. Had they had anything to do with Bash's death? Had the killer thought Bash had them? Suddenly I wondered if this actually might have been a robbery attempt gone wrong after all. Only, they tried to rob the wrong person.

I tuned back to Carmichael. "There's something I think you should know."

He frowned. "What?"

"I was supposed to meet with Bash yesterday."

His eyebrows rose. "You? About what?"

"About the song. 'Hot Waitress.' Bash hired me to find proof that he'd written it. I was supposed to give him an update on my findings yesterday."

"You were supposed to. I take it that means you did not speak with him," he surmised.

I shook my head. "He never showed up. I tried to call him, but there was no answer." I glanced at the house.

Carmichael winced again, as if coming to the same conclusion as to why Bash hadn't answered his phone.

"May I ask what you were planning to tell Bash?" Carmichael asked.

I bit my lip. Honestly, I hadn't been sure what I was going to tell Bash. "I have some tapes," I said slowly. "Of the Deadly Devils' old jam sessions."

"So you did find what Bash wanted," Carmichael said.

"Maybe. I honestly don't know if they contain any information about who wrote 'Hot Waitress' or not."

"Where did you get them?" His eyebrows were drawn down into a deep V.

I shook my head, not sure I wanted to drag Jenna into this. Assuming she wasn't already knee deep. "That isn't important. What is important is that I have them and I was going to meet with Bash about them last night."

Carmichael's eyes went to the house. "Did he know you had them?"

I shook my head slowly.

"Bring them by my office," Carmichael said.

I paused, sizing the man up. But in all honestly, what else was I going to do with the tapes? They weren't technically evidence of a crime, and Jenna didn't want them anymore. I had no idea who they should go to. Carmichael was probably the best person to sort that all out in a legal and official capacity anyway. "Alright," I agreed. "I've got a few things to do right now, but I can bring them by this evening." I figured that should give Derek plenty of time to be sure of what was on the tapes first.

Carmichael's frown didn't budge, but he nodded. "I'll be in my office until seven." With that he shoved his pill bottle back into his jacket pocket and walked away, his shoulders slumped in a way that made me think a brunch whiskey might be in his future.

I hiked the half mile back to my car. I could have pressed to see Aiden, but I had a feeling he didn't know much more than Carmichael had already given me at this point. Forensics would still be gathering evidence, and the ME would be unlikely to give up anything definitive. And the truth was, I really had nothing more to add to his case. I hadn't seen Bash last night, and I had no idea where he'd been or with whom.

And I wasn't yet ready to face that awkward morning-after moment.

My phone rang as I slid into the driver's seat, and I pulled it out of my purse to see Caleigh's name on the readout. I swiped to take the call.

"Hi, Caleigh," I answered. "What's up?"

"Well, for starters," she answered, "guess who slept together last night?"

I had a brief moment of panic, thinking somehow my evening with Aiden had been telegraphed to all my employees.

Until Caleigh finished with, "Jenna and her boyfriend!"

I let out a sigh that I hoped wasn't audible to Caleigh. "So she did go see him."

"Oh, yes, she did. In fact, she just now left his place."

"What's the address?" I asked, rummaging in my purse for a pen to write it down. "Maybe I can get a name off of it."

"Don't bother," Caleigh said, and I could detect a note of mischief in her voice this time. "You already know it. Jenna just left Keith Kane's place."

I blinked at the pleasant street sitting outside my window. "Wait—are you telling me Keith is sleeping with Drake's wife?"

"Uh-huh." Caleigh's voice was positively gleeful.

"You sure it was Keith and not Harry she was there to see?" I clarified.

"Positive. It was definitely Keith I just watched her kiss goodbye."

I let out a sharp breath. "That puts a new spin on things."

"That's what I thought," Caleigh agreed. "Drake had been threatening both Jenna's *and* Keith's gravy trains. I could easily see the two of them conspiring to get rid of their problem together."

"But if that's true, why kill Bash?" I asked, watching another police car turn down his street.

"Well, maybe Bash saw something?" Caleigh reasoned. "That night at the Beverly Hotel. Maybe Bash figured out it was Keith who killed Drake, and then Keith had to kill Bash to cover his tracks."

"It's possible," I conceded, thinking of how Derek had been sure of Keith's guilt in my office the day before.

"And didn't you say he was late to the band meeting that night? Everyone else was waiting for him in the bar?"

"That's right. He was last to arrive."

We were quiet a beat as we thought about that.

"So what do you want me to do?" Caleigh asked.

"You're still in Tujunga?"

"Yeah. I'm parked two houses down from Keith's place."

"Stay where you are. I'll be right there."

* * *

Unfortunately, with Tujunga sitting on the outer banks of civilization in Southern California, "right there" ended up being a good forty minutes later. But I spotted Caleigh's car as soon as I turned onto Keith's street and pulled to a stop at the curb behind it. We exited our vehicles at the same time, and Caleigh shaded her eyes against the sun as she nodded across the street toward Keith and Harry's McMansion.

"He's still in there. No one's come out since Jenna went home," she told me.

I nodded. "Good. Let's go chat with the boyfriend, then."

We quickly crossed the street and walked up the pathway to the wood and iron detailed front door. I gave a swift knock, and we didn't have to wait long before footsteps sounded on the other side. A beat later the door opened to reveal Harry, again dressed in too-tight leather. This time he'd paired the sausage-casing pants with a T-shirt bearing the band's likeness circa their heyday. Like Harry, the shirt looked faded, wrinkled, and like it had seen better days.

"Hey," he said, squinting at me as if he was trying to pull some recognition to the forefront of his mind.

"Jamie Bond," I supplied.

"Riiiight. Lady cop."

"PI," I corrected. "And this is my associate, Caleigh Presley."

"Presley?" Harry turned his attention to Caleigh. Or at least to her cleavage. "Any relation to Elvis?"

Caleigh's face lit up. "Actually, yes! The King is my third cousin twice removed on my father's side."

"Dude. Cool." He grinned at her. Well, at her cleavage.

"Is Keith in?" I asked, looking past him. "We were hoping to talk to him."

Harry nodded. "In the living room." He opened the door wider to allow us entry. "Come on in."

I stepped inside and was immediately assaulted by the stench of marijuana and beer. I could see Caleigh wrinkling up her nose beside me, but her mama had raised her right, and she was too polite to say anything.

"It reeks like pot in here," I told Harry.

What can I say? Derek had raised me.

Harry just giggled. "I know. Gotta love legal California, right? They even deliver that stuff now."

Keith was sitting on the leather sofa facing the giant TV. This time it was tuned in to a news station, the image of Bash's house flashing across it behind a reporter. While the scene was slightly different than the one I'd left—fewer police cars and more paparazzi—I could tell by the snippets of text scrolling across the bottom of the screen that not many more details had been released to the public yet.

Keith turned from the news as we walked in, popping up from his seat as soon as recognition set in. "You again."

"Hi, Keith." I gave him a big smile.

"What are you doing here?" he demanded, his eyes flitting to Caleigh.

"We had some questions to ask you," I said, not waiting for an invitation before sitting in the armchair opposite him.

"About what?" he asked. He slowly lowered himself back to the sofa, but his eyes were still pinging quickly between Caleigh and me as if expecting an inquisition.

Smart man.

"Let's start with that," I said, nodding toward the TV. "What do you know about Bash's death?"

"It's on like every channel," Harry piped up. "They're coming after us, dude."

"They?" I asked, turning my attention to the bass player.

"Whoever killed Drake and Bash. Obviously someone is killing off the band. And we're next!" Harry's eyes were wide and had a little bit of a wild look.

"Chill," Keith told him. "No one is killing off band members."

Which wasn't entirely true. Two band members were dead. And I had a feeling all the rest were liars.

Harry didn't look convinced either, but he clamped his lips shut and sank down onto the leather sofa with a squeak.

"I'm sorry for your loss," Caleigh said, laying the Southern charm on thick. "This must be such a shock."

"Huge. Big shocker," Harry agreed, nodding vigorously.

I turned back to Keith. "And you?"

"And me what?" Keith shot back.

"Were you shocked to hear Bash was dead?"

"O-of course I was!" Keith sputtered. "What sort of question is that?"

"Where were you last night?" I asked, answering his question with a question.

"Here." His eyes darted around the room.

"Alone?"

"Harry was in his room."

"And you were in yours?" I asked.

Keith nodded.

"Alone?" I asked again.

Keith licked his lips. "Yeah."

I glanced to Caleigh. She shook her head, giving me a small, knowing smile.

I turned my gaze back to Keith. "I don't think you're being honest with me."

"W-what are you talking about?" he asked with more pinging eyes, more sputtering, and a lot more fear.

"I'm talking about the woman you were with last night." Keith worked his jaw back and forth a little. "Okay. Yeah. So, I was with a chick. So what?"

"So she's your bandmate's widow. Jenna James."

"Dude!" Harry yelled. "You were with *Jenna*?"

"No!" Keith jumped up from the sofa again. "I mean…" His eyes went from Caleigh to me, as if trying to assess how much we were guessing and how much we knew for fact. "I mean, yeah. Yes. I saw her. So what? She was grieving. I-I was comforting her."

"With your tongue?" Caleigh asked, giving him her Southern belle smile.

Keith's mouth opened and closed a few times, as if trying on a few different lies for size. Apparently none felt like they'd get him out of this jam, as he finally just let out a long breath, seeming to collapse in on himself as he sank back down onto the sofa. "Okay. Yes, fine. I was with Jenna last night."

"*Dude*," Harry said again. Though this time there seemed to be more reverence than shock in the intonation.

"But it's not what you think!" Keith protested.

"Oh?" I asked. "What is it that we think?"

"Look, it's not like this was an affair or a fling."

He was sleeping with his friend's wife—that was pretty much the definition of an affair. But I just nodded for him to go on.

"Jenna and I are in love."

"Really?" Caleigh asked, clearly skeptical.

"How long have you been seeing each other?" I asked. He licked his lips again. "Almost a year."

"Did Drake know?"

"No!" Keith shook his head, grey hair swinging at his sides. "No way. We were super careful. Jenna didn't want him finding out and cutting her off."

"And I don't imagine he'd take too kindly to his friend betraying him either," I pointed out.

Keith sucked in some more air. "Yeah. There was that."
He paused. "Look, Jenna gets me like no other chick does. It isn't
just physical, you know? We have so much in common."

"Like Drake," I noted.

But he shook his head. "No. She's like *real*, you know."

Well, parts of her were. Other parts were clearly man-
made.

"And we're both survivors," he went on.

"Cancer?" Caleigh asked, sympathy in her voice.

He shook his head. "Abduction." His gaze went to the
ceiling. "From up there."

Mental forehead smack. "Don't tell me you're a member
of AAA too?"

He nodded slowly. "I've been probed, man. By aliens."

"*Dude!*" Harry piped up from the sofa, the word taking
on another meaning this time.

I shook my head. "Okay, E.T. stuff aside, what was your
plan with Jenna?"

"Plan?" Keith asked.

"She asked Drake for a divorce," I pointed out.

"Hey, that was all her idea, man." Keith jutted his chin
out. "But yeah. We were going to be together after it was
finalized."

"And she got her alimony settlement. Only she found
that Drake had her followed by a PI."

"Wait, aren't *you* a PI?" Harry asked.

The man was so quick on the uptake it was scary.

"Jenna feared Drake would find out about you," I went
on, ignoring Harry's attempts to catch up, "and then she'd get
nothing in the divorce. So, you killed Drake for her."

"Whoa!" Keith put his hands out in a surrender motion.
"I didn't kill anyone. I was nowhere near the pool when Drake
drowned. I was in my hotel room."

Then it hit me. "With Jenna. She's the hot, stacked
'chick.'"

Keith nodded.

"So *Jenna* was at the hotel the night that Drake died
too?" Caleigh piped up.

"Now wait a minute," Keith said. "Jenna had nothing to do with this either. She was with me the whole time."

Convenient that the two secret lovers were each other's alibis. Or non-alibis as the case might be.

"Maybe you two killed Drake together when Jenna realized that her blackmail plan might backfire."

"Blackmail?" Keith frowned. His eyes went from me to Caleigh. Then to Harry, who just shrugged.

Apparently Jenna hadn't shared that part of her plan with her boyfriend.

"The band tapes," I supplied. "Jenna had the tapes with all of your jam sessions on them."

"Jenna had our jam sessions?" Keith said, almost more to himself than to us. His eyebrows drew down, his eyes going to the floor as he processed this.

Harry frowned. "How did *Jenna* get them?"

"Drake gave them to her as a wedding present," I said.

"Before he realized what was on them," Caleigh added. "Before the song hit big."

"So what is on them?" Keith asked. I detected a distinct note of fear in his voice at what the answer might be. I was tempted to leave him hanging for a bit for lying to me.

"I don't know," I finally relented. "Neither did Jenna. She didn't listen to them. But someone broke into her house to try to take them."

"Dude!" Harry said.

"Jenna told me someone broke in. She didn't say why," Keith said. "Did they get the tapes?"

I shook my head. "Jenna interrupted them before they could find anything."

"Where are the tapes now?" Keith asked, his eyes cutting meaningfully to Harry.

For once, Harry looked stone-cold sober, his full focus on my answer.

"They're somewhere safe."

The two shared a look again. I had a sudden niggle of fear that I might be painting a target on my back. I'd be glad to offload the whole mess into Carmichael's lap that evening.

"Harry," Caleigh said, her big blue eyes turning on the bass player. "You never said where you were?"

"Me?" Harry looked from one face to another. "W-what do you mean?"

"Last night. Keith here says he was with Jenna. If that's true, it sounds like you were alone when Bash was killed."

Harry's face went white. "I didn't kill him!" His eyes went to the larger-than-life display of Bash's house on the TV screen. "It's some maniac out there. Someone killing off Devils!"

Not even Keith looked like he believed that anymore.

"Have either of you talked to Tad Windhorse?" I asked, feeling like our welcome was quickly wearing off here.

Two blank expressions turned my way.

"Tosh Thomas?" I tried again.

"I told you he took off years ago," Keith said.

"That may be, but he's in town now." Or at least he was. "He got in a couple of days before Drake died."

The fear was back in Harry's eyes, and he opened his mouth to say something.

"No!" Keith jumped in, silencing Harry with a look. "We haven't heard from him."

Harry shut his mouth. "That dude was bad news," he mumbled.

"Look, I think we've had just about enough of answering your questions," Keith said, rising from his spot on the sofa. "I think you better go."

Honestly, it was a wonder they'd let us stay as long as they had. Keith followed us as we rose and walked to the front door. He held it open, all but shoving us out onto the porch.

"And stop following us around!" he warned.

Before he slammed the door shut and threw the lock.

CHAPTER EIGHTEEN

———

"I think they both did it," Caleigh decided as we walked back to my car.

"Keith and Harry?" I clarified.

"No, Keith and Jenna." She turned to me. "What if Jenna was afraid Drake was going to get to the tapes before he gave her a divorce and she'd lose her leverage? She decides she needs to be a widow instead. She tells Keith that Drake has the proof he wrote the song and gets Keith to kill Drake for her at the hotel. Then they lie and become each other's alibis."

I nodded. "Only, there was lipstick on the glass in Drake's hotel room."

"Jenna?" Caleigh asked.

"Aiden seems to think so." I leaned against my car. "What about this scenario? Jenna said she confronted Drake about being followed by us. She told me she did it over the phone from her house, but maybe she did it in person. She was at the hotel to meet Keith anyway…maybe she visited Drake first and had it out with him."

"And drugged and killed him?" Caleigh offered.

I nodded. "Or maybe she did the drugging. Then she called Keith to take Drake for a walk down by the pool, where he pushed him in."

"And maybe Bash saw them. Or saw something later that Keith did that made him suspicious. And then they had to kill Bash too."

"Right." I nodded. "They set themselves up as each other's alibis yet again, only one of them—"

"Or both of them."

"—goes out and kills Bash before coming back to the house and pretending to have been here the whole time."

"I like it!" Caleigh said, bouncing in her seat. "Only…"

"Only what?"

"Who broke into Jenna's house to get the tapes?"

Dang. She had me stumped there. "I don't know." I blew out a long breath as I unlocked my car. "But I know there is one person who is conspicuously missing from the entire equation."

"And that is?"

"Windhorse." I quickly filled her in on how he'd been MIA from the Blue Moon the night before.

"Have you tried calling to see if he's in today?" Caleigh asked.

I shook my head and pulled out my phone. I scrolled until I found their number again and put it on speaker. A minute later the sound of ringing met us.

"Blue Moon Lounge?" a man's voice answered again.

"Hi, I'm looking for Tad Windhorse," I said.

"You and everyone else."

Caleigh and I shared a look. "I take it that means he's not there?"

"No. Didn't show up for his set last night, and he's missing rehearsals this morning."

"Does his partner know where he is? Sierra?"

"Wish she did. She's pretty ticked off. Says she hasn't heard from him at all."

"You don't happen to know where Tad was staying?" I asked. "What hotel he was staying at while in town?"

"Hang on a minute." I heard him move the phone away from his mouth as he called to someone else in the room. "Hey, Sierra. What hotel is Tad staying at?"

I couldn't hear the muffled response, but a second later the guy came back on the line. "Who did you say you were again?"

Great question. "His sister. Jamie. I was supposed to meet up with Tad while he was in town."

Caleigh grinned at me and shook her head but stayed silent.

"Right," the guy said, calling to Sierra again to relay my story. I listened to more muffled conversation in the background as they exchanged a few words. Finally he came back. "Sierra said he's at the Pacific Inn on La Brea. Room 212."

Bingo.

"Thanks," I told him before hanging up.

I turned to Caleigh. "Wanna follow me to La Brea?"

* * *

"This looks like a dump," Caleigh said, wrinkling her nose as she got out of her car in the parking lot of the Pacific Inn.

She was right. The place was falling apart and looked like the type of spot where drugs dealers and prostitutes regularly set up shop. In fact, there was a young guy in baggy jeans and a knit cap sitting near a large hole in the ground that was once a pool who looked like he was sizing us up as potential customers. What his wares were, I didn't want to know.

"Let's just talk to Tad and get out of here," I said, locking my car.

Caleigh followed as I took the rickety metal stairs at our right to the second floor. I tried to ignore the myriad of scents coming from the different rooms—everything from cigarettes, to Indian food, to strong disinfectant that made me morbidly curious to know what it had been used to clean up. Loud music played from somewhere down the hall, and I could hear a baby crying from one of the rooms. I counted down until we got to 212.

No scents wafted from inside. No sounds. No movement.

I rapped sharply on the door, listening for any sign of life on the other side.

Nothing came back to me.

"Doesn't look like anyone is here," Caleigh noted, squinting through the dirty window to the left of the door.

The curtains were partially pulled, but being that they'd ripped in several places, there were enough gaps to see the room behind them. I cupped my hands around my eyes as I peered in.

The bed was made. No suitcases in evidence. No clothes or personal effects.

I straightened up, giving the door one more knock just for good measure. Though it was pretty clear no one was home.

"Now what?" Caleigh asked.

"Let's go see the manager," I decided, leading the way back down the clunky staircase.

Caleigh followed me the length of the macadam parking lot to a small office on the ground floor. When we entered, a metal cage separated the bored-looking Asian man in a SpongeBob T-shirt from us. He looked up as we approached, a cigarette dangling from his mouth.

"You wanna room?" he asked, not moving from the wooden chair he was perched on.

I shook my head. "We were actually looking for the guy in room 212. Tad Windhorse."

He looked up at the ceiling. "That the pale guy with the flute?"

I nodded.

"Yeah, he gone."

"Gone?" I asked. I shot Caleigh a look.

The manager nodded. "He leave yesterday. Check out." He paused and narrowed his eyes at us. "Why? He owe you money? He look like the kind of guy got no money. Who plays flute for a living?"

"He didn't say where he was going by any chance, did he?" Caleigh asked.

But the manager shook his head. "No. I no ask questions like that. Dangerous to ask too much."

I could well see that being true in a place like this.

"Would you mind giving me a call if you see him again?" I asked, sliding my card under the metal cage.

The guy shrugged and nodded, but I had little hope of ever hearing from him.

Tad had checked out. I had a feeling he wouldn't be back.

"So Bash is murdered, and Tad skips town," Caleigh said as we walked back across the parking lot.

"Doesn't look good for Tad, does it?"

Caleigh shook her head. "You think Aiden could track Tad down?"

"I think he has a lot more resources than we do," I agreed. I pulled my phone out and shot him a quick text, telling him where Tad had been staying and that he was currently MIA. I didn't expect him to answer back right away, but as I was unlocking my car, his reply came in.

I'll look into it. Thanks. Miss you already.

"You have a huge goofy grin on your face," Caleigh said.

I glanced up to find her smirking at me.

"What did he say?" she pressed.

"That he'll look into it."

"Is that *all* he said?"

I shot her a look. "That's all I'm sharing."

"Bummer." She was still grinning. "Okay, so where to now?"

"Now," I told her, checking the time on my phone, "I have to help Kendall Manchester deliver some bad news to Gammy."

That put a damper on Caleigh's teasing mood. "Sorry. Sounds unpleasant."

I shrugged. "It will be. But it's paying our electric bill, so I'll suck it up."

"Want me to come with?" she asked.

I shook my head. "No, go back to the office. I want you and Maya to find everything you can on Tad Windhorse and where he might hide out. Friends, family. Anyone he'd turn to if he was in trouble."

"Or running from the law?" Caleigh added.

I nodded. "That is a distinct possibility."

* * *

Forty minutes later, I arrived at Sunset Acres. I spotted Kendall Manchester's red Ferrari in the visitor lot as soon as I pulled in, and I eased into a slot next to her. We both exited our vehicles and met up on the sidewalk.

"You ready?" I asked her.

Kendall nodded. "Yeah. Let's get this over with and get that cheating gold digger out of her life."

"Is your gammy expecting you?"

Kendall shook her head. "Oh no. This is an ambush. I didn't want her to give that Alejandro any heads-up to come up with a lie."

"Are you sure she's home then?" I asked, hoping I hadn't driven all the way out there for nothing.

Kendall rolled her eyes. "She's old. Where's she gonna go?"

I could have argued that Ellie was far from immobile, and apparently had ample means, but I let it go, following my client as she wound down the paved pathway between the resort style buildings. "Which one does she live in?" I asked.

"She's in Lavender Lane." She pointed toward the right. "Near the golf course."

I followed a step behind, mentally preparing what I'd tell Ellie. She'd seemed so enamored with Alejandro. Happy with him. It was hard to know you were about to shatter that for someone. Even if it was more the fault of the gigolo who'd cheated on her than the messenger who had photos of the gigolo.

We turned to make a right at a large sign indicating we were entering Lavender Lane, when Kendall sucked in a quick intake of breath and her arm shot out, holding me back. "Jamie!" she hissed.

I froze, my eyes whipping around. "What?"

"Look!" She pointed to a spot near a large oak tree, and I followed her line of sight.

Standing under the leafy branches next to a bed of bright purple blooming lavender bushes was Alejandro. And in his arms was a slim brunette in a tight red dress.

"Ohmigod, he's got another one!" Kendall said, the venom in her eyes unmistakable. Kendall might have been a somewhat shallow millennial, but the anger on her grandmother's behalf in that moment was real.

Before I could stop her, she surged forward, running toward the couple. "Hey! Who do you think you are?"

I jogged after her, watching a surprised Alejandro look up from his latest lover, his expression morphing from shock, to recognition at seeing Ellie's granddaughter, to fear at the way she was barreling down on him.

"I knew it!" Kendall yelled. "I knew you were a no-good, lousy, cheating son of a—"

But the rest of her rant froze on her lips as the brunette turned around.

I stopped in my tracks beside Kendall, both of us recognizing the brunette's features at the same time.

"Gammy?" Kendall said, the confusion clear in her voice.

"Kendall," Ellie said, her eyes going from me to her granddaughter. "What are you doing here?"

"I'm here to tell you that Alejandro's cheating on you," Kendall said, having recovered some of her shock. Though the statement held a lot less conviction than she'd had a moment ago. She licked her lips. "Right?" She turned a questioning gaze on me.

I closed my eyes and said goodbye to my electric bill payment. "No," I said with great reluctance. "I don't think he is."

"Cheating?" Alejandro said. "Me? On Ellie? I would never!"

"But the photos? The redhead in the bar?" Kendall looked at me almost like she was pleading for understanding.

"Photos?" Ellie was no longer looking surprised but more along the lines of angry. "What photos? What are you talking about?"

I sighed again. "Photos my associate took of Alejandro at a dive bar the other night with a redhead." I glanced at Ellie's brunette wig. "Who I assume was you?"

"You were following us?" Ellie's eyebrows drew down in a frown.

"Wait—I'm confused." Kendall held up a finger for us all to pause. "*You* are the redhead?"

"It was a wig." Ellie's hand went to the brunette one she was wearing now. "I was playing Hot Stranger in a Bar."

"Playing..." Kendall's eyes went round as the meaning sank in. "Ew, ew, ew! You were like dressing up for...sex?" Kendall did a mock shudder and made a gagging motion. "Gammy, you're too old for that!"

"Oh, please. I've had more sex in my life than you can count, child."

Kendall looked about ready to die of dramatic disgust.

Ellie frowned disapprovingly at the millennial but turned her attention to me. "Aren't you Mary's granddaughter?"

"No," I confessed. "I'm actually a private investigator Kendall hired. After she saw Alejandro kissing a blonde here at the Acres."

Ellie gasped, her disapproving eye going back to her granddaughter.

I turned to Alejandro. "Also Ellie, I assume?"

Alejandro nodded, a hurt look on his face. "Of course. Ellie is the only woman for me."

"Why didn't you just ask me?" Ellie asked Kendall. "Why did you have to hire some investigator?"

"She thought he was after your money," I explained on Kendall's behalf. "She was trying to protect you." Which in hindsight sounded ridiculous. It was clear Ellie was far more capable of reading Alejandro's character than Kendall was. Or we were for that matter. I shook my head, feeling like a total fool. And an amateur.

"I think we need to have a talk," Ellie said to Kendall, looking every bit the stern grandmother, despite the skintight dress and fishnet stockings. "And as for you," she said, turning to me.

"I know. I know. Stop following you around." It was a reoccurring theme in my life lately.

* * *

"So Gammy just liked to play dress-up?" Danny's laughter filled the interior of my car from my speakerphone as I drove down the 10.

"Apparently," I said, changing lanes. As soon as I'd pulled away from Sunset Acres, his face had lit up my phone with an incoming call, and I'd filled him in on the Manchester debacle. "Neither Sam nor Kendall had gotten more than a glimpse of Alejandro's mystery women from the back."

"So he wasn't cheating at all?"

"He claims not to be." I paused. "And I kind of believe him. They actually seem to be in love."

"Lucky kids," he joked.

"Yeah, well, I'm not sure Kendall took it so well. If things keep going well between them, she's liable to have to share her inheritance with a Step-Gampy."

"The kid's got plenty of money coming to her," Danny reasoned. "Her dad's latest movie is supposed to be the blockbuster of the summer."

"People still go to the movies?"

"They might this summer." I could hear the phone shifting on Danny's end. "Anyway, I was just calling to see if maybe you're free for that dinner tonight?"

The comfortable banter suddenly died on my lips at the invitation. I tried to read into his tone whether this was two friends having a taco or something that might lead back to his place for lipstick-stained wineglasses.

"What did you have in mind?" I asked.

"I dunno. Chinese? Italian?"

"Italian?" I tried not to envision the romantic drippy candles at La Pastoria.

"Sure. What time?" he asked.

I hadn't actually been agreeing. But Danny's tone seemed casual enough. Like a casual friend asking another casual friend out for a little casual company.

Or casual sex.

I licked my lips, shoving that last thought aside.

"Give me an hour. I'm on my way to pick up something from Derek, then I have to make a quick stop in North Hollywood."

"At this time of day?" Danny said. "Better make that at least an hour and a half."

I grinned. "Good point. Eight? At La Pastoria?" I didn't know what made me pick that place, but it just popped out.

"I'll be there," Danny said. And he hung up before I could take it back.

* * *

Twenty minutes later I pulled up to the marina and parked in a spot near the slip where Derek's *Black Pearl* was tethered. I gingerly took a step onto the deck, feeling the uneven wooden boards wobble beneath my spiky heels. A couple of empty deck chairs sat up top, and a half-empty beer next to one told me they hadn't been unoccupied long.

"Hello?" I called.

I heard laughing and movement from down below in response, and a moment later Derek's head popped up from the boat's interior. "James. Hey, kid."

"Hey. You got the tapes?" I'd called him on my way over to let him know I was delivering them to Carmichael.

He nodded. "Yeah. Elaine's just packing them up." He gestured toward the interior of the boat as he climbed the stairs.

"Did you get a chance to listen to them all?" I asked hopefully.

But he shook his head. "There's a lot to wade through. Man, those guys could jam forever."

I felt my hopes sink. "So you still don't know what's on them?"

"Not all of them. But we made copies of them."

"Oh?" That was better than nothing.

Derek nodded. "Elaine thought it would be a good idea to get them all converted to digital. You know. Preserve a piece of rock 'n' roll history and all."

"Elaine's a smart cookie," I noted.

Derek grinned. "Don't I know it."

"Did I hear my name?" came a cigarette-laced female voice. Elaine came up the stairs carrying the shoebox full of tapes. She was dressed in her usual attire of skintight spandex skirt, tight top, and tall heels. Today's was a coordinated cheetah print that brought out the dyed red highlights in her hair.

"Hi, Elaine," I said, giving her a quick hug and peck on the cheek. While she came off a bit rough around the edges sometimes, I knew she had a heart of gold. At times, I'd thought she might even be too good for my dear old dad. Luckily, Derek had yet to find a way to screw up the relationship, so I had hopes she might be my stepmother someday yet.

Elaine handed me the shoebox. "Thanks. We had a rockin' night listening to these."

"I'm glad you enjoyed them."

"Oh, we did," Derek said, grinning as he rocked back on his heels. "That hour-long 'Kinking it with the Band' rendition really set the mood last night."

"TMI, old man," I told him as I took the shoebox from a giggling Elaine.

"Hey, you busy later?" Derek asked. "Elaine made meatloaf. We got plenty for three?"

"Sorry. Plans," I said, giving them both a wave as I walked back to my Roadster.

* * *

It was dark out by the time I finally arrived at the dreary lot of Alvin Carmichael's square building. I parked under the same emaciated palm tree near the back of the lot and beeped my car locked, noting that only a couple of the windows in the building still had their lights on. I quickly crossed the lot and skipped the dodgy elevator in favor of the stairs, making my way to the 3rd floor.

At the end of the hall, I pushed open the doors to Carmichael's suite, finding the reception room empty that evening. Bored Receptionist must have already left for the day.

"Hello?" I called out.

Carmichael's head popped out of his inner office. "Oh good. You're here. Come on back." Then he popped back in, so I had little choice but to comply.

"I've got the tapes," I said, crossing the few paces to the door to his claustrophobic office. I held the shoebox out in front of me as proof. "So hopefully you can figure out who they should go to now and what to do with them, because—"

I abruptly stopped talking as I came into the room and got a good look at Carmichael.

Or, more specifically, at what he had in his right hand. A menacing black gun.

Pointed right at me.

CHAPTER NINETEEN

"What is that?" I asked. Even though it was pretty darn clear it was a weapon. What wasn't clear was why Alvin Carmichael was pointing it at me.

"I hate this," Carmichael said. He shook his head, his expression pinched in a way that made me think he was telling the truth. "It was just supposed to be Drake. But then everything fell apart, and everyone is asking questions, and you!" The gun pointed at me. "You just couldn't leave it alone. I knew you would find out."

I licked my lips, my brain working overtime to try to catch up. "Find out what?"

His eyes met mine, a dark, flat look in them that said any chance at compassion was long gone. "You know what."

I feared I did. "You killed Drake?"

He nodded, his head bobbing up and down so slowly that the intention behind it gave me chills.

"Why?" I asked, honestly curious. Of all the people close to Drake, Carmichael had seemed the only one who didn't benefit financially from his death.

"Because he knew too much." Carmichael shook his head some more. "That song. That stupid, ridiculous song. It was as moronic as all of their stuff. But the public ate it up like good little sheep, didn't they?"

"You're talking about 'Hot Waitress'?" I asked, trying to understand where he was going.

"Yes." Carmichael laughed loudly.

The sudden outburst of emotion startled me, and I realized how close to the edge of sanity the guy was.

"'Hot Waitress.' What a perfectly asinine song. Crude lyrics. Tired melody. So trite it's interchangeable with any other stupid pop song on the radio, but it's suddenly playing on everyone's phones. And it's a hit."

"And a moneymaker," I added.

He nodded. "It was. Oh, if only it hadn't made so much, maybe this never would have happened."

"So you killed Drake over the song?"

"Over the *money*. I told the band not to worry—I'd take care of everything. Distribute royalties like I always had. For thirty years they've trusted me with it. I don't know why Drake couldn't just leave well enough alone."

"You mean the lawsuit?" I asked, still trying to connect the dots as to how it could have driven Carmichael to murder.

"No!" He whipped his wild gaze my way, the gun whipping right along with it in a way that made me freeze in place and concentrate hard on not peeing my pants. "What do I care about that lawsuit? My cut is the same either way."

"I don't understand," I said.

But Carmichael just laughed again. "Oh, it's too late to play blonde now, girl. I know you know all about the song royalties. I knew as soon as you wanted the name of Tosh Thomas's accounting firm."

I frowned. "His accountants?"

"I never thought anyone would notice," Carmichael said. "I mean, the band could hardly do simple math, the morons. And they were all so wasted in those days. What did they know about accounting? What did they *care*? I sent them enough money to keep them in booze and girls, and they were happy. Had been for years."

A picture was starting to form in my mind. "All their royalties came through you."

"Of course they did."

"And you disbursed payments to the band members?"

"Yes."

"And you kept a little for yourself."

"That's how being a manager works."

"But you kept more than just *a little*, didn't you?"

Carmichael's mouth curved up into a slow smile. "See? I knew you knew too much."

Not until just that second. But as soon as the last puzzle piece fell into my lap, all the other pieces suddenly fit together seamlessly, painting the picture clearly for me that had led to Drake's demise.

"Drake's spreadsheets," I said, remembering what Caleigh and I had seen on his computer. "He was keeping track of sales and rankings. Estimating how much he'd be due with each upcoming payment."

Carmichael's mouth scrunched up in a sneer. "Technology. It's made it way too easy for anyone to find out anything. Back in the nineties, none of this information was online. You had the Billboard 100—that's it. Your manager says you sold this many copies, it's how many you sold. You trusted people."

"The band trusted you," I pointed out. "But Drake didn't."

"The guy gets a laptop, and suddenly he's a freaking accounting whiz. He was a rock star. He wasn't supposed to be making spreadsheets!"

"But he did. And he realized his checks weren't matching his sales," I guessed. "Because you were skimming money from the band."

"I earned that money!" he shouted, the gun suddenly waving wildly around the room. "I have ulcers because of them! I've devoted my life to them! They're driving me into an early grave, and what do I get? Ten percent? Ten percent of the nothing they earned off those crappy hair metal ballads?" He shook his head. "No. No, when I saw that first Deadly Devils royalty check, I knew they'd never notice if I took just a little more."

"How much more?"

"Enough!" he shouted at me. "Enough to make my job as their babysitter worth it."

"But when the song hit big, you took too much. Too much to go unnoticed by Drake," I guessed.

"That was my payday. That was what I'd earned!"

"That was what Drake was going to talk to the band about at the hotel that night," I said, putting it together. "He figured out you'd been stealing from the band for years, and he was going to call you out?"

Carmichael shut his mouth with a click, the gun steady on me now. "Yes. He told me it was over. He was going to tell everyone."

"So you killed him before he could."

His eyes took on that dead look again, flat, uncaring, and dangerous. "I had to. I couldn't have him ruining everything."

"So you arrived early at the hotel. You went up to Drake's room?"

He nodded slowly. "I pleaded with him not to tell anyone. Told him I'd pay him back everything and more if he kept it between us."

"But he wouldn't?"

Carmichael's mouth twisted up into a creepy smile that held zero humor and tons of menace. "It wouldn't have mattered if he'd agreed. Like I was going to pay off that moron. It was just a way to get into his room. Keep him preoccupied as I spiked his drink. Keep him thinking he had the upper hand on me." He paused, the smile growing as he enjoyed mentally reliving the scene. "He really was such a fool."

"What about the lipstick on the other glass?" I asked.

But Carmichael shrugged. "What do I know about the floozy he had in his room before I got there?"

"So you didn't have a drink with him?"

"Me?" He laughed again. "As if the great Drake Deadly would offer his lowly manager a drink. No. I was a servant in his eyes. Which was fine. I was happy to serve him his last drink."

I shuddered at the calm in his voice as he talked about poisoning his client of over thirty years.

"Then what?" I asked. "You persuaded him to go down to the pool?"

"He said he was feeling a little woozy. Maybe had too much to drink. I told him I'd help him to the meeting. Only by the time we got downstairs, he could barely walk. And then when we passed the pool…" Carmichael smiled and shrugged. "He might have fallen in."

I felt a chill, as if experiencing the cool water washing over me. Picturing Drake's last moments. As his manager stood over him, watching him go under, and then walking away.

"And Bash?" I asked. "Did he find out you were skimming money from the band too?"

Carmichael sucked in a breath. "Bash was unfortunate. He saw the water."

"Water?" I asked.

"When Drake fell into the pool. It made a splash, and…and some of the pool water got on my pants. Bash noticed they were wet when I arrived at the bar for the meeting."

"And he knew you had killed Drake?"

"Not then. I tried to pass it off as a mishap in the men's room. But the next day, after Drake's body was found, Bash called me and said he knew. He knew I'd been the one to push Drake in."

"Did he know why?" I asked. "That you were stealing from the band?"

Carmichael shook his head. "He thought it had something to do with those stupid tapes."

I glanced down at the shoebox still in my hands. I'd almost forgotten about them in the exchange. "So Bash came to you. I assume it wasn't to turn you in to the authorities?"

Carmichael shifted his grip on the gun, clearly getting antsy with all my questions. "No. He wanted compensation for his silence."

"He was blackmailing you?"

Carmichael nodded. "He wanted me to sign an affidavit saying that before Drake died, he told me that he'd lied about writing 'Hot Waitress.'" He shook his head, eyes going to the tapes in my hands. "They were all obsessed over that stupid song."

They had a lot of financial reasons to be. "Did you give him what he wanted?" I asked, feeling like I was on borrowed time. I couldn't keep Carmichael talking forever. I kept my eyes on the gun as I took a small, tentative step backward toward the door.

"I told him I would give the affidavit to him," Carmichael said. "I told him he could have whatever he wanted."

"Only, you didn't give it to him. You killed him."

He nodded. "Bash did call me yesterday evening. Just like I told you and the police he did. He said he wanted me to bring over the affidavit then."

"Only, when you got there, you hit him over the head instead."

His wicked grin was back. "I thought the Grammy was a nice touch."

"Then you showed up the next morning to pretend to find the body?"

He nodded. "Good way to explain any evidence I might have left behind, right?"

Actually it was. In fact, he'd seemed to think of just about everything.

Including, it seemed, disposing of the nosy private investigator both of his dead clients had hired.

I licked my lips, looking down at the gun barrel, knowing I was running out of time. "You would have gotten away with it," I told him. "Why involve me?"

He scoffed. "You involved yourself! Everywhere I turned, there you were! Asking questions about the band's finances."

I shook my head. "I was asking about the song."

"How much did Drake tell you before he died?" Carmichael demanded.

"About you? Nothing!" I said honestly.

"Right." He narrowed his eyes, and I could tell he didn't believe me. "You had a lot of questions about how much money he was making."

"I thought his wife had killed him for the royalties."

"Then you wanted to know all about Tosh Thomas's checks."

"I was just trying to locate him," I protested.

"Then you showed up at Bash's place."

"He was my client." I shook my head. "Trust me, I had no idea you were skimming money or that you'd had anything to do with the deaths."

He pinned me with a look. "You do now."

Rats. Couldn't argue that one.

"Look, there are ways out of this," I told him, taking another small step backward.

"Stop moving."

I froze.

I licked my lips. "I can help you," I told him. "I know the ADA. He can cut you a deal." I was lying through my teeth. There was no way Carmichael would get a deal after this confession. But if Carmichael could lie to his clients for thirty years, I could do it to a murderer for a few minutes. Especially if it saved my skin.

Only, Carmichael apparently wasn't as easily fooled as his clients had been. He just shook his head. "Nice try. But I see another way out of this."

I almost hesitated to ask… "Which is?"

He pointed the gun directly at eye level. Which gave me a pretty good idea what his master plan was even before he spoke. "You need to go."

"People will be looking for me," I told him, desperation in my voice as images of those people flashed through my mind. My Bond Girls. Aiden. Even Derek nudged his way in there. Tears suddenly sprang to my eyes, despite what a tough girl I was.

And what about Danny? Who even now was probably arriving at La Pastoria, waiting for a dinner date that would never happen. What would he think? That I'd stood him up?

"And those people will find you," Carmichael answered, breaking into my self-pitying thoughts. "Right here. Shot to death over those tapes." His eyes went down to the box in my hands. "I think it sounds entirely plausible that Keith and Harry didn't want that proof surfacing and ruining their newfound income. Which is why they conspired to kill off Drake, then Bash, and finally the nosy PI who was hired to find the tapes."

I felt my skin grow cold. Not only was it a good story— one I'd been envisioning myself over the last few days—but I *had* just been to see Keith and Harry and they *had* all but thrown me out. Caleigh had witnessed it all. And I had a terrible feeling it wouldn't be hard for her, or anyone else, to imagine they really were guilty and had come after me.

"You're going to frame Keith and Harry?" I asked. My voice had an odd ring to it even to my own ears. There was a note I didn't usually hear in my own voice. Fear.

Carmichael nodded, his eyes flat, hard, and determined. "Once the police find this gun in their house, it won't be a stretch."

I looked down at it. He was right. A literal smoking gun was good evidence.

"You won't get away with this," I tried again, even though it held zero conviction.

"I think I will. Who do you think a jury is going to believe—those two stoners or me?"

Him. Hands down. In fact, an hour ago, I would have believed anything Carmichael had told me over those two.

Which meant he had a pretty solid plan.

Which meant I was in pretty serious trouble.

Trouble that was moving closer to me, as Carmichael took a step toward the doorway where I was hovering, the gun straight in front of him, bearing down on me with its menacing black barrel.

"Say goodbye, Ms. Bond," Carmichael said.

I heard a whimper that may or may not have come from me. This was it. My life flashed before my eyes, and it was a short enough replay that another whimper escaped. This couldn't be the end. I wasn't finished.

And I wasn't going down without a fight.

Carmichael raised the gun. He narrowed his eyes.

And I threw the box of cassette tapes at him.

The lid flew off, and dozens of plastic tapes rained down on him. He instinctively shielded himself with his hands, and for a second the gun moved away from me.

A second I did not waste.

I turned and ran. Out the door, back through the tiny reception room, and out the front doors of his office.

"Stop!" I heard him yell behind me, tapes crunching under his feet as he gave chase.

But there was no way I was going to stop. I sprinted down the dingy hallway, hitting the door to the stairwell and flying down two at a time. I practically slid down the first flight, my feet tripping over each other in my haste. I could feel my breath coming fast, my heart pounding with not only exertion but pure, unadulterated fear.

I heard the door to the stairwell slam open again, Carmichael right behind me. But I didn't dare take the time to turn around to look. I wound downward, my heels clattering noisily on the metal stairs.

Then I heard another sound. The loud shot of the gun going off. I instinctively ducked, realizing he was shooting at me. I cursed myself for leaving my Glock in the car. That was the last time a bottle of antacids and a mousy personality fooled me into thinking a person was safe and sane.

Another shot rang out, and I felt searing heat along my shoulder. I stumbled forward, hearing my own cries echo in the cavernous stairwell.

"You're not going anywhere!" Carmichael shouted a floor above me. His feet fell heavy on the stairs as he rushed toward the bottom. Gaining on me. "You're not getting away from me!"

Wanna bet.

I stumbled down the last flight, hitting the outer door at the bottom and slamming into it with all my weight. I pushed through it, the pain in my shoulder throbbing. I saw blood on the door where I'd touched it and had to breathe back a gag reflex. Seeing my own blood outside my body did that to me. Especially when I feared a whole lot more of it might spill out any second if I didn't keep moving.

"Help!" I screamed. Though the only witnesses to it were a couple of crows picking at crumbs in the deserted parking lot. They flapped their wings, taking flight, and oh, how I wished to do the same. Just fly away to safety. But my only means of escape was my Roadster, parked at the edge of the lot under the gangly palm tree.

And it was way too far away.

Another shot rang out, ripping through the night air like a firecracker.

Carmichael was right behind me.

"Stop!" His voice was high and filled with wild rage. "Stop right there or I shoot!"

I stopped. What could I do? My car was several yards away, and my legs were no match for a bullet's speed. I felt hot tears on my cheeks. I hadn't even realized I was crying, but there they were. My breath was coming out jagged and halting, and my entire body was shaking.

I slowly turned around to face Carmichael. If he was going to kill me, he was going to have to look me in the eyes to do it.

"Stop moving!" he yelled, spittle flying from his thin lips. His sparse hair was standing on end, a sheen of sweat visible on his face. His pupils were dilated with rage and some wild, unchecked mania. "Stop right there. Stop talking, stop moving, stop running, and just let me shoot you—"

A pair of headlights cutting across the parking lot stopped him midsentence.

Mostly because they were aimed right at him. And moving at high speeds.

Before I could even react, I watched in horror as the car attached to them surged forward, slamming into Carmichael's body and tossing it like a rag doll across the parking lot. He landed with a sickening thud several feet away, the gun clattering to the pavement behind him.

I blinked, my heart frozen in my chest as my gaze pinged from Carmichael's prone form to the car, its engine idling a few feet away. A car that, I realized as my brain slowly began to recover from the shock, was actually a very stylish mint green Jaguar.

"Ohmigosh," Jenna James said, exiting the driver's side door. "Ohmigosh, he was going to kill you! He was going to shoot you!"

I nodded dumbly. "I think he did shoot me," I said. I looked down at my shoulder and saw a red stain spreading there through my sweater.

And then I promptly passed out.

CHAPTER TWENTY

———

By the time the paramedics arrived, I had a tentative grasp on consciousness again, and I listened to Jenna give them a slightly hysterical account of what she'd witnessed. Apparently, after I'd left Keith's house earlier that day, he'd immediately called Jenna and told her that I knew everything about their relationship. Which hadn't made Jenna too happy, considering she'd already warned me off of following her before.

As payback, she'd tracked me down—thanks to a couple of calls to my office. The first had been answered by Maya, who had politely told her she could leave a message. Unfortunately, the second one had come in when Maya had stepped out to the restroom, and her social media crew of teenagers had helpfully answered the phone and told Jenna I was scheduled to meet with Alvin Carmichael that evening.

Jenna had shown up at Carmichael's with every intention of telling me where I could stick my nosiness, when she'd pulled into the parking lot and witnessed Carmichael about to shoot me. On instinct, she'd floored it.

I should have been angry at the teens for giving out my location and at Maya for hiring kids in the first place. But all I could muster up was supreme gratefulness at not only Jenna's timing but also her lead foot.

Once the paramedics had stopped the bleeding from what they informed me was a deep flesh wound, they bundled me into the back of the ambulance just as two cop cars pulled into the parking lot. I watched a uniformed officer get out of one and meet a paramedic near Carmichael's still form. The slow shake of the paramedic's head was enough to tell me that the manager wasn't getting up again.

Luckily I didn't have to stick around to see the state of the body, as the ambulance bay doors shut and I was whisked away to the ER. A dozen stitches and a couple of really nice pain pills later, I was contemplating a long nap when a familiar voice floated to me from the doorway of my treatment room.

"Hey."

I pried my eyelids open to find Aiden standing there. His luscious lips were curved into a small smile, though his eyebrows were drawn down in concern.

"Hey, yourshelf," I answered.

His grin grew. "Sounds like they gave you some good pain medication."

"Why do you shay that?" I slurred.

He shrugged. "You just look relaxed." He stepped into the room and approached my bed, his hand reaching out to brush a few stray hairs off my forehead.

His touch was soft and warm and felt nice enough that I might have closed my eyes and made some happy moaning sounds.

I heard a low chuckle rumbling from his throat. "How much did they give you, Bond?"

I opened my eyes lazily. "Just the right amount."

"You're making me a little jealous that I'm on duty," he joked.

I breathed in, trying to get my head to connect with my body again. "Carmichael's dead," I told him.

His joking demeanor disappeared, the smile dropping instantly from his face. "I know. I've been to the scene."

"Jenna hit him with her Jaguar. Even though she wanted a Bentley."

He nodded. "We've taken Jenna's statement."

"She's not in trouble, right?" I asked. "I mean, she saved my life."

"No, she's not in trouble. Defense of others."

I felt more relief than I thought I would at hearing that. "Good. 'Cause she's not a bad person. Even the aliens love her."

Aiden gave me a funny look but let that one go. "How's your shoulder?" He glanced down to where a white bandage was taped to my upper arm.

"I don't feel a thing," I told him honestly.

He chuckled again. "I hope that continues when the drugs wear off."

I rolled my head on the pillow to face him. "I thought about you," I told him, the pain pills pulling some honesty from me. "When Carmichael was going to shoot me."

Emotion washed over his features, and I could see his nostrils flaring with the effort to breathe.

"I thought that I should have told you," I said.

His sandy eyebrows drew down over his warm brown eyes. "Told me what?" he asked softly.

"Why I can't say I love you."

Even through my drugged haze, I could see the words hit him like a physical blow. All his years of training as a lawyer couldn't keep his face impassive, the hurt from reaching his eyes.

"I'm sorry," I whispered.

He shook his head as if trying to shake away the emotion. His hand went to my hair again. "It's okay. You're hurt. You're tired. We'll talk later."

All of those were true.

I closed my eyes. "It's Danny."

"Jamie, we don't need to talk about this right now," he said. A note of urgency lay in his voice. Like he was desperate to keep the words from coming. As if as long as I didn't voice them, he could ignore the truth.

"He's more than my friend, Aiden. He's always been more."

I heard him suck in more air as if he were the one suddenly drowning.

I opened my eyes to meet his. "I can't say I love him either," I told him.

A hint of relief crossed his face.

"But he's why I can't love you yet." I licked my lips. "I'm sorry," I said again.

I stared up into his sad eyes, not sure what he was thinking. Finally he let out a long sigh. "Yet. You said yet."

I felt the corner of my mouth curving upwards. "I did say yet, didn't I?"

He nodded, a forced smile on his lips, even if his eyes still held that hurt in their depths. "I'm a patient man, Bond."

"Good. 'Cause I'm really shleepy. I might need to resht for a few yearshhh," I said, feeling my eyes starting to close again all on their own.

I felt Aiden's soft lips skim my forehead. "Good night, Jamie," he whispered.

And then he was gone.

* * *

"You know, I totally thought you stood me up," Danny said, crunching on a tortilla chip outside Bosco's Cantina. Thanks to the unseasonably warm weather bringing us into the high eighties for a welcome respite from winter, we were sitting on their outdoor patio, a couple of frosty margaritas in front of us and bowls of chips and salsa between us on the table.

"Serves you right," I told him, sipping from my drink.

"Ouch." He gave me a look of mock hurt. "What did I do wrong?"

I grinned at him. "You're a flirt, Danny. You toy with women's emotions. And someday, you're going to have to put your money where your mouth is."

"Is that an invitation?" he asked, raising one eyebrow at me in a boyishly wicked expression.

I leaned across the table, giving him a come-hither look that many lesser men than him had fallen for. "You couldn't handle me."

He threw his head back and laughed. "You're probably right, Bond."

I winked at him over the rim of my glass. "I know I'm right."

It had been two weeks since I'd been discharged from the hospital, and my shoulder was healing into what proved to be a really cool scar with a really harrowing story to go with it. And thanks to Carmichael's confession to me and my subsequent multiple statements to the DA's office in triplicate, Aiden had been able to wrap up both the murders of Drake Deadly and Bash—or Grover Tanenbaum, as it turned out his real name was.

My cases hadn't been quite as neatly wrapped in a bow, though I had given Jenna back the retainer check Drake had originally made out to me. It seemed only fair, being that she'd saved my life and he'd hired me under false pretenses. Bash's cash? That was a different story. I'd deposited it. Hey, I'd closed the case, brought the guy's killer to justice, and I had, in fact, found the tapes I'd been hired to find. Even if they had ended up all over Alvin Carmichael's office floor and taken into evidence.

"So where are your Bond Girls today?" Danny asked, slurping his drink.

"Well, Sam is out with Julio." I paused. "Senior."

Danny raised an eyebrow. "*Out* as in on a date?"

I shrugged. "Jury's still out. But I don't think Sam is minding the attention. And I know Julio Jr. isn't."

"Well, good for them." He sipped again. "And Caleigh?"

"At a potluck at Sunset Acres."

Danny snorted, almost spewing his drink. "She's partying at the retirement village?"

I nodded. "Apparently she made a couple of friends there. She said they remind her of her grandma at home. In fact, she's even going to be one of Ellie's bridesmaids this summer when she ties the knot with Alejandro."

"Wow." He nodded. "Poor Kendall."

I shrugged. "She'll get over it."

"So you hear from Jenna recently?" Danny asked, scooping salsa onto a chip and glancing at the pink stucco clad apartment building across the street.

I nodded. "She just bought a vacation home."

"Oh yeah?"

"You'll never guess where."

He shrugged. "Cancun?"

"Area 51." I grinned as Danny laughed again. "She and Keith intend to spend the winters there, watching the skies for visitors."

Danny slurped his drink. "Hey, if they're lucky, maybe they'll have a freaky lizard threesome and write a book about it."

I threw a chip at him.

"What? It wasn't a bad book."

"Don't tell me you bought a copy of Dave's masterpiece?"

Danny nodded. "You can borrow it anytime." He winked at me.

"Pass," I said, sipping my drink.

"Okay, so what I want to know," Danny said, leaning his elbow on the table, "is if Carmichael killed Drake over royalties, who was it that broke into Jenna's house looking for the tapes?"

"Well, it turns out that was actually my client. Bash." Yeah, one more reason I was keeping the wad of cash.

After the police took Jenna's statement when she hit Carmichael, she came clean to them about everything, including the break-in at her house. Aiden had immediately dispatched a forensics team to her house, where they found out that not only did her housekeeper cut corners, but that Bash'd had a dandruff problem. They'd found skin cells that matched his on the floor inside the family room.

"My guess is he was desperate to find those tapes," I told Danny. "After Drake was killed, he must have assumed—like I did—that it was because Drake was going to show the band proof that Drake had written 'Hot Waitress.'"

"So he figured Drake had kept the proof at home?"

I nodded. "Bash probably wanted to find it before anyone else could and destroy it. He hired me, but when I wasn't getting results quickly enough, he broke into Drake's house to see if he could find them himself."

"Only, he didn't know Jenna had them in her car," Danny said.

"Right. When he failed there, he decided to blackmail Carmichael to invent proof in the form of the affidavit."

"So, were they?"

"Were they what?" I asked, sipping my drink and licking salt off my lips.

"Were the tapes proof that Drake wrote the song?"

I grinned. "No."

Danny made a disappointed sound in the back of his throat and tilted his head against his colorful wooden chair. "After all that, they didn't even contain anything?"

I shook my head. "I didn't say that. They actually *did* contain the jam session where *someone* wrote 'Hot Waitress.'"

"Someone?" Danny asked. "You're killing me here, Bond. Who?"

"Harry Star."

"The bass player?" Danny laughed, the same shock I'd felt at hearing his name evident on his face.

When Derek had called me to say he and Elaine had finally found the "golden recording" where one of the band had introduced the idea for "Hot Waitress," I'd been on the edge of my seat to know if it had been Bash or Drake who'd penned the first lines. Harry had never even been on my radar. Then again, to be fair, Harry had never even been on *Harry's* radar as the original songwriter. When I'd played the digital recording of the jam session the following day for Keith and Harry at their place in Tujunga, Harry had seemed as shocked as anyone. He'd been so stoned then—and pretty much since—that he hadn't even remembered being the one who'd come up with the idea. Keith hadn't either, admitting that all the while, he'd assumed it was Drake.

"So what's Harry going to do? Push for full rights?" Danny asked.

I shrugged. "I've got no idea. That's for the Devils to work out." I paused. "Well, the remaining Devils anyway."

"Speaking of remaining Devils...ever find out where Tosh Thomas slash Tad Windhorse ended up?"

I nodded. "Albuquerque."

"New Mexico?"

"Caleigh found out his real name is Ted Tiberon and he had a sister there. She tracked him down to her place."

"So why did he take off?" Danny asked, his eyes cutting to the apartment building again as he sipped.

"Caleigh said he was scared." I swallowed a bite of chips and salsa. "Once she told him that we knew he was at the Beverly Hotel the night Drake died, he admitted everything."

"Lay it on me," Danny said, leaning his elbows on the table.

"Well, for starters, Drake didn't just come to see him at the Blue Moon to bury that hatchet. Drake actually told him the same thing he planned to tell the rest of the band—that Carmichael had been bilking the band of profits for years. Tad said he didn't believe it, but Drake told him to come to the hotel, where he'd be showing the entire band proof in the form of his spreadsheets."

"So Tad did show up for the band meeting?"

I nodded. "He did. He said he arrived early and went out into the courtyard garden to meditate before the meeting. After he got his zen on, he said he was walking back to the bar when he passed the pool and saw Drake's body floating there."

"He didn't tell anyone?"

I shook my head. "He says he freaked out and just took off. He thought that, with their past, he'd look guilty."

"Which he did," Danny pointed out. "And then when you showed up asking questions about Drake's death at the Blue Moon…"

"He got even more freaked," I finished for him. "Tad realized even his new name and identity wouldn't shield him then, so he ran."

"Even though he was totally innocent."

I shrugged. "I guess even innocent people do dumb things. He said he didn't want to get involved in the whole mess and ruin the good vibes he'd been trying so hard to cultivate the past few years."

Danny shook his head. "I don't get meditating. How is sitting there *not* thinking about things supposed to give you clarity about how to think about things?"

I laughed. "I don't know, Danny."

He gestured across the street. "Think this guy is gonna show?"

I glanced at the pink apartment building. We'd been waiting for the last hour for my latest client's husband to show up to meet his mistress.

Yep—a nice, normal cheating client. Just like I'd hoped for.

Okay, well, he wasn't 100% normal. Turned out that Maya's teen social media gurus *had* actually managed to get our videos to go viral…among a certain population at least. Specifically the population who liked to dress up in animal costumes when engaging in hanky-panky with members of the opposite sex. Furries, I was told they are called, and our man in a bunny costume being berated by his wife had hit a note with them. I was currently hoping to catch Genevieve Cusler's husband Bill, who liked to meet women while dressed as a bear.

Hey, it paid the bills. And possibly enough to get some *real* social media management soon.

"I hope he shows soon," I said, shielding my eyes from the midafternoon sun. "I think I'm starting to get a sunburn."

Danny grinned at me. "Pink cheeks look cute on you."

"Pink cheeks look 'cute' on baby dolls. Grown women are not cute."

Danny shook his head. "Sorry, kid. I think you're cute, and there's nothing you can do about it."

"Hmm." I sipped my drink to cover the fact that my cheeks were, in fact, tingeing pink and it had nothing to do with the sun.

"So." Danny leaned his elbows on the table again, giving me a hard stare. "Tell me what's going on with you and Ken Doll?"

Oh geez. "Who?" I asked, playing dumb while I got ahold of the blush thing.

"You know who I mean, Aiden."

I set my drink down. "We're really going to talk about him?"

He nodded, his hard stare unrelenting. "What's the deal there? Do I have competition, or has Ken Doll run his course?"

"Please don't call him that."

"Don't avoid the question. Do I have competition?"

I put my binoculars up to my eyes, covering the emotion I could feel trying to edge its way in. "What am I, some prize?"

I could hear Danny chuckle. "Oh yeah. You are *some* prize."

I stuck my tongue out at him, though I still didn't trust myself enough to make eye contact.

"Come on, Bond," Danny said, his voice low. "You know you're a lot more than that to me."

The deep, husky tone in his voice had me pulling the binoculars down and facing him.

Gone was any mocking laughter or teasing grin. His expression was dead serious.

I licked my lips, a million responses turning over in my head.

"Panda bear."

Danny frowned at me. "What?"

I pointed across the street. "The furry."

Danny followed my gaze to see Mr. Cusler, dressed in a panda suit that was making it hard for him to gracefully exit his Prius in the apartment building's parking lot.

Danny shook his head and laughed. "Panda bear."

I threw a twenty on the table as the panda made a beeline for apartment 204, where we knew his mistress was waiting. I grabbed my purse, slipping the binoculars inside and pulling out my camera.

"Hey, Bond," Danny said, stopping me just as I was leaving the table.

I paused and turned to face him.

"You're going to have to make a choice some day, you know?" Danny said, the teasing grin back.

I shook my head, matching his teasing smile with one of my own. "What makes you think I haven't made a choice already, Flynn?" I gave him a wink.

Then I jogged across the street to the pink apartment building. Domestic espionage waited for no woman.

Even a Bond.

ABOUT THE AUTHOR

Gemma Halliday is the #1 Amazon, *New York Times & USA Today* bestselling author of several mystery series. Gemma's books have received numerous awards, including a Golden Heart, two National Reader's Choice awards, three RITA nominations, a RONE award for best mystery, and two Killer Nashville Silver Falchion Awards for best cozy mystery and readers' choice. She currently lives in the San Francisco Bay Area with her large, loud, and loving family.

To learn more about Gemma, visit her online at
www.GemmaHalliday.com

The Jamie Bond Mysteries

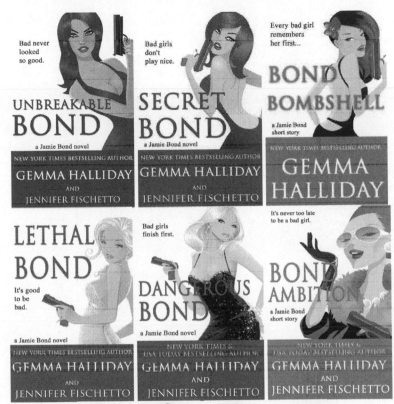

www.GemmaHalliday.com

Made in the USA
Columbia, SC
25 January 2021